HERO

WOLVES OF ROYAL PAYNES

KIKI BURRELLI

———

Join my newsletter
And stay up to date on my newest titles, giveaways and news!
Want a free—full length— wolf shifter Mpreg novel? Join my newsletter when you get Finding Finn!

———

Join the Pack! Awooooo!
Come hang out with your pack mates!
Visit Kiki's Den and join the pack! Enjoy exclusive access to behind the scenes excerpts, cover reveals and surprise giveaways!

EXPERIENCE THE WOLVES OF WORLD

Wolves of Walker County (Wolf Shifter Mpreg)

Truth

Hope

Faith

Love

Wolves of Royal Paynes (Wolf Shifter Mpreg)

Hero

Ruler

Lovers

Outlaw

1

JAZZ

ONLY IN PORTLAND could you find organic beeswax lip balm sold at a stand directly next to rows of decorative butt plugs. Some had jewels, glittering in pretty pinks, greens, and blues. Others had tails attached to the end. I paused at one that had a simple rounded cap with an image of a red X like you would see on an old pirate map.

X marks the spot.

"How much?" I asked the little old lady sitting behind the booth. From the corner of my eye, I caught sight of my hair, stained brown instead of its usual orange-red.

The woman peered up at me. She looked like she spent her weekends baking cookies for her grandchildren's bake sales. "One of my finest. One hundred percent stainless steel." Her eyes dragged up and then down my body. "It's pretty heavy and not for beginners, sweetie."

I hated it when people used pet names before they knew a person. Sweetie. Hon. Babe.

Blech.

But, this old lady was interesting, which already made her cool in my book—nothing worse than a boring stick in the mud. And she was kind. She hadn't been judging me with her warning but cautioning me. I understood. My stupidly round eyes and fiery curls made me look years younger than my actual age of twenty-three. Even though I had brown curls today, I had the body of a broomstick. Or shovel handle. Either worked. I didn't rely on my muscles to live, and it showed.

"How much?"

Before she could answer, I felt the telltale heat at my nape. If I turned my head, I'd see one of my ghosts lurking in the crowd, trying not to be seen. I couldn't be too annoyed. I'd egged the ghosts on, but how could I have known when Hollister had contacted me asking if he could give out my number that this time, this group, would be different?

Every other team my father had hired to try and find me normally didn't make it within fifty miles of catching me. And if they had, it was because I was bored and had allowed it. But these guys were relentless. I'd lived with a target between my shoulders from the moment they'd gotten hold of my cell phone number. And they were intelligent too, which sucked for me.

My father had wised up, deviating from hiring run-of-the-mill meatheads with guns to the freaking Teenage Mutant Ninja Turtles—if the turtles were angry brooding men led by a stupidly gorgeous, arrogant man.

Though the five—six, counting that evil dog that had nearly bit me the last time—were always on my heels, I'd never felt more alive than I had these past few weeks. My life wasn't about floating around and partying with the friends I had scattered over the country—while fun, a person can only party for so long. I had a goal, a purpose. Stay one step ahead, stay free, stay smart.

I dropped down to my haunches, balancing my arms on the tabletop. "I hate to ask you, but is there a man behind me staring like he's trying to drill a hole? Please don't be obvious when you look."

This wasn't her first sting operation, clearly. Her gaze slid over and then back just as quickly. "There is. He looks like a pretty strong guy. Are you in trouble, son?"

Not as long as I slip free. I knew my father hired these men to find me, but for the life of me, I couldn't figure out *why*. He hadn't especially cared for me growing up. He'd said I was the result of an impulsive night and that my mother had dropped me off on his doorstep before running. She hadn't wanted the trouble of raising a baby. My father hadn't either, but at least he had people to pay to raise me.

Our relationship hadn't improved since then.

I grabbed the slip of paper I always kept in my pocket. When I opened my hand, revealing the paper to the woman, she saw a picture of the men's leader. Knox. "Do you see this man behind me?"

She studied the illusion I projected. Though the photo came from my mind, every detail of the man's face was perfect. I didn't know how I could do what I did, just that I'd always been able to. If I got my hands on something—as long as it wasn't bigger than a large dog—I could make it look, and sometimes act, like anything. A piece of paper became a photograph. A stack of business cards became enough money for me to have a good night out, and then some.

"I don't see him," she said. "But I think I see a few others watching you. A man with a dog."

I sighed with relief even as she spotted more men on my tail. These guys were rough, clever, and kept me on my toes, but if Knox was here, I needed to be worried.

Knox.

Only an asshole would dare to have a gorgeous name while walking around like every good boy's wet dream. I wasn't a good boy, but I could pretend for Knox.

Stop it, Jazz. You're going to get caught. He doesn't care about you; he just wants to catch you.

I was Stockholm-Syndroming myself. *How pathetic.*

Knox wasn't some guardian angel sent to make me feel not so alone. I was pretty sure he and the rest of his team were some kind of ex-military, mercenaries. They were too smart to not be.

I had to remember Knox had been hired to find me. The moment he did, he'd turn me over and move on to the next job. "I'll take the plug." I reached for my wallet where I kept my real money.

I wasn't above stealing, but not from little old ladies trying to earn a little extra cash. I stole from my father or companies nested under the umbrella of his huge conglomerate. Clubs, restaurants, hotels chains, spas—there was an endless list that stretched across the country.

"Seems odd a young man learns he is being followed and immediately buys a sex toy."

I winked as she handed me the plug wrapped in brown paper. "Odd, that sounds like me." I threw a quick look over my shoulder.

The mountain moved in. They'd spotted me, I'd spotted them, we both knew we saw the other. My plan came together as I mapped a route out of the large outdoor bazaar. I knew my weaknesses as well as my strengths. I wasn't a fighter. Any one of those men could snap me in two like a twig while I tried my hardest just to leave a mark.

But I could be slippery. I could find cracks and crawl through them. And I had a certain lovable knack for chaos.

I'd been running for most of my life and had learned early on: always plan your exit, and never double back the way you came. I wouldn't be caught in a room with only one door, not unless there was a window to jump out of.

I straightened and tensed to move. "On second thought, can I get one of those lip balms too?" I asked.

The woman blinked several times but recovered. "Which flavor?"

"Pina colada, please." I'd imagine I was relaxing on a tropical beach instead of running away from men hell bent on ruining my casual Saturday fun.

I handed her the money, giving her extra for being so nice, and then slipped through the gap between her booth and the booth next to hers. One of the men said something, probably some mission code word that meant, *hurry up, he's getting away.*

I ran by a man walking several dogs of all shapes and sizes. Digging the plug from the small bag, I unwrapped it and cupped it between my hands before dropping the plug and letting it roll away on the ground behind me.

The dogs howled and barked, snapping to get at what looked like a large tabby cat sauntering by them without a care in the world. The dog walker lost control of the leashes as the dogs tugged him to the middle of the sidewalk, piling on top of their new furry friend.

By the time the dogs had calmed down and the walker got them pulled back, the cat would be gone and nothing more than a truly adorable plug, but by then, so would I.

Though I was sure of the plan, I still ran, hazarding a brief glance back where the mountain glared. His mouth moved in rapid shapes that were likely a string of curse words as he tried, and failed to get through the throng of chaos in front of him.

The one with the dog had his hands full as well. My illusions didn't just look like other things; they smelled like them as well. If I made a turd look like a pie and put it in a person's hand, they'd believe it was a pie until they put it in their mouth. Cujo was as distracted as the others.

But these guys never attacked alone. That was part of what made them so difficult. They came at me as a team, every time. Which meant...

I skidded to a stop, the Wonder Twins taking up the square of sidewalk several yards ahead. With hair as black as oil and bright blue eyes, they were difficult to miss. Sometimes, they carried swords with them. I'd spotted the handles once or twice in our time together and assumed they'd realized a crowded market place wasn't the best place to show up visibly armed.

Visibly being the operative word there.

I searched the area, spotting a police officer on top of a large brown horse. It could have been something fancy like an Arabian chestnut stallion, but to me, it looked like a brown horse.

Snagging the paper in my pocket, I held it, making my hand tremble as if in fear. "Officer, p-please help me."

The man on horseback narrowed his eyes at me, possibly his bullshit meter going off, but I pushed the paper closer to his nose.

"I have a restraining order. Those two men are not supposed to be within a hundred yards of me. Please, help." Sometimes, looking younger than my twenty-three years was useful.

With the proof of my story right in front of him, bullshit meter or not, the police officer looked from me to the Wonder Twins. "Wait here," he told me as he made a clicking sound with his mouth and his horse walked forward.

"Yes, of course, I'll wait..." I waited for him to get farther away, and closer to the twins, before heading off down an alley I'd spotted.

If I wasn't positive the wonder twins were going to do nothing to the police officer but be annoyed by him, I wouldn't have sent him over. I didn't want people getting hurt, or worse, killed, because of me. That had partly been the reason I'd told Hollister it was okay to send my information along. I didn't know the men at that time, but if they were asking my friend about me, they were in harming distance of him. Better they got the information they wanted and focus their attentions on the real target.

Looking left, right, and behind, I checked to make sure none of them had spotted me. It had sucked covering my red hair; it was one of the things I liked about myself. But it also made me too easy to spot. At least this way, no one had their eyes on me as I pranced down the sidewalk on the other side of the street, skipping toward the alley I knew went all the way through and opened on to the other side of the block. I pulled out the lip balm, twisting off the cap to slather a layer of fruity coconut beeswax onto my lips.

"Mmm." I smacked my lips together, sliding the tube in my pocket.

Before I could make the turn that would bring me freedom, a strong hand emerged from the darkness between two buildings and grabbed mine, pulling me into an off-balance spin. Disoriented, I slammed against a rock-hard chest as the growling man pulled my hands behind my back. His large, firm body pressed against mine while my shoulder blades smashed against the unforgiving concrete of the building behind me. Not only did he have my hands restrained, his thick fingers tightened over each wrist, and he kept my hands apart.

I needed two hands to do what I did. I knew that. I'd never told anyone else that. And somehow, this man who had been following me for months knew that now too. I must've slipped and been too obvious.

Or his relentless observation was starting to pay off.

"Getting sloppy, Jazz," Knox murmured. "'Target secure. Convene to the rendezvous point." He spoke into the small headset pinned behind his ear.

While I'd thought I'd been zigzagging through them, the bastards had been herding me to where they'd wanted me.

"I'm disappointed. Diesel said this plan would work, and I told him you were too smart to fall for it." He tsked me, his grip never loosening. His voice was like a summer storm. Swelteringly hot, sharp as a crack of lightning, but also deep and soothing like thunder rumbling in the distance.

Maybe everyone wasn't soothed by thunder and lightning, but I wasn't everyone.

Though having this man this close made my body go haywire, I attempted not to let it show. "Maybe I just like getting close to you," I shot back, my voice too breathy for the tease to count.

Knox smirked. Lips that full should've been illegal on a man like him. *What would they look like curled in a real smile?* I'd never know. Knox only ever smirked or scowled when he looked at me. His silver eyes traced my face, lingering at the bags beginning to form under my eyes.

I could make most any object look like anything else, but I couldn't do a thing to magic my appearance. Not in a way that was travelable anyway. My appearance, I had to maintain the old-fashioned way with sleep, dyes, makeup, and creams. And lately, I hadn't gotten a whole lot of sleep.

"You changed your hair," he grumped. "I don't like it."

Though I wasn't a fan of it either, I bristled beneath the implication that he had a say in how I looked. I'd shave my hair off if I wanted to and was ready to say as much. But when my mouth opened to unleash a heated retort, the words that came out weren't at all what I'd planned. "How do you like me? Helpless?" I made a show of trying to tug my hands free.

His grip was too strong for me to expect to pull away, but my repeated tugging made our bodies collide softly together. My dick sprung to life, and I would've been embarrassed, except Knox's cock did the same.

Worth it.

"Is that lip balm in your pocket, or are you happy to see me?" I purred. His length didn't feel a thing like the small tube. The heat and hardness made it impossible to mistake his erection for anything but what it was.

His lips twitched in what looked like the barest hint of a smile. That couldn't be right. Knox didn't smile. I was convinced he didn't have the facial muscles for it. He eased his body back, allowing a breeze's width of space between us.

Clueless to what he was planning, I watched, breathless, as he pulled my right hand to the front of my body. He pinned my arm there with his other shoulder before slowly sliding his hands into my front pocket.

His fingers didn't linger in my pocket. He grabbed what he'd been aiming for and pulled the tube clear of my jeans. Tucking the plastic into his front pocket, he returned my right hand to my back, the grip on my wrist no gentler than it had been.

Every solid inch of him stamped against my front. I managed to keep my eyelids from fluttering and the moan from escaping, but I could do nothing about the way my dick twitched like a dog lifting its nose to a pleasant smell in the air.

"Now I know that's not lip balm." Knox let his gaze drop low between our bodies so there was no mistaking what he was talking about.

Insufferable dick. It wasn't my fault there wasn't a lot of time for loving when you were being chased by mercenaries. At this point, a well-built filing cabinet would turn me on. I couldn't admit to any of that. I wouldn't give him the satisfaction of knowing he had any effect on me. This was a job to him.

I let my eyes go round—full doe mode—and peered up at him. I had to look up to see into his face anyway. I sucked only the corner of my bottom lip beneath my teeth. "Why are you so obsessed with me, Daddy?"

A growl rumbled through his chest. Fuck, I liked that more than I should, especially since I'd never met another person who could growl like Knox. The sound wasn't an angry man's approximation of a growl; it was real, deep, and sank into my bones.

"The hissing kitten finally wants to purr?" His strong jaw and sharp cheeks loomed closer. Knox had the type of face that always looked ready for a shave. He never had a beard, but I wouldn't call him clean-shaven. His cheeks were as rough as the rest of him.

"I can do more than purr—" The rest of my taunt dried in my throat the moment my brain pointed out how close Knox's face was, how close his lips were. He watched my eyes, occasionally glancing lower to my mouth. He was fucking with me, I knew that, but my stomach flipped all the same.

My body didn't care who was touching it, just that it was being touched.

His lips drew closer, filling each of my senses with him. His scent wasn't as much comforting as it was *wild*. When I inhaled, I pictured a huge dark cloud rolling ominously over a dark blue ocean. He smelled like a storm, but there was more to it. I detected a hint of leather and the sharp freshness of cut cedar. His wasn't a scent that came from a bottle, but from his life.

Instantly, I was curious about the version of Knox that wasn't chasing me. Where did he live that he smelled like this? What did he do there? Did the five of them live and work together? I had questions—a dangerous thing when coupled with my relentless curiosity.

But even my questions were silences as his lips hovered even closer. I could've stretched my head forward and bridged the gap, press my mouth against his.

Just because I could didn't mean I should. A kiss from *this* man would only make running away from him that much more difficult. Already, alarm bells sounded in my brain. The mission wasn't as much to get out of his grasp but to stop the kiss that would surely turn my life into a tailspin I wouldn't be able to pull out of.

I did the opposite of what my brain told me to do. Annoyingly, it was also what my body wanted. Those two jerks didn't see eye to eye when it came to Knox. I went loose, limp, and pliant. Knox's grip tightened to accommodate for the way I sagged into him. I licked my lips and angled my face higher, allowing Knox open access to my mouth.

For a split second, I thought I saw something flash in his gaze. Not mean or taunting, nor arrogant or domineering. Something *possessive*.

But the look was gone as quickly as it had come, and Knox's mouth inched closer. He'd loosed his grip on one wrist; that would have to be enough. I sighed into him, but the moment our lips should've touched, my knee collided with his groin.

He didn't let go as I'd hoped, but he grunted and jerked back, giving me enough room to duck under his arms. I spun my wrists, grimacing at the burn, but it was necessary to twist my arms so the narrowest part lined up directly behind his thumbs. I yanked like they'd explained to do on the self defense video I'd watched a few days ago.

Amazingly, it worked. My wrists slipped free, stinging from the force of his hold but my own to move as I liked.

He snarled and made a swipe for my waist. I jumped back, evading his grasp but also tucking myself further down the alley and away from the street. Unlike the alley a little farther down the sidewalk, this one didn't go all the way through. I was stuck. An angry, sexy beast stood between me and freedom.

Even now, tense and stiff with irritation, he made my insides quiver. I had a type: nice, fun-loving guys who weren't interested in anything that wasn't surface level. Knox wasn't a surface-level kind of guy. He was the type of man that would burrow under your skin and wrap himself around your bones.

He was hired to capture you.

Thankfully, my brain chose that moment to speak up before I did something stupidly insane, like fall back into his arms a second time.

Reaching into my pocket, I pulled out the sheet of paper, fashioned it into a gun behind my back, and stuck the barrel against my temple.

Knox froze, his hands outstretched. "That isn't real, brat," he growled, his nostrils flaring.

"Isn't it?" I found his gaze. "Are you certain?"

He may have been watching and figuring things about me, but he couldn't know everything. He couldn't know that while the gun was nothing but paper, it would smell like a real gun. If I pulled the trigger, it would sound like a real gun.

His uncertainty kept him from lunging forward, but he remained between me and the exit. "You'd never do it," he taunted. "You love your own pretty face too much."

That stung in an unusual way. He'd called my face pretty, which I enjoyed, but he'd also implied I was some sort of vapid kid. Little more than an unruly child throwing a tantrum.

I cocked the gun. The click of the hammer sliding into place was deafening in the muted alley. Something that looked like actual fear danced behind his eyes, gone in the next moment. My finger rested against the trigger. Though I knew the gun was fake—I'd made it— I'd begun to believe I could feel it against my head. A thrill of fear skittered up my spine.

"Do you want to risk it?" I asked softly. "Do you think you'll get paid by my father if you drop me off with a hole in my head?"

His entire body coiled like a spring poised to leap into action.

I stared him down, unsure of what I would do if he called my bluff. I wasn't in danger; he couldn't be one hundred percent sure of that. He would be next time, that was for sure. Every trick I used on Knox and his team, only ever worked once.

He'd made a decision, clear by the way Knox's body

relaxed. He stepped back, placing his hands against the wall.

I stumbled forward in my haste to get free. The gun to my head, his hands on my wrists, his scent in my head—I was disoriented by nothing but *him*. This day would be a lesson in nothing but how important it was that I keep my distance. Maybe I'd been toying with them a little, lingering these passed months mostly in the Portland area. I got attached and almost got caught because of it.

I didn't breathe as I crossed Knox. Nothing stopped him from reaching for me a second time except his uncertainty. He didn't move, though, and I made it to the mouth of the alley, peeking up and down the sidewalk before I planned my getaway route.

"Jazz." Knox let my name linger on his tongue.

Don't turn. Don't listen. Just go. You don't want to hear it.

That was what my brain thought. My body grabbed the corner of the building and lingered.

"Next time I see you, I want your hair back to how it was. And you put another gun to your head, conjured or not, and I'll paddle that ass."

2

KNOX

My cock throbbed watching the little flirt scamper out the mouth of the alley. I knew the gun hadn't been real and was reasonably positive pulling the trigger would've done nothing more than produce a loud sound, but seeing Jazz with that gun to his head had done something to me I wasn't prepared to face.

Not while standing in a rancid alley surrounded by the smells of urine and trash. We'd been chasing Jazz for months. How could any of us have suspected five mercenary alphas who had completed missions in the world's shittiest nations would have trouble picking up a twenty-three-year-old guy on his own?

You don't want to fail them again, that's all.

Sure, that's what I would tell myself. Our team could use a morale boost. We'd been running on less than empty for the past five years.

The comm in my ear opened. Faust's slow cadence filled my ear. "Can someone explain to me why I'm watching our mark run the opposite way? Knox, confirm, is the target secure?"

I growled out a curse. I'd failed them again today anyway. "Negative. Target is not secure."

The only reason the comms weren't cluttered with curses was because of training. The curses would come, and I would deserve them.

"We're throwing it in for now. I'm coming to get you."

When there was no confirmation, I barked, "Confirm."

"Affirmative." The crisp word was flung at me from four very irritated alphas.

I checked the perimeter, though it was unnecessary. In a place like this, we posed the greatest danger. As I stepped out onto the sidewalk, blending in with the flow of pedestrians, the tube of lip balm jostled in my pocket.

I gripped it, nearly snapping the plastic cylinder in two before ripping it from my pocket. The end smelled fruity and tropical, but it also smelled of Jazz.

His lips had glistened. Was this stuff why?

I pulled the cap off, bringing the wax to my nose. My cock pressed against the inside zipper, straining to get toward that scent. It had been a long time, for all of us, and Jazz's scent—rosemary, lemon, and warm vanilla—felt like a soft stroke up my length.

We'd never come as close to capturing the young man as we'd come today. I bit back the smile that always threatened my lips when I thought of Jazz.

I should've been nothing but irritated by his antics as the others clearly were. We'd signed up to apprehend a man's runaway son, not a nymph with magic powers. But the kid was damned impressive. He thought on his feet, and he was fast. Even without that magic trick of his, he would've been a difficult catch. I missed seeing his red hair today. I'd dreamed of his red curls, something I would never admit to the others. After first contact, that night, I'd dreamed of his soft thighs opening, guiding his hips down as his body swallowed my cock. He'd moaned with each upward thrust, his curls bouncing in time with our lovemaking.

I snarled and shoved the lip balm in my pocket while reminding myself of all the reasons that couldn't happen.

Punk, insufferable, cruel, and a little shit. Those been Jazz's father's exact words when describing his son. He'd claimed to be the over-indulgent father to a brat who had grown up with too much money. He'd told me Jazz had gotten in over his head, that he'd begun dabbling in the black market—specifically selling weapons to people he had no business interacting with. He'd painted himself as a well-meaning father who was just looking out for his son's best interest.

He was full of shit. But his lies didn't make sense. Anyone who spoke with Jazz for more than a few seconds could tell he wasn't cruel or insufferable. Naughty? Yes. But in a way that felt more like he was testing his limits than anything else.

I hated knowing only half a story. When I caught Jazz again, and I would, I'd just ask him before handing him over. He would have to go back eventually. Jazz's father had paid us half already, and once we secured Jazz and returned him, we'd get the other half and would finally have enough to devote all of our attention to what really mattered.

Faust waited for me at the Hummer. Dog sat at his side glaring at the pedestrians passing by. "What happened?"

I growled. I wasn't the original leader of our team. Mercenary work had been Pierce's idea. But he was dead now, and these guys needed someone to follow. "Nothing." I exhaled sharply. "He outsmarted me."

More accurately, he played chicken with something

apparently I cared more about than he did. I wasn't sure where the "paddle his ass" comment had come from, but I meant it. I never wanted to see Jazz with a gun against his head again.

We loaded up, and I flipped the Hummer around, going the opposite direction. At the stop light, the back doors opened, and the twins slid in on either side. Dog growled and jumped to the row behind him. He didn't share anything with anyone but Faust.

"What the fuck, Knox?" Jagger snarled while Huntley just stared. They weren't blood twins, but if it weren't for the scar running the width of Jagger's throat, telling them apart would be almost impossible. After so long together, they even smelled the same.

"He got away," I growled.

"Got away? Or did you let him go?" Huntley shot him a knowing look.

Maybe years ago, before everything that had happened, these men would've understood what I'd gone through. The terror I'd felt. I'd stared down the asshole of Satan himself and laughed, but I hadn't been able to outwit a kid nearly half my age. "I told you what happened."

On the night we lost not only our chosen team leader but our pack, homes, friends, and family, the five of us had survived, but only physically. Whatever spark in each of us that allowed a body to be more than muscle and instinct had died that night too.

Since then, vengeance propelled us. My thirst for revenge was the only thing that got me up some mornings. Then we took the job to find Jazz. What had started as a distraction and means to secure funds had become an obsession. But not one the others shared.

And if they thought I wasn't as devoted to finding who

was responsible for murdering our family, then they wouldn't follow me.

Things hadn't always been this way. Loyalty had once bound us. We'd been a brotherhood. Now, we were shells of our past selves.

Taking the exit out of the city, we drove under an overpass, and there was a thud on the roof. The tires vibrated, threatening to swerve out of control. I spun the wheel, yanking the Hummer into neutral until the tires rolled normally again.

"I told him to stop jumping on the Hummer," Faust snarled along with Dog.

The back door opened, filling the vehicle with turbulent wind as Diesel slid from the roof to the back seat while the Hummer sped down the highway.

I could've slowed down and made his time easier, but, as Faust had explained several times to him, he was going to bust the shocks if he kept up the habit.

"Tell me we're going back," Diesel snarled, ignoring the way Dog's lips curled to show him his teeth.

"We're going back." I needed to get Jazz's scent out of my head, and we all needed to concentrate on what was really important.

———

UNDER TWO HOURS LATER, I turned down the unmarked road toward our new home base. The way was paved, but the concrete had been so poorly maintained there were large, uneven cracks amid deep potholes.

The brush on either side was in serious need of a trim. Or a chainsaw. Thick blackberry bush stalks thwacked the windshield and sides, making Faust growl.

"Ruining the paint job," he muttered under his breath.

I'd see him out here in the next couple of days aggressively chopping down any bush that dared to hit the Hummer. To the rest of us, it was a means of transportation, but machines spoke to Faust on a level that none of us could match.

I took the final corner, revealing the angry Oregon coast in the distance as I pulled up to a crumbling water fountain. The fountain was in good shape compared to the enormous structure behind it. The sign out front was peeled, the wood mostly rotted, but the words Hotel Royal Paynes were still legible.

With four wings, over a hundred bedrooms, a ballroom, industrial kitchen, indoor pool, and original furnishings, the place had come as a steal. We'd burned anything too musty or ruined, cleaning and repairing the rest. Ninety percent of the building was still unlivable, but we had space to live and work, and all the rest of the building needed was some hard work and know-how.

Mr. Paynes had built the premier resort on the Northern Oregon coast decades ago on a tip from one of his financiers. He'd poured every penny into the place, believing he was getting in early on an economic boom that would triple his investment in the first year. But that boom never came to the quiet coastal city. Rockshell had less than a thousand residents, and this hotel slowly turned into the type of place teenagers dared their friends to go into.

"Home sweet trash hole," Huntley muttered. He and Jagger opened their doors at the same time.

The Hotel Royal Paynes was a trash hole, but I'd made the decision anticipating the building would offer the men a distraction. Nothing could replace our old pack. We'd lived isolated out of necessity but also preference. When Alpha

Carrier had died, there'd been six alphas poised to take the lead over the pack and fulfill the role of pack Alpha. Pierce had been the one to suggest mercenary work as a means of supporting our pack.

Adjusting to the sorts of jobs the rich paid the scary to perform in the night hadn't been easy for them all. Despite his massive size and scary appearance, Diesel'd had the hardest time adjusting. He'd once confessed that after coming back from each mission, Diesel needed to shower in scalding hot water for hours before he could hold his pretty boy—his pet name for his omega and mate. Technically unclaimed while Diesel had been waiting for his mate to be ready to make the step to omega, Quinlan had represented everything that was good in the world. He'd been a sweet human, adopted by our pack from infancy. He and Diesel had grown up knowing what their future held. That Diesel had been slow to violence, utilizing every other option first.

Diesel said nothing as he yanked his door open and got out. His irritation was palpable, each step sending out a shockwave of anger. As large as a bear, his long hair and beard hung in chunks over his tight, broad shoulders. He looked like a man of nightmares.

When Quinlan had died with the pack, so had everything warm and loving inside of Diesel.

"He's going to leave," Faust said with his head turned away and toward Diesel. "If we don't have a breakthrough soon, he's going to leave."

Diesel wouldn't last long on his own without an ounce of self-preservation.

"We have half the money. We have a nearly functioning headquarters, and we're amassing the equipment we need. We can start running the tests." We'd already done as much footwork as we could. Picking through the rubble of our home had taken the better part of a year. The five of us had buried every person we recovered, though many of the bodies had been too badly damaged for us to tell who was who.

The end result was the same. No one on pack lands could've survived the destruction. No one understood what could've caused so much damage in such a concentrated area.

That same week, we'd been in Columbia when a mission went wrong. Our leader, Pierce, had been killed entering first on location of our last mission. We'd been returning to pack lands to break the news of his death to our people...

I'd never forget that smell.

Faust got out without replying, whistling sharply for Dog to follow.

Before I knew what I was doing, I had Jazz's lip balm clenched in my palm. I balanced it on the dash, letting Jazz's essence fill my nostrils, anything to keep away the stench of death. I inhaled, exhaling harshly.

The team needed a win, and I'd let this Jazz thing get out of control. The next time we made an attempt to capture him, I would go alone. All the others wanted to do was pore over the reports from that night, review witness testimony by those who lived in the area. We'd read the reports already—had them memorized—but that didn't stop the others from examining each word, looking for a meaning that would break the case open. No one had missed the explosion. People said it had lit up the night, bringing hell on earth.

The type of work we did to support the pack had made us a few enemies—but none of them were responsible for that night. We'd checked—*thoroughly*. The guilty party was still out there, living, breathing, eating, drinking, *laughing*.

"I've seen your face when you say his name. Maybe the others don't recognize the look, but I do." Diesel stepped from the shadows near the entrance to the hotel.

"What are you talking about, Diesel?"

Most of Diesel's face was obscured by his scraggly hair, but what I could see of him was tortured. "You look at him the way I looked at Quinlan." Just saying his omega's name made him wince. He didn't speak it often—in front of other people.

My throat constricted. I needed to assure my packmate that our mission was still the same, but the words tasted like bile. I pushed them out anyway. "He's a job, Diesel."

Diesel growled. "Yeah, right. And that's just lip balm."

3

JAZZ

I should have left Portland.

I would.

But not tonight.

After my near disastrous run-in with Knox, I'd emerged on the other side certain of one thing.

I needed to get laid.

Thankfully, the process wasn't all that difficult. My twinkish shape and unruly red curls normally brought men to me. Not the other way around.

I shook out my hair, lifting my chin obstinately as I thought of Knox and how I'd nearly humped his leg like a dog. I'd gone back to my hotel that night and showered, watching the brown water stream down my skin. I hadn't washed the temporary color out because Knox told me to. I liked my red hair. It served as a warning.

It was still early when I took a seat at the bar. Later in the evening, there was a drag show planned, and I figured that was when this place would really pick up. No matter. I didn't need a large selection. I just needed a man with a dick who would let me forget about my troubles for a while.

Maybe it would have been smarter to leave town, find a new place to settle for a while and *then* get laid, but it would be easier this way. I'd be able to relax and stop looking over my shoulder. Mostly, I hoped a good dicking would knock Knox out of my head. When I closed my eyes, I saw him. His steely, piercing gaze, the rough line of his jaw, the way my fingers itched to touch the scruff at his cheeks.

He was pure sex, and I was desperately obsessed. I flipped a quarter between my fingers—an old nervous habit. Living on my own, I had a lot of down time, and a little phalangeal dexterity seemed like the perfect time waster. Coupled with my natural ability for small illusions, a little sleight of hand came in...well...handy.

"What can I get you?" the bartender asked with interest. He let his elbows rest on the bar top and he leaned in, bringing his face closer to mine. "What are you thirsty for?"

I forced a coy smile, not feeling all that responsive. I didn't know what was wrong with me. The bartender was cute in that "let's spend the dawn hours smoking, drinking, and talking philosophy" sort of way.

"Cosmo, please." I slid an actual twenty across the bar—this place was far too charming to belong to my father's blob of businesses—noticing a dark shadow over the money, cast by a figure that had appeared at my right.

My stomach flopped over. It was him. It was Knox. He'd come to—

I turned my face toward the other man with a blinding smile stretching my lips. I wasn't trying to be sexy; I was just stupidly happy that he was here.

Except the man at my side wasn't Knox.

My blood had gone carbonated, making my limbs feel light. Now, all that fizz flattened, and gravity weighed on me.

"Let me get that for you," he said, smoothly sliding my money back toward me.

I was here to get laid. This guy looked like he wanted to volunteer. I'd be stupid to refuse him, even if I wasn't feeling that same spark. If I was honest with myself, I'd admit that no one in the world had ignited a spark like Knox, but in this case, honesty was not the best policy.

Honesty would keep me hung up on a man who really didn't give two shits about me, unless his concern was about the money he'd be paid for a job completed.

"Thanks," I said softly. "I was wondering when I'd see a gentleman around here." That wasn't true. I hadn't been wondering that. Who wanted a gentleman when they could be fucked hard by a sex demon? My cock stirred, but not because of the guy next to me.

"You don't sound like you're from around here," the man said, taking the vacant seat next to me.

I brought the tart cocktail to my lips, swallowing my wince along with the burn. "I'm just passing through."

"And looking for a little fun?"

I had no problem cutting right to the heart of a matter. I was here for sex; I wouldn't feign innocence simply because he'd highlighted that fact. I swallowed down my unease, turning in the chair so I faced him. "If you're offering..."

"He isn't."

The voice that haunted my dreams for the past three days was right behind me. I spun on my stool along with the man beside me. We both had to look up to see into Knox's face. His brooding, unhappy face.

The carbonation returned, a response from my body that I had no control over. If I were smart, I'd cause a quick distraction and run. Instead, I sat there stunned along with my new friend.

"Excuse me..." The man looked from Knox to me. "You know this guy?" He pointed as if I could in any way be confused about which man he spoke about.

I should've answered him, but my heart felt like a racehorse seconds after hearing the crack of the starting pistol.

Holy balls, I wanted to leap on Knox just to see if he would catch me. Either way, I'd have more of my body plastered against his, which was my only goal.

You're a fucking idiot, Jazz. Stay away. Think of an escape.

Instead of saying any of that, I heard myself say, "I do."

Knox's eyebrows lifted infinitesimally. But, since the rest of his face was set in a perma-scowl, I noticed the fleeting expression. "This is the part where you leave," Knox said to my companion.

I wondered briefly what would happen if the man refused. I didn't want to see violence but was curious as to the lengths Knox would go—for a job. *Remember that, Jazz.*

The other man scooted his chair legs back, raising his hands in front of him. "I'm just here for company and drinks."

Knox didn't reply. He crossed his arms over his chest and waited.

"So I'll just go fuck off over here then." The guy picked his drink up and headed down toward the other side of the bar.

A few more people had shown up, and more would come the closer the bar got to its evening entertainment. My would-be lover would find someone else's arms to fall into tonight. And I would...

Probably not be getting laid.

I frowned, grasping my drink by the stem. "That was rude."

"Were you going to fuck him?" Knox asked, still standing like a dark cloud over my plans for the night.

I set my glass down, and Knox tensed.

"Keep your hands on the bar top, Jazz, where I can see them. And answer my question."

I left my right hand against the stem of my martini glass, my fingers caressing the narrowest section while I set my left palm down about a foot away. "Is this how you want me, Daddy?"

I'd been trying to tease him, but this time, the Daddy thing was ill-advised. My ass clenched against the seat, and I choked down a soft moan. What little alcohol I'd consumed was enough to loosen my limbs. My brain demanded I run—do something other than sit here and let myself be captured—but my body refused. According to that jerk, I'd come here to get laid, and the very man I wanted to sleep with was standing behind me.

Knox sat down, spinning the chair so he could see most of the room while looking at me. He hooked his left foot against the bar of his stool, creating a boundary wall with his bent leg. "I won't ask a third time."

Technically, that was him asking a third time, but I didn't point that out. I was too busy trying not to pant in his presence. I shrugged like I couldn't be bothered. "I don't know what we would've done. You made him leave before I could find that out."

Knox vibrated, his chest rumbling with a low noise that was like a feather stroking my dick. "Put down your drink. We're leaving."

I didn't think he was worried about hauling me over his shoulder and carrying me out. Even if I screamed bloody murder, I'd be concerned for the people around us, not Knox. Why tell me we're leaving then? Did he expect me to go willingly? Keeping my face down, I cast my eyes around the room, looking for an exit. The front door wasn't too far, but I was pretty sure there was a squeaky door in the back kitchens. If I could get over the bar—

"Don't try it, Jazz," Knox warned, his lips close to my earlobe. "This game ends tonight. It's just me here, but I won't stop until I have you." He leaned in closer, and the heat coming off his body brushed against my right side. "Run if you want. You're mine."

"How much?" I barked, so loudly a few people turned our way. The tables were really filling up now. The drag show was more popular of an attraction than I suspected. "How much is my father paying you?" I clarified at his blank look. I'd almost forgotten. Again. He hadn't meant I'd be *his*. He'd meant it more of a "I'll catch you" sort of way, but try telling that to anything on my body that was below the belt.

Knox frowned. "A considerable amount. He must really care for you."

I let the air in my lungs push out between my lips. "Pfft. He wants to lock me up and throw away the key. Can't make trouble that way."

My words didn't clear his frown. "We're dancing," he grunted, sliding off the stool and grabbing my hand.

"I don't feel like—"

Knox wasn't listening. He tugged me off my stool and toward the dance floor. I didn't know what sort of dancing Knox had planned. The music was upbeat, and I couldn't see him busting out any of the moves I saw on the dance floor now. I stretched my other arm back for my drink. I needed some liquid bravery to handle this man.

Knox grabbed my wrist before I could bring the cup to my lips. He shook his head slowly. "You don't need this shit."

"What? You don't drink?" A man like him? I'd believe him if he told me his mother's breast milk had been whiskey.

"I do. You don't need to." He pulled me closer, keeping one of my arms wrapped around his waist so I couldn't get my hands together. The slip of paper burned a hole in my pocket.

I could make everyone think it was a bat or a mouse. That might start a stampede for the door. But what if someone got hurt in that stampede? This place was too busy now for me to cause any sort of mayhem without endangering someone.

The second Knox pulled me into his arms, my brain short-circuited. He held me close. I couldn't lean back far enough to get my hands together between our bodies, and he was too muscular for me to clasp my hands together behind his body. At least, around the shoulders he was, and that was where he kept my arms, like two high schoolers, swaying at the first dance.

Except the gentle rocking motion Knox established didn't match the music in the slightest. He didn't seem all that concerned by that fact. He made the world how he wanted it and would likely invite anyone who had an issue with that to fuck off. "If you weren't running, you could go to school. Isn't there something you want to do with your life?"

If he thought he would somehow convince me that going back was the right choice, he should save his breath. "I won't go back," I said as firmly and clearly as possible.

His brow furrowed like this was unexpected news.

I leaned in, nose to nose. "I'll kill myself before I go back there."

Knox snarled loudly, jerking me closer. His hardness prodded my lower stomach, and I gasped.

Delicious tendrils of anticipation burst from the spot, lighting the rest of my body on fire.

"Why?" he seethed. "What does he do? Does he beat you?"

Did he sound like he hoped I would say yes? No, that was insane. I was only grasping at straws.

"No. He doesn't beat me." I lifted my chin. I wouldn't let this man or any other doubt the truth I knew in my heart.

"Then what, Jazz? Tell me why you won't. Give me a reason." His tone sounded pleading, but this man didn't plead.

I knew my answer wouldn't make sense to him. It never did to anyone. "The second I get home, he'll lock me up in a beautiful room with a television, computers, a gaming system, movies... Staff will bring my food—but they'll be the only people I ever see. I won't see my father again. He doesn't want me. And I don't mean we've grown apart. He's never wanted me. I'm just something to hide to him." I shook my head so hard my curls smacked my face. "I won't go back there. I won't go where I'm not wanted." I waited for him to say something mean, to tease me for not enjoying the type of life others might long for—kept like a cat no longer wanted.

I couldn't be locked up, though. Not in that house. Not with him. I didn't know how to explain it any better.

Knox pressed his forehead against mine and inhaled slowly. On his exhale, I found myself copying him. "You don't want to be caged," he whispered. "You've got too much fire to live within the same four walls."

What. The. Fuck.

No one had ever responded like that—understood exactly what I was trying to say. Most people, if this subject was broached at all, just looked at me like I was some rich snob.

Our feet had stopped moving a while ago. Knox gave up all pretense of dancing and held me close. I blinked rapidly, staring at his rugged face like it was the first time. This man was a living contradiction. Hard but soft. Gentle and rough. Mercenary... "Who are you?"

His steel-gray eyes burned with desire, and my heart did a cartwheel of joy. Until now, I couldn't be sure how much of his response was because of me and how much of it was because I was a body pressing against him. "I'm the man who's going to kiss you."

Then he did.

Holy jalapenos—he did. I didn't know a kiss could make a person *feel* this way. He wasn't just pressing his mouth against my mouth. His kiss sunk into my soul. I felt him all over, my skin coming alive, singing for more of his touch. His lips vibrated with the growl sounding low in his chest. The noise was inhuman but no less sexy because of it. He made the small hairs on my neck stand straight up, but not in fear. Every part of me strained for more of Knox's caress.

When he leaned back, I expected the spell to be broken, but he peered down at me with gentle eyes. "I like your hair." His whisper danced over my cheek.

I did it for you.

There, I said it. Maybe not out loud, but I admitted to it in my mind, and that felt just as dangerous. *He will leave you the second he has his money.* His earlier protests ignored, my brain was brutal now, desperate to get through to me.

"Okay, everyone, it's the time you've all been waiting for! Crowd in, fight your neighbor for the best seat in the house, and prepare to have your balls blown off!" Dressed in a floor-length, red sequin gown, the queen at the mic thrust her hands out on either side of her in a sweeping display of jazz hands.

The people inside surged forward, crowding the spot where we'd been dancing.

Knox scowled, but not even he could quell the excitement of drag queens giving it their all on the stage. It was like watching a herd of antelope surround a lion, while paying it no attention at all.

Bodies bumped into us, and I took advantage of the hustle, slipping my hand into the loosest pocket. I snagged a leather wallet as Knox spoke over the heads of those around us. "Grab my hand, Jazz. I'll lead us out. Don't be stupid."

Stupid? Stupid was listening to a single thing this man said. Stupid was mistaking how horny he made me with proof that I could trust him. I'd already been stupid. Now I was being smart. I nodded, pressing the wallet between my hands before sliding it into Knox's waiting palm.

He squeezed his fingers around the wallet, feeling my four fingers, my thumb. I even added a little illusion of weight so it felt like I tugged at him. Unlike sight, smell, and sound, conjuring weight and movement never lasted longer than a few moments. It was long enough. Knox stepped in one direction, leading my wallet hand, and I took off in the other.

The trick lasted for seconds before Knox figured me out, but by then, I was already several feet away from him, winding through a crowd the way only a man my size could. Knox was a boulder, manually forcing the flow of people to divert around him. But I was a pebble, and I slipped outside before Knox was halfway to me. I heard him yell something, but I wasn't going to ask him to repeat it. I turned and ran down the city street in the direction of my hotel. I believed

Knox when he said he wouldn't stop chasing me, which meant I needed to run now.

Had Knox figured out where I was staying? Portland was home to several hotel chains owned by my father, but there were still only so many. Even if he knew, I'd get there before him. I'd grab what I could and run out the fire escape if I had to.

So deep in my plan of escape, I didn't notice the street I'd used to get to the bar had since cleared out. Before, there had been lots of other people walking around, working in the office buildings on either side. Now, it was just me.

I kept running. If Knox didn't get me, then I had no need to fear anything on this street. At about a block from my hotel, my foot snagged over something on the sidewalk, and I fell forward, slamming my chin into the pavement before I rolled to a stop.

I groaned, relatively certain I hadn't broken anything but needing to stretch my limbs out slowly just in case.

"Get up," a harsh voice demanded.

That wasn't Knox. It wasn't any voice I'd heard...and yet...

"Get on your fucking feet," the man snarled.

I jerked my head toward him, my angry retort stuck to my tongue as I spotted the lethal gleam of a knife. My mind blanked, and all the fight whooshed from me. This wasn't a piece of paper or a rock disguised as a knife. This was an actual implement of pain that he would use to hurt me. And apparently, I was a big fucking baby because my tongue twisted in to a hundred knots, and my spine felt like the consistency of foam.

All my gusto, all my bravery, it all leaked from me like air from a tire. I sank down to the sidewalk, though I was already on the ground. I made a squeaking noise, wishing I could make my hands stop shaking long enough to do something. It was just my luck to run from the frying pan and into a fire. Who else could possibly run from a kidnapper straight into the arms of a mugger?

The man jerked at my elbow in an attempt to get me to stand, but I was dead weight. The knife jostled in his other hand, slipping forward to cut my forearm. Blinding white pain made me scream, but the man didn't care. He tugged at my injured arm, sending more pain up my arm as I bled all over the sidewalk.

"Your father—"

I never found out what this person had to say about my father. He yelped first and slumped to his knees. I couldn't even manage to slide back on the sidewalk. My muscles were too frozen with fear. He yelped again, and that time I heard a whistle, the force of impact. Blood blossomed on the man's shirt from both his shoulders.

Knox towered over the fallen man, a throwing dagger in his hand with three more glinting at his belt. I cradled my head in my hands, rocking as my arm bled, staining my shirt.

When Knox leaned over to touch me, I screamed. He ignored it and pulled me to my feet, stretching my arm out slowly to assess the damage. "He hurt you," Knox growled, turning away long enough to kick the man groaning on the ground.

I didn't understand what was going on. I understood the fear; I was a baby. I ran not because I was good at it, but because I had to. I wouldn't last a second in a fight, and when the chips were down, I didn't rise to the occasion either. I folded.

"I have you. You're safe." Knox offered me warmth in his arms. I leaned into it, letting his strength seep into me. "You're safe," he soothed, rubbing my back.

I heard a click the moment before I felt cool metal at my wrist. My head jerked down to the handcuffs Knox had put me in.

"Please, don't—" Had I thought he would do anything else? Hold me? Comfort me? Tell me everything would be okay? Why? He only wanted the money. He needed to turn me in to get the money. I knew that. And yet, my heart still broke when he pulled out a syringe and a small vial filled with clear liquid.

The safety I'd felt vanished. Knox loomed over me like a beast, his face transformed into something I'd see in my nightmares. "You're a monster," I mumbled, my bottom lip shaking.

Knox said nothing as he filled the syringe.

"I'll do anything," I begged. "I'll double what he's paying you. Knox!" I meant to scream, but I didn't have the air left in me.

Nothing would change Knox's mind anyway. He pressed the needle to my skin and pushed down.

As my sight went dark, a tear slid down my face.

Knox wiped it away, holding me as the drug took hold. "I'm sorry, kid."

4

KNOX

JAZZ SLEPT ON HIS BACK, though the number of times he'd tried to roll, I assumed he preferred sleeping on his side. He would look cute like that, snuggled up with his arms drawn close.

His arms were up above his head now, cuffed to either side of the headboard with his fingers wrapped together on each hand with an elastic bandage. I'd bandaged the cut on his arm—not so deep it needed stitches. The sedative should've been completely out of his system. I hadn't liked administering it while he'd been so upset. He'd cried in my arms, and I could do nothing to fix it because I was the asshole who'd made him cry.

Now, I had four other assholes shouting at me about how I hadn't taken Jazz immediately to the drop-off site.

That hadn't been a random mugger Jazz had run into. They were too close to Jazz's hotel. The man had acted too quickly. I wasn't more than a few blocks behind Jazz, but by the time I'd gotten to him, he'd already been on the ground bleeding.

My blades should've gone through the fucker's throat

instead of only wounding him and cuffing him to an exposed pipe.

He'd known Jazz was staying there. He'd known, waited, and would've done much worse to my boy had I not gotten there.

I frowned at my choice of phrasing. Jazz couldn't be my boy. Not only was he our ticket to being able to concentrate fully on investigation and research, but my heart had hardened about the time I'd buried the last of the bodies of our old pack.

What little consideration left in me was spent on my team. I didn't have any more room to care.

But room or not, the pretty man sleeping peacefully was a mystery. How could he do what he did? His abilities reminded me of those mates, the ones who lived with Faust's friend—Nash.

I'd ask Faust to contact him, but not until Jazz woke up. He'd been so afraid, so heartbroken. I needed to see his face. And ask him a few questions.

His father was a fucking liar. I knew that much already. He'd painted Jazz out to be a troublemaker who didn't care who he hurt. But Jazz had frozen with real fear at that knife. That reaction hadn't been the reaction of man steeped in violence.

The redheaded angel sleeping in my bed wasn't a hardened criminal. He was wild, but in a way that needed to be cared for and guided. I'd started chasing Jazz for the money, but something wasn't adding up, and I was beginning to feel like a pawn.

I loathed that feeling.

Jazz turned his head, trying again to roll to his side. The movement brought a wave of curls against his forehead, and I reached forward as if by instinct to brush them aside.

Jazz's eyes opened—not slowly as he carefully woke, but suddenly. He gasped, the air sounding painful as he dragged it down his throat. His hands were fists, and he pulled at his restraints like he didn't care how the metal links dug into his wrists. He kicked his legs out, slamming his heel against the side of my head before I wrangled his limbs down.

"Get off me! Don't fucking touch me!" he snarled, his breaths coming in panicked heaves.

"Jazz, breathe, Jazz. You're safe—"

"Knox?" Jazz blinked repeatedly, looking around the room like he was seeing it for the first time. "I thought...the last thing I remembered was you taking me back to my father."

And thinking he was waking up in his father's home had made Jazz react that way? I couldn't say I loved that tidbit of knowledge.

"You're not. You're with me still."

Jazz's eyes narrowed with suspicion and distrust. In all the time I'd spent chasing after him, he'd never looked at me like that. "Why?" he spat.

I deserved that ire. He'd been afraid and crying, and I'd shot him up. The least I could do now was tell him the truth. "Because your father lied to me, and I need to know why."

Jazz rolled his eyes, and I squeezed my fists to keep from cupping his face and kissing away every ounce of disrespect. "He lied because he's a liar. There, your questions are answered."

I cocked my head to the side. My boy was trying to look brave despite his position. Only Jazz could be tied up but still haughty. "Why? Why lie about that stuff? Especially when a single conversation reveals his deception?"

Jazz scoffed. "He didn't hire you to talk to me."

So Jazz's father thought I might never realize he'd lied about the type of guy Jazz was?

"I mean, the quality of the men he's sent before you..."

It shouldn't have come as a shock hearing Jazz had been running from people trying to capture him for a while. "How did you get away?"

Jazz smiled. One side of his upper lip rose a little higher than the other giving his grin a cocky edge. "They never got close. None of them. I got stupid." He lifted his gaze, finding my eyes. "I won't be stupid again. Drop me off. I don't care. I'll get out, or I'll die trying."

My gut clenched, and I sprang forward, cupping Jazz's cheek as I'd wanted to. "Stop saying that."

His nostrils flared and his chin jutted out obstinately. "I have to pee."

It was likely he did. He'd been out for hours. He was probably hungry and thirsty too. I fished the cuff key from my pocket and unhooked his left hand first, then the right. When I cuffed his hands together—fingers still bound— behind his back, he tried to jerk free.

"What are you doing? I have to pee. That requires hands."

"I know." I led him to the bathroom. My room was on the second floor of the hotel. In its heyday, it was probably an expensive suite. We'd only gotten the plumbing going in a few spots in the old building, but my bathroom was one of those spots.

I flipped on the light. The sight of the toilet made Jazz dig his heels into the floor. "What do you expect me to do? Hang it over the bowl like a carnival game? What happens if I reach the top first? Do I get a prize?"

"No," I grunted, fighting to keep my lips from curving.

"The situation should be clear. You are trouble. You are more trouble when you have use of your hands." I jiggled the chain linking his cuffs. "Now, you're less trouble."

"You can't mean—?"

"You wanted to be slippery and force me to chase you for weeks. This is the repercussion."

"You're punishing me?" Jazz yelled indigently.

"If I was punishing you, you wouldn't have to ask to make sure. I'm allowing you to accept the consequences of your actions. I can't trust you. Until you show me I can trust you, your hands stay cuffed. Now do you want to go or not?"

Jazz's face drooped into a pout. His bottom lip swelled as he stuck it out. He was adorable.

And he was pissed.

"Ugh, fine," he grunted, turning back to the toilet.

I let him step away, and he waited, looking sharply over his shoulder.

He was impatient too.

"Come on, hurry. I really have to go." He punctuated his whine with sharp jerks of his body that were very tantrum-esque.

This sort of behavior should not be rewarded, but he had been out for a while. I took position behind him and reached around his waist.

Jazz gasped. "Wh-what are you doing?"

"You do want your dick out of your pants before you piss, don't you?"

Jazz forced out a laugh. "Oh, right. Yes. I forgot. Okay, I'm ready."

Jazz took a deep breath that I didn't all the way understand, but the poor guy had waited long enough. I made quick work with the button and zipper. I forced every unappealing memory to my mind, picturing horrible, gruesome scenes we'd stumbled upon in the field.

"Okay," Jazz whispered. "I'm done."

I tried picturing the most heinous, gut-wrenching missions a second time, but it was no use. There wasn't a memory horrible enough to eclipse the fact that I held his dick in my hand.

"They say, if you shake it more than twice, you're just playing with...me," Jazz murmured, the corner of his mouth twitching in a lightning-fast grin.

He grew hard in my hand. I'd had time to tuck him back, zip him up, but I didn't. Instead, I held on as his cock came alive, filling my palm with lusty intent. He curved his spine, jutting his ass back against my dick.

"Admit it, this had nothing to do with repercussions. You only did this so you could put your hands down my pants," Jazz purred, his voice throaty and deep while he rotated his ass over my erection.

My erection twitched against his ass. "No, brat. What else am I supposed to do when I hold such a naughty boy's pretty dick? Any man would get hard."

Jazz gasped, such a sweet, soft sound.

I laughed, wishing I could have watched his face when he'd made that sound. I wanted to see his expression light up with something that wasn't just a shield. I wanted to see Jazz's true face.

My wish was answered. Jazz turned his head, giving me his profile as he grinned. "What happens if I ask for a shower?"

Oh, my boy plays with fire. How couldn't he know how much I wanted him or how desperately my dick strained to get to him? "Try it."

My lips brushed against the shell of his ear, sending a visible shiver down his spine.

I teetered on the edge of control, too close to simply tearing his pants off and claiming him against the bathroom wall to be trusted. "C'mon."

I tugged him to the sink, pinning him between my body and the porcelain as I washed my hands. Concentrating on the familiar action allowed me to block the fact that my dick throbbed, salivating to sink deep inside the luscious ass directly in front of me. Drying quickly, I brought him back to the bed, choosing not to cuff his arms to the headboard again and instead letting him hold them cuffed in front of his body. His fingers were bandaged. Any time I'd been able to study him using his ability, he'd needed to *wrap* an item in his hands. It hadn't mattered if he could grasp all the way around the thing, only that he held it with both hands.

Jazz sighed loudly. "What am I doing here, Knox? I'm pretty sure my father wouldn't meet you in a place this...in need of care, and the money is the only reason I'm here right now. So...why am I *here* right now?"

"Because you don't add up. And I don't like things that don't add up."

Jazz nodded, his entire affect heavier than just five minutes ago. "So, when you soothe your inner accountant, you'll send me to my father?"

Fuck no. I jerked back from the sudden vehemence his question ripped from me, dragging a deep growl with it.

Jazz narrowed his eyes. He couldn't know we were shifters, but he had to know we were *something*. Then again, so was he. His father hadn't mentioned his ability explicitly. Only that he was *hard to get a hold of*.

"Maybe. I won't know until I get there." That was a

prick response, but there were too many variables still in play for me to give him a nicer answer. I wouldn't lie.

Betrayal flashed in his pretty brown eyes. "Thank you for your honesty." Jazz turned away, rolling to lay on his side, facing the other direction.

I hated the feeling swelling in my chest. My inaction grated at me, but there was what I wanted to do and what I needed to do to keep our team together. I couldn't do what I wanted—what my every instinct demanded. "I'll get you food," I murmured like a coward before stepping out and locking the door.

I spotted Dog from down the hallway. He sat in the kitchen with his back against the wall like a sentry keeping watch. He still felt a little ashamed over falling for Jazz's fake cat. His one ear stuck straight up. He had hearing in both ears but had lost part of the right in a dog fight when he was a puppy. Spotting me, he barked once, sharply.

I walked into the kitchen, finding Faust on his hands and knees. "Do I want to know?"

Faust may have had a love for machines, but when he got bored, he *tinkered*. It was never good when Faust tinkered. "I'm not pulling anything apart," he responded dryly. "I think we have rats or mice. I keep finding shreds of paper."

I shot an accusing glare to Dog, who growled to let me know what he thought of being blamed.

"This old place definitely has rats, but why are you on your knees?"

Faust leaned back, pulling himself out from under the sink. Balancing on the balls of his feet, he shrugged. "I thought I heard one."

We were all alpha wolf shifters accustomed to a life of grueling work that had tested our physical and mental limits. We all hadn't had as difficult a time as Diesel adapting to our new way of life, either. The twins had taken to mercenary work like ducks to water. Considering their rough starts to life, it made sense. Those two had a lot of internal rage, and, since the attack, it constantly simmered just below the surface.

None of these men could adapt well to a life of sitting around and waiting. "I need you to do something for me," I said, waiting for Faust to stand before continuing. "Your pal, Nash, his mate and the other mates—they can do stuff, right? Stuff like what Jazz can do?"

"Yeah, I'd asked him for tips on how to deal with the extra abilities, and he refused to tell me. Said he'd been sworn to secrecy."

I could only imagine one person who would've done that, but I couldn't fault him. He was a good friend to Jazz, and that was enough to make me smile.

"Knox?" Faust frowned, my happiness such an unexpected thing it alarmed him.

Dog barked twice, and I looked to the hallway. Dog wouldn't bark for no reason. He stood at attention, his eyes never wavering from the hallway I'd come down.

Fuck.

I tore out of the kitchen, sprinting down the hallway where I unlocked my door.

I yanked the door open, stomping closer to the mattress. The *empty* mattress.

It didn't take long to piece together what had happened. The chair I used at my desk had been moved directly under the air vent. Jazz must have stood on top and pried the vent open some how. I growled as a rich, coppery scent hit my nose. Blood.

Searching the rectangular opening, I spotted a dark red

smear on two of the corners. Jazz had hurt himself opening this vent, and now he was somewhere in the ducts.

He wouldn't find a way out of that dusty maze, but he could explore farther than we'd repaired and severely injure himself. He needed to be found.

"Faust! Diesel! Huntley! Jagger!" My team assembled, coming from scattered corners of the hotel.

"Let me guess," Huntley drawled. "You lost him."

I growled loudly, and Huntley took a sharp step back. I needed to calm down. My team didn't deserve my ire.

And I *had* lost him.

"He's in the vents. If he takes a wrong turn, the whole thing could give out from under him. Diesel, I want you to take the east wing—"

"When I find him," Diesel rumbled darkly. "Do we turn him in or kill him to be rid of the trouble?"

My fist lashed out, colliding with Diesel's face. Though the punch had cracked the bridge of his nose, I hadn't hit him hard enough. Yet.

Faust dove toward me, squeezing his arms around my middle as he kept me from charging forward. Huntley had Diesel in a similar hold, while Jagger stood in the middle acting as backup.

"Is this it? You choose that fucking guy over us? Your team?" Diesel yelled over Huntley's head. The man was a juggernaut. If he'd wanted through Huntley, he could've gotten through.

That meant he wasn't lost. Not yet.

I shook out of Faust's hold, making eye contact so he knew I had better control of the rage that still burned. "I'm not choosing anything. I simply can't recall when we decided threatening those weaker than us was something we do now." Yes, we'd done seedy, shady shit, but we were selective and only ever took jobs against those who deserved it. We'd never taken an innocent life and had saved countless.

Diesel sagged over Huntley's shoulders. His face turned gray, and he looked to the ground. "I'll take the east corridor," he mumbled, leaving immediately after.

I watched him go, still seething from the threat. This was wasted time, though. Our disagreement took moments that could've been spent searching for Jazz. "Anyone else have a question?"

I cast my gaze onto the others. Faust shook his head, while the others shrugged.

"Then move! I don't care what he makes you think you see—we need to find him now."

Huntley and Jagger shifted, taking off down the hallway, barking and snarling like two hounds of hell.

Faust clapped me on the shoulder before heading out silently, Dog on his heels.

I started at the bedroom, tracking the venting to where it split in a Y in the corridor. The right side had a bulge on the outside, likely a dent on the inside from where someone had set their knee down. I stalked down the right side, keeping my eyes up as I ran.

His scent was sweet, like lemons in the sun, and it made my nose tingle. I fought a driving desire to find him simply so I could bury my nose in those curls.

I stood at another split in the ducts. The venting sagged where it branched. If Jazz had made it down this way, he was lucky he hadn't crashed through in that spot. While searching the surrounding ceiling for clues, the twins tore down the corridor from the west.

Jagger tossed his wide wolf head, pointing toward the duct above me with his muzzle.

Jazz's scent grew stronger. At the same time, it sounded like a bowling ball was attempting to crawl rapidly down the vet.

My gut clenched. Jazz was fleeing now. He knew he was being chased, and he was afraid. That meant he wouldn't be as cautious as he'd been the first time.

Tracking his movement, I made sure to remain directly under him until he reached the split. The ducts shook and creaked before finally giving away, throwing huge clouds of dust and plaster into the air. The venting turned into a tube, depositing Jazz in my arms, kicking and screaming.

"Your dogs are a menace!" he snarled. Huge clumps of dust and webbing clung to his curls. His hands, still hand-cuffed and bound at his front, bled from where he'd torn his fingernails. "Let go of me! Let me go!" Jazz screamed.

I hauled the pint-sized menace over my shoulder and let my hand fall once over his ass.

My palm stung, and Jazz stilled instantly.

He'd put himself in danger. He'd caused unease in our team. There was a laundry list of reasons why Jazz needed a solid spanking—more than just the one. He'd probably never been appropriately disciplined in his life. But the moment my palm had collided with his cheeks and the sting had spread, Jazz hadn't fought or called me names—he'd *moaned*.

5

JAZZ

I wiggled, trying to find a way to sit on the chair that didn't remind me of what had happened in the hallway.

Or how I'd reacted to it.

It was too much to hope Knox hadn't heard my moan. The sound had come out of me at a time I hadn't known to safeguard against it. I still didn't understand it.

My elbows dug into the desktop while Knox made me sit with my hands up. He'd uncuffed my hands, but since I'd *proven he couldn't trust me*—his asshole words, not mine—he now resorted to new measures.

He tore off the strip of duct tape from the roll with his teeth, flattening the end of the strip around the kitchen mitt covering my hand, wrist, and part of my forearm.

"These are going to get wet," I whined. I was already caught, in pain from my most recent escape attempt, and likely headed for my father's house, where he'd lock me up and throw away the key. I deserved a little whine time.

Knox paused to growl at the bandages on my face and arms. "When you can't wear the mittens, you'll wear a spreader."

I frowned. He couldn't mean like what I thought he meant. A spreader? Like, a BDSM thing? I looked at Knox for a long time. If I were only given a handful of words to describe the man, scary and terrifying would be high on the list, but so would rugged and handsome. Who was Knox when he wasn't chasing after me? What did he do? Chase after other men?

I bristled at the idea and tugged my mittened hand from his grasp. "I won't let you put something on me that you've used to fuck other people," I snarled.

Knox didn't respond. Instead, he lifted me from the chair, spread me awkwardly over his lap, and spanked me five times in quick succession before sitting me back in the chair.

Fuck, that hurt. But it didn't *only* hurt. His hand on my ass made me feel other things too, even while the heat of his spanks blossomed over my skin. I exhaled shakily—still an embarrassing noise, but better than a moan.

"You need to ask questions before you jump to conclusions," Knox murmured. I had to be imagining the way his breath shook as well.

He looked like a brick wall, immovable, unchangeable, but was I affecting him? I had in the bathroom. His dick had sprung up, letting me know exactly what I would miss out on. And I'd be missing out on *a lot*.

"Okay, how many other people have you fucked using it?" There, that was a question. One with an answer that really wasn't my business. If he thought I'd let him use something he'd used on hundreds of others—

"None, brat. I had Faust weld it for you."

On cue, there was a sharp knock on the door, and Faust stepped in. He held a thin metal bar with two rings that had been welded to either end. "This'll do the trick."

He swung the pole around so he held it vertically, the other end braced against the mattress. "Unbreakable—at least, for the purposes you have planned. Wide enough to keep the wearer out of any tight holes and ribbed for his pleasure."

Knox growled at his partner's joke, but I grinned. It was funny. And now that I knew this wasn't some sexual hand-me-down, I supposed there were worse ways of being restrained. I'd prefer the bars to the kitchen mitts. I couldn't do anything with these things covering my hands.

Seeing my grin only made Knox growl louder. "Nothing needs to be ribbed," he snarled, but he sounded so aghast, neither Faust nor myself could keep from laughing more.

"I'll leave you to...whatever this is." Faust gestured weakly at my hands, the second mitt waiting to be secured and the rolls of tape—duct tape and medical grade—surrounding us.

"Good," Knox snarled.

Faust shut the door with a smirk.

I slumped over the desk, leaning my weight on my elbows. "You two are really cute together."

Knox scowled, but for half a second, it looked like he was fighting to hold it. He silently wrapped my other hand, checking the cuts he'd already bandaged before sliding the mitt on. "You'll wear these most of the time and the spreader when your hands need to air out."

Hearing him plan how I'd be restrained throughout the day didn't fill me with as much anger as I thought it should. Perhaps because it was Knox and I was already an idiot when it came to him. None of my responses were what they should've been. "Awful lot of trouble to go through just so you can satisfy your curiosity."

"It's for your own good, brat."

That was rich. Being tied up, unable to use my hands even to go pee—that was for *my* good? "How so?"

Knox sighed, leaning back to survey his work. I lifted my elbows, waving my hands around in front of me. They felt weird, and I wouldn't be able to use them to do a single thing, but it was nice to be able to move my arms around however I wanted. "We made a deal. Half up-front, half when we deliver you."

Was he trying to tell me he was bound by a stellar work ethic? "This sounds like an awful lot of trouble for some money. I can pay you. Whatever he offered. I'll double."

Knox shook his head. "No, brat. I don't want a stack of cash that will turn into rocks hours later."

I shut my mouth with a smile. Was it fair for him to be smart and sexy? I didn't want for money in my life, but not because I had any of it. "What do you need the money for anyway?"

"Not your business," he grumped, cleaning up the mess he'd made from the desk. "But if I have to explain to the guys that not only are we not getting paid for the foreseeable future, but they have to share their home with a boy who can't behave, they are going to have a lot of questions. I hate questions." He said the word questions like it meant something violent.

I'd been fixating on his use of the word *foreseeable*. Did that mean he wasn't planning on sending me back now? But that it could change? Or that he hadn't made his choice yet? I knew enough that I didn't think I was in immediate danger, which allowed me to relax—at least when it came to worrying I'd be hauled off at any second.

"Well, if I'm going to be staying here while you figure things out. I'm gonna need my stuff. I don't suppose you checked me out of my hotel room?"

Knox glared.

"I need clothes. And lotion. The air here is making my elbows chapped. And I wouldn't say no to a nice body wash, a hair mask." I got distracted listing the items I wished I had at that moment. I hadn't left anything behind that I couldn't replace, so I didn't need to worry about losing anything sentimental. I didn't have anything sentimental. My stomach growled, and I paused, waiting for Knox's reply. "What if I prom—"

Knox pressed his index finger against my lips. "Stop saying that word, I don't think you know what it means."

My mouth curved before he could remove his finger.

He ripped his finger from my lips like I'd burned him. "I'll get you food. You, stay."

I wouldn't be trying for the vent again. Even if I hadn't been neutered, the passage had been tight and full of so many spiders I was still sure they covered me. "Yes, sir." I gave a salute that likely looked ridiculous, given my puffy hand. "Do you have any pizza?" I called out as he left.

He shook his head, but I wasn't sure if he was answering me or just that exasperated.

When he returned, he had a bottle of water and an apple. "We don't have a lot in the kitchen. Mostly we hunt for our meals." He spoke as close to mumbling as I'd ever heard him.

I leapt off the bed, reaching for the water bottle before noticing my hands.

Knox's eyes flared, tightening as he realized the same thing I had. Knox would have to feed me. He recovered quickly, cracking the lid and spinning it off the top of the bottle before he put the spout to my lips.

I kept my mouth open and waiting, moaning when the cool water hit my tongue.

He set the bottle down, looking from my mouth to the apple before he reached for his waist, sliding out the gleaming handle of a dagger.

I flinched from the sight, but Knox kept his movements slow. "I forgot that you..." He gestured absently with his forehead to the knife and then me.

Was he trying to bring up my massively embarrassing moment of panic from before? When I'd spotted that man's knife and froze?

He quickly peeled and then sliced the apple into smaller chunks, wiping his blade on his pant leg before sliding it out of sight. He set the first bite-sized chunk at the front of my mouth, and I chewed slowly.

"Thanks," I whispered, hoping he would know I wasn't thanking him for the apple. He could have been cruel or arrogant, but he'd noticed I was afraid and did something about it.

No one had ever protected me like that.

When I'd had as much as I wanted, he wiped my face and then washed his hands. "That wasn't enough food. I'll get you more in a bit. Don't worry."

I grinned, keeping my face down and away so he wouldn't see it. "I wasn't worried."

Knox's stare burned into my cheek. I met his gaze, my eyes watering from the intensity of his gaze. I looked away quickly, feeling as if I'd seen into something I wasn't meant to. "You'll eat more food. I'll send one of the guys out."

He sounded so serious, I didn't even try to say something funny back. I just nodded as he grabbed my mitt. He led me out of his room and down a long corridor that stretched in both directions. At one time, this place must've been beautiful. Now, the wallpaper peeled, and the hardwood trim was rotted, but it wasn't hard to see the elegant floral pattern and gleaming wood they'd once flaunted.

Though gorgeous, the place held a constant musty smell, making me think we were near water. I coupled that observation with the way Knox had always smelled of the sea and determined we were near the ocean. Just call me Detective Jazz. But Portland wasn't that far from the beach, and at that point, there was the entire coastal border to consider. I'd been knocked out during the trip here. If I knew how long we'd traveled, I'd be in much better shape.

"You're on the North Coast, Oregon," Knox told me.

I lifted my chin because I'd been found out, and that made me a tiny bit embarrassed. "Why tell me? Aren't worried about me escaping?"

"Nope," he replied arrogantly. "You broke out of my room last time. You were nowhere near escaping. We would have caught you no matter what."

"Wow, dick much?"

Knox tugged on one of my curls, giving me vague grade school flashbacks. But I hadn't gone to grade school. And none of my tutors had made me feel like *this*—and thank goodness. That would've been so wrong. So, so, so wrong.

With each *so* my chin felt heavier, bringing my gaze lower and lower down Knox's body.

He wore the type of clothes you didn't notice until you made it a point to look at them. His olive green utility pants were tapered where they met the top of a black combat boot —no surprise there. His pants hung at his hips with a belt that had no right to look so complicated. After all that, his simple black t-shirt might have been boring, if it weren't for the chiseled edges of his muscular chest and arms.

Knox cleared his throat, and my gaze shot up to his knowing gaze.

At least he hadn't caught me staring at his crotch; that had been only a few seconds ago.

He turned a corner, reminding me I hadn't been paying attention to the route as much as I'd been paying attention to the fine way Knox filled out those—

"I'll just open a window," Faust said loudly, alerting me to the fact Knox and I were no longer alone.

The new room was interesting enough to drag my attention from Knox's body. Shaped like a half circle, I faced a sloping wall of windows that stretched the length of the wall to my front. Some were broken and boarded while others were cracked, but enough windows were still intact to show off the spectacular ocean view. They weren't just near the sea; they were almost in it.

The rest of the room wasn't as impressive but was clearly a work in progress. Old tables and chairs were stacked in one corner, many of them in disrepair. In the center, they'd pushed together a string of folding tables, creating a central space that held several computers and surveillance monitors. Several of the monitors looked like they were recording spaces inside or just outside the building we were in, but a few of the other screens showed locations I couldn't place.

Faust, returning from the window he'd cracked open, stepped in front of the screens, blocking most of them from my view.

The other two, Huntley and Jagger, sat in the corner. One had their feet propped up on the table, while the other had his head bent over a stack of black-and-white photos.

Curiosity brought me closer, but before I got close enough to see the picture clearly, Knox tugged me back. "You'll sit here."

He plopped me down in the corner, out of the thick of it

but in a chair that was more comfortable than all the other chairs looked.

"Has the report come in yet?" Knox asked Faust.

"I expect it any minute."

I made eye contact with the dog from across the room. I smiled. The dog turned his head and sighed. "What's your dog's name?"

Faust jerked his head from his dog to me. "Dog."

Well, okay, Things were going to be like that then.

Dog met my gaze again. I offered him a hopeful smile this time. He'd tried to bite me before but perhaps now we'd bond. We were both beasts, both kept collared by a man claiming to be their master.

Knox hadn't *actually* claimed to be my master, but he certainly was bossy. I also didn't have a collar, or a leash... and now why did I want one? I shook my head like that would knock loose the hedonistic thoughts. There was no use. I couldn't think of Knox for any length of time and not have the thoughts turn to sex.

While the others talked, I took in the room. The wood molding was mostly crumbling, but there were random strips of gold. With this view, decorated in gold, this room must've been a sight. "Where did this place come from? Why was it abandoned?"

"It's a hotel," Huntley grunted.

"Yes, but where did everyone go? Is this *The Shining*?"

Faust smirked. "Do we need to be worried about ax-wielding psychos?"

I didn't think these guys worried a whole lot about that sort of stuff. Individually, they were larger than life, each with his own special skill set. Together, they felt invincible. But that didn't scare me like it probably should have. I was restrained; the mitts on my hands wouldn't allow me to forget that. I was not free to move around however I liked. Other than that, though, I wasn't having that bad of a time. My fingers hurt from my escape attempt, the cut on my arm throbbed a bit—for the same reason—but that had been my choice.

Things got lonely moving from place to place. I went out, made new friends—or rather, acquaintances. I had few actual friends in the cities I frequented. This was nice. Just existing in a shared space with other bodies.

"Speaking of ax-wielding psychos," Jagger mumbled.

Diesel entered immediately after, shooting Jagger a look that might have made me pee my pants if I'd been on the receiving end. Jagger just smiled.

These people were nice to be around but also a little crazy.

Diesel plopped a pile of paper bags on the table along with a cardboard drink holder. He propelled the bags like missiles towards the others, who caught them easily, digging into the contents immediately after.

The room filled with the deliciously greasy smell of fast food and the sounds of crumpling wrappers.

Faust unwrapped one of his burgers, peeled the patty from the rest of the hamburger, and dropped it down to Dog, who sniffed it several times. I thought he wouldn't eat it before he let out a long-tortured sigh and began nibbling the corner.

"I didn't know what he liked." Diesel dropped the remaining bag in front of the table near Knox. He set a beverage cup down next to it.

I hadn't felt like any of them, other than Knox, liked me a whole lot, but Diesel especially seemed annoyed by my presence. Knox had said he would send someone to get food, not that he had sent someone, which meant Diesel had gone on his own, and he'd bought me food.

And in this strange new world I was in, that was as good as a declaration of best friendship.

Knox wheeled me and my chair closer to his table. Here, I looked like part of the group, instead of the strange mittened man in the corner. Leaving his own bag untouched, Knox unwrapped my sandwich: grilled chicken instead of hamburger. Covertly, I looked around the room, seeing no one else had a grilled chicken sandwich. Everyone else seemed to be happy with the same meal: an ungodly number of hamburgers and mounds of fries.

Knox brought the sandwich to my mouth, and I took a small bite. My face burned, not because I was being fed by my walking fantasy but because I felt another set of eyes on me.

I peeked over at Diesel, who watched me and Knox intently. His eyes tightened, his mouth twisting into a grimace of pain before he turned away and sat next to Faust, facing the other direction.

Knox lifted my cup, but when I pulled on the straw, the liquid didn't shoot up. It was thick. A milkshake.

No one else had a milkshake. Granted, I was looking at tiny acts of decency and blowing them up into declarations of friendship, but it didn't feel meaningless. The sandwich and milkshake meant something, but I didn't know Diesel well enough to know what.

"It's in," Faust announced.

Everyone but Knox put down their food. The only reason he didn't was to keep feeding me.

"Why do we think this place won't come back with *sample inconclusive* like all the others?" Huntley asked.

Faust never looked away from the screen. "Because this

time, we sent it to BioCo. They are the world's leader in compositional analysis. They have a flawless identification rate." His eyes darted back and forth as he read. Seconds later, he slumped back.

"What does it say?" Jagger continued eating his sandwich as though he'd already decided the information wasn't worth his full attention.

Judging from Faust's body language, it wasn't.

"Inconclusive?" Knox asked.

"Not technically," Faust finally answered. "Thank you for contacting us, your sample caused quite a stir, blah, blah, blah. After many routine tests, the sample came back inconclusive. They said they continued, running the more advanced tests...*the compound, though unidentifiable, reacts most like sulfur dioxide. The compound is* not *sulfur dioxide, as it contains a crystalline structure that should not be possible. We request...*" He stopped reading aloud and began scanning again. "And then they just ask us to bring them more to study, like the others."

"It's *most like* sulfur dioxide?" Huntley repeated, unimpressed. "Then what the fuck *is* it? How have we sent this shit to every university and laboratory in this country, and nobody can fucking tell us what it is?"

He sounded angry enough that I was relieved neither twin had their sword.

Knox rolled my chair slightly more behind him as if sensing my concern, or their anger. "This is good. None of the other places could tell us that much. We have something to go off of."

"An unknown chemical compound that may or may not have been used in the destruction of our homes." Jagger rubbed his neck, directly over his scar.

"We know it wasn't there before the land was

destroyed. It was there after. That's evidence enough for me to believe this compound had something to do with the destruction." Faust ripped another burger from his grease-spotted bag.

"But how?" Diesel growled. "Was it dropped from the sky? Planted? There's nothing more than they can tell us? Twenty-five thousand dollars, and all they can say is what it's most like?" He stood, moving to the windows where he paced—like a caged lion—back and forth. "Five years," he muttered. "Five years and we're no closer. We've done nothing!"

Diesel grabbed the nearest chair and flung it against the opposite wall. It slammed against it, denting the plaster and shattering into splinters.

I turned to Knox. His brow furrowed with concern. "Not nothing, Diesel. We're doing it the same way we do everything else. Learn the situation. Divide and conquer."

"I'm done learning. I'm done waiting for tests that never tell us anything. Someone killed our pack, our family and friends, my mat—everyone."

Pack was an odd word to use, and it hadn't been the first time. I looked to Dog and then the rest of them. When I'd crawled through the ducts, it had sounded like an entire pack of dogs had been chasing me. But there was still just the one. What were the odds that they had other dogs they only let out when their kidnapped hostages make a run for it?

I already knew they weren't *all* human, but then, I didn't think I was either. How else could I do what I did? But my father was a grade-A, one hundred percent, human male douchebag. Of that, I was sure.

Of course, I knew what any shrink would say if I suggested my mother was an otherworldly being. *Romanti-*

cizing a lost parent is—I knew how it sounded. I didn't talk about this stuff with anyone for a reason.

I stared at Dog. Could he turn into a person too? If so, why was he always in his dog shape? Maybe his human shape was hideously ugly.

I cocked my head to the side, scrutinizing Dog further.

Dog spotted me, laid his ear flat, and growled.

"He doesn't like eye contact," Faust said.

This dog didn't like anything, but I didn't point that out. Faust had also proven my suspicions true. How else would he know so much about the creature unless it turned into a person?

A quiet, sane voice *deep* in the back of my mind whispered that I was using wacky, not real logic, and that there were a hundred other reasons why Faust would know something like that, but I was convinced.

Were they all mixed breeds like Dog? I looked Knox up and down. He wouldn't be a dog; that didn't sound right. No. Knox was a...

Wolf.

The second the word formed, I knew it. Like hearing the spindles of a lock clicking into place, the door opened, and I could clearly see what Knox was. What they all were.

How? No idea. But I knew *what*.

Except Dog.

Unless he was just a dog. This was getting confusing.

"What does Dog turn into?" I asked.

I hadn't been paying attention to their conversation, but it all stopped so they could stare at me.

Faust looked from Dog to me. "What?"

"If you all turn into wolves, what does Dog turn into?"

Faust, Huntley, Jagger, and Diesel all glared at Knox.

"Don't fucking look at me, assholes. I didn't tell him," Knox snapped.

I smiled because, knowingly or not, they'd confirmed my suspicions again. They could turn into wolves, and Dog was possibly just a dog. I'd let the jury deliberate more on that one. "Knox didn't tell me," I said with an air of importance. "I figured it out."

All but Faust and Knox looked like they didn't believe me. I didn't need them to. I'd figured something out, and it felt good.

I craned my head up to Knox. "So when you said you mostly hunt for your food, you weren't talking about fishing or like shooting an animal."

"Why would we use guns?" Huntley looked positively disgusted by the idea.

"You eat the meat raw?" I asked.

They all shrugged. Apparently, no one here thought that was unusual. I supposed if they were only wolves, living in the woods, they would eat all their food raw. But still...

"Do you test for worms?"

Faust snorted, while the twins made a barking noise that sounded most like laughter.

"We don't get worms, brat," Knox said, though his face didn't match his tone. He growled like usual, but his face looked brighter...lighter somehow. Almost like he was very near to smiling, which would be odd, since I didn't think his lips were elastic enough to stretch into a full smile.

"Do you have *special* feelings about fire hydrants?" I asked sweetly.

Faust let out a real laugh.

Knox shoved the sandwich in my mouth in reply. I smiled as I chewed. It was a little cold now, but it still tasted good, and Knox had been right earlier. That apple hadn't been enough. As I took the final draw of my milkshake, crackling through the creamy mixture to the bottom of the cup, something very important occurred to me.

We'd been in this room for some time. Despite their earlier irritation at my presence, no one had made mention of my father. No one had looked at me like I was nothing more than a human dollar sign. I didn't know if this had all happened on purpose or if it was accidental. Maybe they'd just been preoccupied with their investigation. This could all mean nothing. Or it could mean everything.

I hoped it meant everything.

6

KNOX

Rain pelted the windows. The clouds had moved in that morning and were here to stay. But the gloomy weather couldn't dampen Jazz's spirits.

"Pizza!" Jazz shouted for joy.

His happiness was worth the looks I'd get from the other guys. I'd explained my concerns to them in the days since, and they all agreed something fishy was going on between Jazz and his father. But, they weren't all as eager to get involved as I was. Diesel was positive I just needed to get laid.

Jazz used his mitten to fling the pizza lid open. He'd gotten pretty good at using them in place of hands, and when he couldn't do something, me or Faust were around to help. "Double pepperoni, extra cheese!"

I'd known that was his favorite. "It's to share, brat."

Jazz's forehead wrinkled in an expression that bordered on murderous, but it cleared a moment later. "I guess that's okay. If I ate it all, I'd just get a stomachache."

That would be something, seeing a man Jazz's size try to put down a pizza the same size as a truck tire.

Jazz reached for a slice, remembering his dilemma a moment later. His expression fell, torture replacing joy.

"Okay, okay," Jagger mumbled. "You don't have to look like a kicked puppy." He lifted a slice, placed it on one of the paper plates that came with the pizza, and balanced the plate on Jazz's outstretched mitts.

Jazz walked carefully back to where I sat, taking the seat next to me without being told. In the handful of days he'd been here, he seemed to prefer staying close to me. At first, I thought it was fear of the others that drove him into my protection, but, as the days went on, I realized he just liked staying close.

So much of our day was already spent together. After the first time, I allowed Jazz the use of a single hand when he needed to use the restroom so he could handle his business on his own, but everything else, I did for him. Me or one of the others helped him eat, drink, and move anything he couldn't manage with his mitts. At night, he slept with me in my room. I took his mitts off to give his hands time to breathe, but he slept with a thin chain linking him to the headboard. He could roll on his back, front, and both sides, but he couldn't get more than a few feet away from the bed.

I frowned at Jazz sticking his tongue out like a frog trying to coax the slice from the plate to his mouth. Picking it up, I held it out for him to take a bite while the others grabbed their own.

A part of me enjoyed having someone soft to protect again. It was the closest I'd felt to being an Alpha in a long time, and while I didn't hate the feeling, I didn't deserve it either.

I couldn't tell if this new acceptance of Jazz from the others was a truce or something else. As long as I kept everyone fed well, for the time being, we could live in harmony—or at least without constant complaining.

"How many should we save for Diesel?" Jazz asked while he chewed.

We could live in near harmony anyway. After that first day of having Jazz at the hotel, Diesel had made himself scarce. The food he'd bought Jazz had been an apology. The Diesel I knew would never have suggested killing an innocent person to be rid of a problem. But he wasn't entirely the Diesel I knew anymore. His omega was dead. Nothing would bring Quinlan back, and despite that, a part of me had thought that when we started getting answers, the real Diesel would reemerge.

But what if that Diesel—the one with an endless well of patience and kindness—was gone forever?

Jazz skipped across the room, the plate clapped between his mitts. It was empty except for his pizza crust, which Jazz dropped on the ground four feet away from where Dog was sitting. He scooted the crust closer to the dog with his foot. "Here you go, puppy."

He didn't pay attention to the way the *puppy* growled low with his sharp teeth bared. My hackles rose, the wolf in me rising to the challenge.

Dog wouldn't bite unless Faust allowed him to, and that fact alone allowed me to remain seated.

Dog needn't have bothered growling; nothing could deter Jazz. "There you go, you grumpy pants," he said affectionately before returning to the pizza box.

"His farts are going to be awful," Faust moaned.

This time, Huntley lifted a new slice for Jazz. Instead of setting it on the plate, he held the slice in his hands and moved it toward Jazz's mouth in a jerky motion. "Choo,

choo, here comes the train." He kept the slice just out of Jazz's reach.

Jagger and Faust smirked, and I watched Jazz's face. He grinned at the teasing, but irritation made the apples of his cheeks pink. Huntley stood between him and pizza. That wasn't a safe place to stand. Clearly, Huntley didn't know how much Jazz talked about pizza.

"Give it to me!" Jazz barked, launching forward like he meant to tackle Huntley from his chair.

Huntley hadn't expected Jazz to leap at him like a gazelle fleeing a lion and jerked back in his chair, causing the chair legs to groan before snapping beneath the odd angle. The slice of pizza he'd taunted Jazz with fell from his hand and landed toppings down, against his chest.

Faust laughed loudly along with Jagger, but Jazz rushed forward, attempting to offer Huntley his arm.

"I'm sorry! I was only trying to fake you out."

"You succeeded," Jagger bellowed.

Huntley jumped to his feet, wiping at the mess on his shirt. "Serves me right for underestimating my opponent." He sized Jazz up. Hilarious, given their disparate differences. Huntley stood and nearly seven feet of highly-trained muscle, and Jazz was a redheaded wisp of a thing with mittens on his hands.

Besides, Jazz looked more upset than Huntley that he'd fallen. We fucked with each other, mercilessly and often. Before Jazz, there had been days when we'd only spoken to each other to call the other rude names. But Jazz never let the teasing get to him and, more often than not, defended whoever was being teased.

He liked to be helpful. Which why he was currently on his knees trying to clean up the pizza bits that had fallen. But he had a problem accepting help for himself.

Instead of asking for help, Jazz's MO was to run. Chasing him had been difficult for that reason. Jazz had an ability to sense danger before it fully presented itself. By the time it did, he would be gone already. That answered how he'd been able to stay one step ahead of his father for so long. Jazz had filled me in. His father had been trying to catch him since he turned eighteen, though Jazz had left home the day he'd turned thirteen. My jaw clenched tight any time I thought of thirteen-year-old Jazz, wandering the country alone.

It wasn't until Jazz turned eighteen that his father started sending men to catch him. The same number of years that we'd spent trying to discover who was responsible for killing our pack, Jazz had spent on the run, pausing only when he had a long enough head start between himself and whoever was after him that week.

I'd just add these questions to the rest of the pile of mysteries. Why wait until your child was a legal adult before trying to force him home?

"Okay, well, one of you has to take me," Jazz said from the door. I'd been too lost in thought to notice him moving across the space.

Huntley, Jagger, and Faust looked at me. I must've been asked a question. "What?"

Faust smirked. "I mean, if no one else will take you, I can."

Take him?

"I don't care which of you does it, but one of you needs to take off my mitt and stand on the other side of the door listening to make sure I don't try crawling through the toilet." Jazz stepped out to the hallway.

Faust leaned forward in his chair like he planned on following Jazz.

I growled sharply.

"Hey, you weren't offering." Faust shrugged. "Poor kid has to go."

"I still do!" Jazz hollered from the hallway.

I caught up with Jazz halfway to the bathroom, the guys snickering at me the whole way. Jazz stuck his mitt out for me to remove, and I held it while he went inside. He could try to use the free hand to undo the other, but such a task would come with some pretty obvious noises, and besides, I needed to start giving him opportunities to prove we could trust him.

He washed up and came out, holding his arm up patiently.

As I reattached the mitt, he silently watched my hands work. He didn't complain or whine. When his eyes lifted to my face, I felt his gaze, but he was just as silent. What did he see? A monster? A man?

I wanted him as much now as I had the first time I'd pressed him against me. But was that all I wanted? My way with his body?

And why should these urges feel any different than any other time I'd wanted something? Maybe it was just the way he took everything in stride. He'd found out we were wolves and, so far, had zero questions about that fact. The questions could still be coming, but I figured he was just good at accepting things outside of his understanding.

Hiding what we were in a world that might turn on us if they knew was easier than anyone expected. Especially in recent times. People were so convinced men couldn't turn into wolves that when it happened, they latched onto any excuse to keep from the truth: the world wasn't what they knew it to be.

"You've been very good, Jazz." That sounded too much

like what you'd say to a well-behaving animal. "You've earned a reward."

His face lit up before quickly dimming. "Is this some kidnapper's trick? Promise me something so I'm compliant? If you're just going to dangle it over my head so I jump when you tell me to, then don't bother."

He crossed his arms over his chest and leaned back against the wall.

My frustration had nothing to do with what Jazz was saying and everything to do with why. "Dammit, boy, I'm not trying to trick you."

"Sure. Is this the old bait and switch? Promise me something awesome, but really it's a piece of trash?"

I would've laughed at that if my protective instincts weren't going haywire. "Who hurt you?" We hadn't researched the teams that had been sent after him in the past. He said none of them had gotten close, but what if...?

Jazz's eyes darted to mine, likely drawn by my tone.

I wasn't joking, but he wanted to believe I was.

"Hurt me? Mr. Magic Fingers?" He unclenched his arms so he could wiggle his hands on either side of him. If they weren't bound, the fingers would've been wiggling as well.

He was trying to distract me, either with humor or his cuteness. I wasn't above fixating on either of those traits, but at the moment, I needed him to know that I was not on that list of people who he couldn't trust.

What if you end up sending him back?

The thought was enough to propel my hands toward the wall. They landed on either side of Jazz's head, and I leaned in.

Jazz gulped and looked up at me, his eyes wide. He licked his lips.

I hadn't meant to kiss him until I watched his tongue peek out. My lips collided with his.

His mouth was soft and tasted sweet. But his body was pure fire. He lifted his arms, winding them around my neck as I deepened the kiss.

Seconds ago, we'd stood in casual conversation, but the memory of that moment was gone, replaced by a desire that burned through us both.

I cupped his nape with one hand and gripped his thigh with the other. He curled his leg around my ass and whimpered as his hips gyrated.

Holding him felt like waking up after a nightmare to realize everything you dreamed about hadn't happened. I hadn't had a dream like that in a while. When I woke up, everything was the same.

I eased our mouths apart, allowing Jazz's leg to find its balance before releasing him. It took Jazz a few extra seconds to stop his hips and open his eyes. Passion made his gaze unfocused.

My forehead pressed against his. "Answer the question."

Jazz sighed slowly and let his gaze fall. He seemed to need an extra second to find his words, so I gave it to him. "What's my reward?" he asked softly. Stubbornly.

I frowned. Why wouldn't he just tell me who hurt him? I'd make sure they never hurt him, or anyone else, again. Even though I wanted to know, I wouldn't do exactly as Jazz had suspected and use his reward as a tool.

He'd earned it through his actions to this point. Whether he answered my questions now had no bearing on that fact. "I know you lost your clothes and hate the soap—"

"You mean rock?"

"It's a natural method that leaves behind no scent."

"It's a rock. Anyway, continue," he said sweetly.

"Tomorrow, we're going shopping."

Jazz's eyes lit up, and I committed the expression to memory. I hated dampening it.

"But there will be rules."

Jazz frowned, some of his earlier suspicion returning. "I hate rules."

I stepped back and wiped my hands together. "Then I guess we don't have to go. You could tell me what you want, but I thought you'd enjoy being there much more. I guess I was wrong—"

"No! No you weren't!" Jazz rushed to my side. "I'll follow the rules. Whatever you want, *Daddy*."

I groaned silently. He needed to stop calling me that if only so I didn't lose my control and show him exactly how *daddy* I could be.

7

JAZZ

The Rockshell Shopping Outlet was no Mall of America. The outlet had one clothing store, but there ended up being a fair selection of men's clothing and, as I'd learned when I passed a shirt with a sequined panda riding a glittering rainbow in the juniors department, some of those clothes would fit me too.

I couldn't be sure until we got home and I was able to try all of this on.

"Exit is clear." Huntley's voice murmured in my ear.

In Knox's ear too, I supposed. We were both wearing small earpieces. The wire Faust had attached around the back of my ear had been so thin I couldn't see it at times. Once Faust had stuck it on, I couldn't see it at all, but I could hear the twins waiting in the Hummer, keeping an eye as Knox and I completed the very dangerous mission of buying clothing and beauty supplies.

The headset was the first of Knox's stipulations for allowing me outside of the hotel. The second was that my hands would remain bound. He'd wrapped them with thin, soft bandages and then medical tape, looping my arms inside the front pocket of the hooded sweatshirt I wore.

I looked like a man constantly in contemplation, but I got to be outside in the fresh air, and that was reward enough.

Sucker could've gotten away with just letting me step outside.

"Don't go far." Knox took the receipt the cashier handed him while I lingered by the exit.

I didn't have use of my hands, so I couldn't help Knox carry any of the bags he'd lined both arms with. I waited as he asked, watching Knox interact with other people.

It was a bit like watching a polar bear go grocery shopping...or a lion attend a yoga class. The man was too wild to be in a place as domestic as this, but there he was, thanking the cashier like a regular person.

It was bizarre.

"We're coming out," Knox said quietly while shifting the shopping bags to one arm so he could lead me with his free hand at the small of my back.

"Isn't this a little overkill?" I asked, catching the eye of a pretty brunette woman scanning a shelf of jeans.

I smiled, and though her eyes narrowed at first, she smiled back.

I stretched up, and Knox hunched down, offering me his ear. "I think you're making the locals nervous."

Knox shook off my concern but kept me pressed into his side. "I don't care," he grunted.

"Has anyone ever explained to you the concept of honey, flies, and vinegar?"

Knox pushed the door open, guiding me into the drizzly gray day. The clouds and gloom weren't so bad when I could sit in the operations room and watch the waves crash against the shore.

My hair was damp, and if we stayed out here much longer, my sweater would eventually get soaked too.

I shivered, flinging my hair off my forehead. I tried twice more, unsuccessfully, before switching tactics and trying to blow the curl off my face.

"Can Jazz stop acting like a windstorm?" Huntley growled.

Oh, that's right. The mics. "Sorry."

Knox led us to the building wall, under a canvas awning. He set the bags down, brushing my curls back gently before tucking the hair on both sides behind my ears. "Better?" he whispered.

Better? Knox was touching me; of course I was better. I didn't think that was what he meant, though. "Yeah. Um. Thanks."

"Why don't you wear it with your hood up?" he asked, sliding the loop of fabric over my head.

I stared at him, the answer obvious.

Knox's eyes tightened, drawing his eyebrows down. "You can ask. If you need help, Jazz, ask me."

As much as I loved the way his breath kissed my cheeks as he spoke, something in his tone had me shying away. It was too knowing, too intimate. "Yeah, okay."

Knox didn't stop frowning, but he did step back. "Do you want to go anywhere else but the drug store?"

I shook my head. We'd been at this for over two hours. Knox had bought me more clothing than I'd ever had at one single point in my life. Inside the store, I'd let the fluorescent lights and that new retail smell take me over.

Now, I regretted asking for so many things. "I'll go through everything at the hotel and decide on only the things I really want, okay?" I hoped that would reassure him.

One look in his face told me it hadn't.

I changed tactics. "This is too much. I'd never be able to carry it all at once."

Knox went from frowning to a full-on glower. "C'mon."

He still kept me close, though his body language had changed. He moved stiffly and kept his eyes on our surroundings. The way these guys acted, it was as if we were shopping in a war-torn country, not a small coastal town.

The moment we stepped into the drug store, I walked a little faster. The clothes were great, and I was excited to have them, but after a week of using the stone Knox called soap, I was desperate.

They had hand soap, but the one time I'd tried to use it as body wash, it had left my skin tight and itchy. Knox had explained it was some kind of super-strength formula that they made in the hotel.

And none of those guys were worried with keeping skin soft and supple.

I let my nose guide me and hurried forward to the row of soaps and body wash. I turned around, waiting for Knox to catch up. As he sauntered forward, the same brunette woman from the clothing store came in. I supposed with a town this size, there weren't a lot of other shopping options.

Knox grabbed a basket. Smart man.

I turned back to the shelf and attempted to read the labels without being able to touch anything.

"Is this the kind you like?" he grunted, jerking his chin forward.

I'd used this brand before. Their stuff smelled great, like

lemon meringue, and left my skin feeling soft. I nodded, and Knox proceeded to sweep one of each thing into the basket.

"Knox! That's too much. I don't need the body wash, after-shower oil, and the lotion. That's overkill."

Knox looked from the contents of the basket, to me. His jaw was still tight, and his steely gray eyes flashed with an emotion I couldn't pinpoint. "Will you use all of this?" He gestured vaguely to the bottles laying on their sides.

Eventually, yes, I would use everything that Knox had in the basket. That didn't mean he needed to buy it all for me. "Probably. Let me choose three. That's fair."

Knox turned from me, sauntering farther down the aisle.

The hairs on my nape rose, and I looked around, finding that same brunette woman only one aisle over, examining an endcap display of fiber supplements.

"Jazz," Knox called out.

I found him halfway down the aisle. He didn't like me getting too far away from him. That hadn't been a rule. The mic at my ear had a tracker in it, and it wasn't like I could take it off myself. If it wasn't a push, I couldn't open a door by myself.

Staying near seemed to be more like a "Knox's rule" sort of thing.

"Is this the kind you use?" Knox asked, standing in front my preferred brand of shampoo and conditioner.

"How did you know?" I asked as I nodded.

"It smells like you."

Technically, I smelled like it, but I liked that Knox gave me that ownership. He'd stopped in front of this brand because it smelled like me. Why was that comforting?

"Just the shampoo and conditioner are fine. The small bottles. I can ration and—"

Again, Knox dropped the entire line, from the deep conditioning mask to the clarifying spray, into the basket.

"That's too much!" I didn't know why I fought this. The man wanted to buy me things. I loved things. But, every item felt like a promise, a commitment of time. It wasn't the commitment that I didn't want; it was the grief. When all this was over and Knox had made his decision, there were only two things that could happen. Either he'd turn me in to my father and get the rest of the million—I'd asked Knox how much I'd been worth to my father—they were owed, or he would decide my father was the shifty one and let me go.

Neither of those options included me continuing to shower in Knox's room. I'd already resigned myself to the fact that I'd never be able to use any of these products again after Knox. I wouldn't be able to separate one from the other.

"You can't just buy me everything," I added when it didn't look like he'd heard me at all.

He rotated, standing slightly curved over me. I sighed silently. My heart seemed to beat a little calmer whenever he was close like this. "I can buy you what I want. This is my reward to you."

"But I don't need—"

"I'm taking over," Knox announced.

Taking over? Had he ever not been in control?

"You can wait at the end of the aisle if you want, but I'm getting you what you need, Jazz."

That was just the thing. I didn't *need* any of this. It would been nice to have. My time in the hotel would be a little easier with these items. It would feel a little more like home.

And that was the problem.

I swallowed down a lump in my throat. "Fine," I

muttered, walking the other way mostly so he couldn't see I was about to cry.

Knox growled low under his breath, but it reached me like a sound bullet. My thighs clenched together. I scowled. One person shouldn't affect another so much. This wasn't fair on so many levels.

I reached a row of hair supplies and paused. I wouldn't say no to a package of hair ties. At least those were small and easy to take with you when you lived on the run.

A wet curl broke free from the prison of my ear and stuck to my forehead. I didn't want the twins to think I was doing another impression of a wind tunnel, so I tried using my elbow to push the hair up. It was awkward with my hands bound, but I'd succeeded in swiping away the curl at the exact same time the brunette woman who had followed us from the other store rushed over.

"Are your hands *tied together*?"

I shoved my hands back to center but was helpless to stop her from grabbing my elbow and pulling up my sleeve. It didn't hurt at all, but she got an eyeful of the entire situation and hissed.

Knox appeared at my other side, his eyes hard. "Let him go," he growled.

"Ready at the entrance." I had a clear view down the aisle and through the store windows to the Hummer idling by the curb.

Huntley and Jagger sat in the front seats, both staring at our trio.

"I won't," the woman replied. Her voice didn't shake, but her lip did. She was scared.

"This isn't what it looks like," I attempted to explain. This was probably exactly what it looked like, and I was in foreign territory trying to persuade someone without the use of my powers. If I had my hands, this lady would be whistling down the next aisle by now.

"It looks like a young man being restrained and ordered around by..." Her eyes landed on Knox, and she looked him up and down, but the action didn't seem to have the same effect on her as it did on me. "I've seen you around town." Her forehead wrinkled. "One of you better say something, or I am calling the cops."

"Huntley has a shot, Knox." Jagger's words sounded in my ear, calm and casual like he was talking about what they'd have for dinner after, not killing a woman whose greatest mistake was caring.

I stepped to the side, putting myself between the woman and the Hummer. Knox growled, stepping behind me.

"Negative," he murmured at a volume I only heard because his mouth was so close to my head.

I couldn't trick the woman, but maybe I could tell her the truth. "Please don't call the police. My hands are restrained, but it's not entirely what it looks like."

While I spoke, Knox tugged me away and toward the exit, nullifying everything I was saying with his actions.

The woman just followed behind. She wasn't yelling or making a scene, but she also wasn't letting Knox pull me more than a few feet away. "What is it then? If it isn't what it looks like?"

"It's none of your fucking business," Knox snarled. He'd reached his limit on patience. His shoulders were tight, his neck strained.

The woman flinched but didn't back down. She exhaled, centered herself, and lifted her gaze, finding Knox's. "It's my business if he's in trouble."

"What is wrong with this lady?" Huntley hissed over the

comms. "Jagger's running a scan. You think she was sent here?"

Knox couldn't answer them without causing more questions.

The woman pulled out her cell phone.

"Okay, wait, everyone stop." I tried to lift my hands, remembering the next moment that I couldn't—and that was sort of the point of this conversation. "I can tell you're a good person Ms...?"

"Hallie," she replied stiffly.

"If you're not going to step out of the way and give me a clean shot, at least get her last name," Jagger hissed.

I ignored him. "Hallie, I'm Jazz. This is Knox. Yes I'm tied up, but that doesn't have to be strange, does it? A decade ago, seeing people with colored hair was strange, and now look. I am not under duress, and we're going to go through the cashier's aisle slowly and calmly to prove that. You can come."

Hallie cocked her head to the side. Her gaze was softer when she looked at me after staring at Knox. "Fine, okay. Let's go." She gestured like a tour guide toward the cash registers.

Knox moved stiffly forward, his free arm latched around my waist. He hauled the basket onto the conveyor belt, and we waited our turn, Hallie standing behind us the whole time.

I could only imagine what the cashier thought as he scanned our items. None of us spoke. Knox was visibly furious while Hallie's eyes narrowed at him.

Knox paid in cash before wrangling the bags in one hand.

Now that my plan had been carried out, I wasn't entirely positive what it would prove. I thought if she saw us doing normal things in a totally unafraid way, she'd be convinced I was fine.

"Now lose her," Huntley grunted.

"Or step out of the way," Jagger added.

"How come I haven't seen you around Rockshell?" Hallie asked.

She crossed the line of *concerned citizen* a while ago, and though the woman was nosy, it came from a place of caring. For me, anyway. I couldn't be angry about that.

Knox could.

"I've seen *him*, grunting around town, but not you. I won't find you on a missing poster, will I?"

Anything was possible.

"Take my number," I blurt out. "Will that make you feel better?" Or at least good enough to let us out without Knox doing something he would regret—maybe—and before Hallie called the cops.

She leaned back, looking less like she was waiting for the right moment to grab me and run. Could that be what was putting Knox on edge? No, it was probably the fact that he couldn't use his skills. Knox was a tactical man. A fighter. But he'd tried intimidating Hallie away, and that hadn't worked. He likely felt neutered by the situation.

Join the club.

"Okay. But if you don't answer, I'm sending the police. I know you're staying up at the old hotel. No idea how or why. The place must just be a pile of mold by now."

Knox grunted like he agreed with her assessment while I wrestled with not feeling offended on behalf of the hotel. The boards were cracking, most of them rotted out. And the carpet was bare in most places, the hardwood scuffed, the plumbing sometimes ran brown—if it ran at all—and they would find random leaks when it rained, but the place had character.

And it had sheltered me for a week. That wasn't nothing.

"Give me your phone. I'll put in my number." Hallie stuck her hand out, highlighting the biggest flaw in my plan.

I didn't have my phone. I didn't know where it was. I'd had one at the bar. I woke up without one and had never bothered asking for it.

I turned to Knox, his unhappy expression telling me he didn't like this plan and also that he'd realized my dilemma. He cleared his throat. "You can have my number."

"I don't want yours," Hallie snapped.

"We share," I lied to help speed this along. Other people were beginning to stare, and the tenuous control I had on the situation slipped further from my fingers with each passing second. I rattled off Knox's number, having already memorized it from the brief text exchanges we'd had before he'd caught me.

Hallie typed the number into her phone and pressed call. The woman had trust issues, but then, every person I'd met lately seemed to. When Knox's phone rang in her pocket, she smiled with the slight relief. "Okay. I'll call later."

It sounded like a promise and a threat.

"Thank you," I said because really, the world needed more people like her—with slightly lower levels of aggressive caring.

Knox led me out, his hard body all but vibrating with excess energy. When he looked into my face, his expression was soft. "How did you know my number?"

I shrugged, unsure of why I was blushing. "In the beginning, when you were trying to persuade me to give myself up." Before I'd led them on a chase that lasted several months. "I didn't save you as a contact, so your number came up, and I guess I memorized it."

Memorized it. Waited by my phone for him to text. All the normal, not insane things.

Knox lifted me in the back seat of the Hummer, stowing our bags before sliding in beside me. I'd scooted to the opposite side, next to the door, but he slid me over the leather to the seat next to him. His body covered mine for as long as it took him to buckle my seatbelt. I held my breath. I couldn't handle a concentrated shot of Knox at the moment. Not without my body reacting in embarrassing ways. Huntley rolled down a window as he smoothly pulled the Hummer out onto the main road.

Knox hadn't answered. He was still staring at me, but at least he'd leaned back, and Huntley's window supplied me with fresh air. His phone rang, and he frowned, checking the screen before his scowl returned.

Forty-five seconds without a scowl. That had to be a record.

He answered with a low, *'This is Knox,'* before dissolving into a string of uh-huhs and mm-hms. He hung a few seconds later. "She's coming over Friday," he grunted.

Huntley and Jagger twisted their heads back to look at Knox like he'd turned into someone they didn't know.

"She's fucking persistent," Knox bellowed. A moment later, "She's bringing food," he said as if that made anything better.

———

"I CAN'T TELL if I like these more or less than the jeans." I walked the length of Knox's room in a pair of tan slacks Knox had bought.

The beauty supplies were already in the bathroom. I tried not to think about the bottles. About how many there were or about how I wouldn't be around to finish any of them.

But that thought made my mouth heavy, so I pushed it out, determined to keep this moment light.

After Knox broke it to Faust and Diesel that we'd be having yet another guest, he hadn't exactly been on anyone's good list. I'd suggest the fashion show to distract him.

And because I really wanted to try the clothes on.

Knox had even unbound my hands so I could put the clothes on without needing help.

"What do you think?" I asked over my shoulder when Knox still hadn't offered his opinion.

"Both good," he grunted.

I turned back to the mirror, angling to the side to check out my ass. "But which is better? I have no reason to keep both."

The question only made Knox angry. He'd fought with his team today, because of me, again. He didn't want my questions about pants.

I hurried into the bathroom, shutting the door behind me as I slipped out of the new pants and into a pair of sweatpants. I didn't normally sleep with a shirt but had since coming here.

I ended up pulling the hooded sweatshirt on from earlier before going back out. Knox sat in the same spot on the edge of the bed and watched my approach. I hung my arms out before I'd fully gotten to him, and I waited for him to wrap my hands for bed.

He must've still been angry from before because he just sat there, staring at my hands.

"Do you have everything you need?" I asked after a few seconds. He kept the tape and everything near his side of the bed but hadn't made the move for them. "Knox." I jiggled my hands in front of him.

Maybe he'd been lost in thought. Something was clearly up, and I started to get worried when Knox lifted his face.

A storm brewed in his gaze, tortured but heated. Guilt and desire. "You could've tried to leave with that woman today."

I blinked, the idea never having occurred to me until he brought it up. I shrugged, uncomfortable with how vulnerable recognizing this made me feel. "You were being nice, buying me some stuff. And... I don't know. Other than the mitten thing...it hasn't been that bad here. You don't hurt me. You don't let anyone else hurt me. And I'm not alone. I'm not looking over my shoulder."

I made my life sound worse than it was. There had been fun times, really fun, actually. But they'd never lasted, and I'd never been able to stay. Was that why I hadn't tried to run with Hallie? Because I wanted to stay?

Admitting that felt like admitting to something too intimate. Knox liked feelings as much as questions.

When Knox finally moved, it wasn't to grab the tape but his wallet.

"What are you doing?" My voice was too high-pitched, like my brain recognized danger I had yet to notice.

"I'm sorry."

If he'd said any other words but those two, my heart might not have begun pounding as it did. "What do you mean?"

"You can go. If you want to go, I won't keep you here,

Jazz. That woman, as annoying as she was, was right. I don't want you to feel like my *hostage*." His throat constricted, forcing the word from Knox's mouth into the world.

He was setting me free. This was my White Fang moment. But it felt so much more like he was rejecting me. "You want me to go?"

Here I'd been worried about not seeing the end of any of my hygiene products when really, I wouldn't be around to open most of them. They wouldn't all fit in my bag.

Shit. I didn't have a bag.

Knox's face tightened into a grimace. "I want you to feel like you can, if you want."

That didn't make any sense, but my face felt very hot, and I was trying so hard not to cry that I couldn't concentrate on piecing together what he'd said. "Okay."

"Okay?"

Was I supposed to say something else? Thanks for the couple of days of warmth? Thanks for letting me sleep soundly for the first time in my life? Thanks for...sending me away?

Knox growled low and lifted me off my feet, crushing me to his chest. "I'm not kicking you out, boy. I'm saying you're not my prisoner. You don't have to stay here."

"I don't have to go?"

That brought a growl that shook both our bodies. "You don't want to?"

The longer he held me, the easier it was to force my breaths even, to focus. "Why do you think I didn't try to get away?" I shrugged.

I was in his arms, our faces centimeters apart when I wrapped my legs around his hips. My whispered words like a confession.

"You were the best part of this whole thing. If I'm going

to be chased by a violent band of marauders—" I tried laughing, but it came out airy and little hysterical. "I like being here. But I get that you guys have your mission and..." I didn't know how to voice what was in my heart. "I don't want to get in the way."

That was as close to the truth as I could manage.

"You aren't in the way." His gaze dropped to my lips.

A declaration of love it was not, but with his dick against my stomach, hot, firm and heavy, I wasn't in the market for declarations. I whimpered, overcome by a fierce wave of desire that had my hips humping against him. "Knox," I gasped.

"I want you," he growled like it was his turn to confess.

I let out a soft satisfied sigh. "I can tell."

His face was all thunder and lightning until he blinked, and worry replaced the storm. "I'm not gentle, Jazz. You deserve gentle."

I inhaled his alluring scent, but this time, I understood it. I could picture Knox living with his back to the sea, his eyes on the past. But that wasn't where he looked now. "It isn't a requirement. Not like I'm a virgin or anything."

Knox's fingers gripped my butt cheeks tighter. "I know that, brat."

Despite his words, he still looked like he was trying to calm himself down after learning I'd been with other men. Had he thought... ?

"You knew that, right? This isn't like a *you're tainted* sort of thing because that would be some bullsh—"

Knox kissed me, cupping my jaw as he balanced my ass against his other palm.

Though the man only had two hands, one mouth, one tongue, two lips, I felt them everywhere. His touches were free flowing, like water covering my skin, soaking me with his heat. His desire. I couldn't help but absorb him.

"I can keep control," he said, though he had to have been speaking to himself because I'd never doubted that he wouldn't. He worried that I was breakable, but I wasn't.

At least, not unless you think he's ordering you away.

I'd deal with that uncomfortable level of dependence later. I bit his lip hard enough that he hissed and yanked back. "I won't break. I won't run. And I don't want you to keep control."

He put both hands on my ass again, kneading each fleshy handful. His silver eyes bore into me like he was trying to see through the skin and bone to the thoughts in my brain.

And then he threw me.

My butt landed first, and I bounced, shrieking as Knox caught me. He ripped my sweater over my head, chest-bumping me so my arms flung up. His arms tightened around my lower back as he set me gently against the bed. He bent his head and licked my lips, never pausing the kiss as he continued down.

"That feels amazing." I shuddered, my skin tingling where his tongue had been. His mouth dipped lower, licking along the sensitive ridge of my neck to my nipple.

His grip on my thigh was *just* this side of pleasure. The small bites of pain made me gasp, and with each sharp inhale, my dick twitched like a fist knocking against a door. Except my dick wanted out, not in.

He yanked hard on the string keeping my sweats up.

"Hey, these are new!" I squeaked, but Knox didn't look like he cared much about clothing.

"I know. That's why I didn't tear them off you." With

one hand cupping my nape and his fingers pressing against my hipbone, Knox held me exactly as he wanted.

His teeth found my nipple at the same time he gripped the base of my cock. There wasn't hesitation or uncertainty, no moment of floundering as he removed my clothing.

My life of moving around a lot meant a lot of one-night stands. They were always mutual, but I was never able to move beyond that beginning awkward stage where you both kind of wish the other would look away while you wiggled out of your clothes. With Knox, there was no awkward stage.

He kissed me like he had every right to. He gripped my dick like it belonged to him. And as he pumped me once with his dry palm, I was inclined to agree.

"Red curls," he murmured, but he wasn't looking at my hair.

Not the hair on my head, anyway. He leaned in, burying his nose in my *down there* hair before inhaling deeply.

Scandalized and aroused, I froze.

He peered up, offering no explanation for his actions, though I had an idea it was a wolf person thing. Without blinking, he held my gaze as he inhaled a second time.

My dick twitched, spitting out precum that slid slowly down my shaft and onto Knox's waiting tongue.

His growl of pleasure was my only warning before he swallowed my length. I hit the back of his throat, and my hips jerked forward. I hissed, drawing back, but Knox would have none of it. He followed the movement of my body, squeezing and sucking while taking large draws against my cock that felt like he was demanding my cum to rise. It was the most aggressive blowjob I'd ever received, and I panted to keep from coming so soon.

I bit my lip, squeezed my eyes shut, sang the national anthem, and *still* fought the urge, trembling at the edge of oblivion.

"No," Knox growled. "Look at me."

I did. His silver eyes glowed, as demanding as the rest of this powerful man.

"Look at me," he repeated, softening the words into something that might've sounded like a request. If you squinted. His mouth returned to my shaft. The soft skin of my dick still glistened in his wake.

I jumped as his fingers slipped between my cheeks. He must've had lube nearby because his fingers were slick. Keeping his touches light and teasing, he danced around the puckered rim. These gentle caresses were nothing like how he'd been dominating my body seconds before, but he was no less in control.

"Your pretty hole is aching for me."

I grunted, nodding. Hopefully, that was enough of an answer because I couldn't manage much more.

"I'm going to fill you up. Right *here*," On cue, he slid his finger in, my body giving way much easier than I would've expected. Probably because my hole really was aching for him and had been clenching and unclenching for most of the evening.

Despite how much I wanted it, his fingers were thick, and I grimaced when he added a second.

"Look at you, my good boy, taking my fingers so you can take my dick." He gripped his erection, bringing my attention to the fact that he was suddenly naked—I couldn't claim to know when that had happened—and holding the largest cock I'd seen in my lifetime.

He must've seen the doubt in my eyes because he

growled, dipping his face low. He rubbed his cheek against my balls like a cat. "You'll take it," he hummed.

Though encouraging, his words were more a statement of fact. I *would* take it. But he'd be here when I did, and that was enough for me to know I'd be safe.

Somehow this man who had chased me, cuffed me, and drugged me had become my safe harbor. He'd kept me restrained, but he'd protected me as well. Fed me, washed me, teased me, and given me someone to talk to even in the wee hours of the morning when I couldn't sleep.

Knox worked three fingers in, smoothly sliding in and out. I felt ready. I bucked my hips to get his attention, but he didn't stop, keeping the thrusts solid but steady, not too deep.

"Knox, I'm ready. I need you."

"Not yet," came his growled reply. "I can't hurt you." His voice sounded strangled and odd enough that I blinked a little of the haze away, enough that I could see him, concentrate on his face. His expression was primal, his eyes flashing like light reflecting off water. "I'll never hurt you."

He didn't mean just now, at this moment. His gaze was too intense for that. He brought his lips around my cock, demanding I come as he thrust in a fourth finger. With that action, Knox pushed me out of the driver's seat of my own body. He was in control now. When he wanted me to moan, I moaned. When he wanted me to tremble, I trembled, and when he wanted me to come—

I climaxed with a strangled cry, clenching around his hand as I did.

"Your pleasure tastes like candy," Knox groaned. I'd assume his words were mere dirty talk if it weren't for the way his tongue cleaned my dick and balls, making sure he didn't miss a single drop.

His splayed hand covered half my chest as he rubbed down my ribs. He shifted on the bed, moving to a more upright position and stretching my legs open to accommodate his wide body.

I braced my elbows beneath me, trying to take a more active role. So far I'd been tossed around and manhandled, which wasn't at all a bad thing, but I didn't want Knox to think I didn't give as well as I took.

Knox noticed and grinned at my new position. I didn't understand the smile. He climbed upward, pressing me deeper into the cushion below. He couldn't have been letting his full weight down, but enough that there was no mistaking the man's body pinning me, claiming me.

I felt breakable beneath him, a fragile thing when compared to his raw strength. Clinging to his shoulders, he moved me again, this time with deeper intent. I knew what he had planned a moment before it happened, but that didn't prepare me. He thrust forward with a deep roar, sheathing himself completely and making me grateful he'd been so adamant about prep.

There was no moment to breathe or adjust. His ass clenched as his hips flexed, his skin slapping against mine with each forward drive. I came in seconds, but I didn't know if Knox noticed. His eyes shone pure silver as a snarl escaped his lips.

That was, I didn't know if he noticed until he brought his hand between our bodies and swirled his finger in the clear fluid. He brought his finger to my mouth, and I sucked it eagerly. I didn't care that he fed me my own release. I'd take whatever Knox gave me.

He growled before the headboard slammed against the wall. As he rutted into me, coaxing my body to yet another orgasm, I finally understood why he'd been so worried about control, why he'd taken so long to prepare my hole. He fucked like a wild animal, an apex predator in complete control. The primal roars, growls, and snarls called to something deep in my soul, a wildness I'd discovered while cradling his body with my thighs.

I wasn't in the position of power, not by a long shot, but I didn't feel powerless.

I felt loved.

My back bowed off the bed, and though I'd come so many times already, this orgasm raced up my spine like it was the first after a long drought. "Knox!" I screamed when it was still going. My orgasm wasn't an explosion to the peak and then a gentle descent. I rocketed to the pinnacle of pleasure—and stayed there. "Knox," I whimpered.

"I'm here. I have you," he murmured, his words deep like crunching gravel. I couldn't hear gentleness in his tone, but gentleness wasn't something Knox could give me right then, only safety. He slammed forward. His fingers spread over my spine, pressing between my shoulder blades.

Stuffed deeper than I'd ever been before, I held tight, my dick finally limp when Knox's roar sounded over my head. I couldn't move as his dick throbbed inside me, filling me with wave after wave of liquid heat.

"So good and tight," Knox whispered. Already, his voice was different, softer. "You did so well," he chanted, touching me all over as if to make sure I was in one piece. "Jazz..."

Maybe my body was, but inside, I'd shattered into a million pieces. This hadn't been just sex. It didn't feel like the beginning of something light and casual. Nothing about Knox was light and casual.

"Jazz isn't here right now. Someone fucked him silly."

The right side of his mouth lifted in a pleased grin. "Silly, huh? That's a good starting-off point." He leaned over to kiss my forehead, and I couldn't believe earlier this night I'd been afraid he was kicking me out. His bed was warm and smelled of him. Though covered in sweat and fluids, I never wanted to leave it, and he didn't make me.

He cleaned me up with a warm wash rag. I helped as best I could, but my arms and legs felt too limp to use for long. That made Knox smile, and when he was finished, he shut off the light like this was a normal evening. He got in bed, holding me in the curve of his body, like nothing had changed.

But as I lay there, listening to his steady, even breaths, I knew one thing with absolute certainty: nothing was the same anymore.

8

KNOX

I squeezed Jazz's fingers as we walked through the front entrance. I'd traded binding Jazz's hands all day to constantly holding them, but he didn't complain.

"I'm pretty sure she saw Huntley and Jagger before. They don't need to hide too," Jazz said with a frown.

The others had been *displeased* when I'd informed them of our upcoming visitor. Diesel hadn't shown himself in days, and I didn't see that changing until after today's lunch at the earliest. The twins had gone hunting, which wouldn't sound so unusual except for the fact I'd since stocked the kitchen with actual food. I didn't like the idea of being unable to provide Jazz with anything that he needed —food included.

I understood what their absences really were: protests that I'd dared to plan something other than earning money for our investigation or investigating. We'd lived with one goal for too long. Finding who had destroyed our pack was still our number one priority, but it didn't have to be the only thing we lived for. It couldn't be.

Their distrust stung, but I reminded myself I was

solving a problem. Whatever that woman thought was going on between Jazz and me, he wasn't in danger, and it wasn't her business. Those were the only two things I needed her to understand after today.

Faust stood to the left near a clump of rhododendrons I'd been meaning to yank out. They grew too close to the foundation, which, despite the rest of this place, was solid. The Hotel Royal Paynes, while a poor business decision from inception, had been built as sturdy as a rock.

Faust looked over his shoulder at us—Dog must've been inside protesting as well— stuffing something in his pocket at the same time. He caught my eye, but we'd both heard the car pull down our driveway—it was a little impossible not to with that muffler—so whatever he had to say would have to wait.

Faust winced. His affinity for machines made it difficult for him to stand idly by when he came in contact with an engine in trouble.

Hallie's car pulled around the final bend, her side window snagging on a blackberry bramble that had grown in after we'd chopped them back. Her old, boxy blue Volvo sounded no better from close up. When she pulled to a stop beside the crumbling fountain, her engine sputtered and choked, hissing like it had given up on life when she cut the power and opened the door.

She climbed out. Two thick braids swayed with the movement as she hung over her door, peering up at the hotel as she pushed her aviator sunglasses up her nose and over her forehead. "This place looks as bad as it did when I was a kid. Smoked weed for the first time right over there." She sighed wistfully.

My eyebrows dipped. The building was still under repair. We weren't finished with it. I'd known when we'd bought the place that the building was something of a local legend. We'd cleaned out enough beer cans and liquor bottles to know it had been a popular hangout. But it wasn't that same place anymore. Maybe it wasn't home—that had been destroyed—but it was a place we slept, and that made it important.

Jazz squeezed my hand, letting me know I'd been quietly growling.

Before, when my men and I had worked to support our pack, we'd taken pride in our homes. There wasn't a house or structure on pack lands that wasn't perfectly maintained. With the money our alpha team had pulled in and our people's know-how, we'd become entirely self-sufficient. This hotel wasn't any of that, but it was where I kept Jazz.

All I could see now when I looked back at the hotel were the cracks, chips, and rust stains.

"I'm glad you came," Jazz effused. "Now you can put all your worries to rest."

"I wasn't worried by the time you all left." Hallie climbed over the driver's seat to grab something sitting on the passenger side. "Door's broken," she chirped at our questioning looks. She held out two glass casserole dishes. "This is more of an apology. A peace offering. I've got lasagna and cinnamon rolls. Homemade."

"Cream cheese icing?" Faust perked up.

"Yes." Hallie nodded, looking Faust up and down. "Now who's this one?"

"My name's Faust," he replied, his gentler tone reflecting how much he wanted at those cinnamon rolls.

Doubt settled over Hallie's round features. Her eyes hazel eyes narrowed. "You live here too?"

Faust leaned his weight back, realizing he wouldn't be getting to the tray of desserts any time soon. "We're—"

"Cousins," Jazz supplied eagerly.

I arched my brow at him, but he just blinked those pretty brown eyes at me. Slinging a possessive arm over his shoulders, I faced Hallie. "Yep, cousins."

"And those two from the car? From last time?"

If it worked once... "Cousins too."

"Four cousins living in one house together? With Jazz? That sounds really strange." She stepped back, closer to her car. Her heart beat a little faster than it had only a minute ago.

I wasn't the only one to recognize her uneasiness. Jazz didn't even need heightened senses.

"It isn't as bad as what you're thinking," Jazz replied brightly. "Knox and the others have actually done a lot of work inside. It's still in progress, but the place is so big. There's a ballroom and indoor pool—though it's mostly filled with frogs right now. Still, I could go a whole day wandering without seeing one of them."

That wasn't even a lie. Neither of us had seen Diesel in days.

"How about I show you around?" I let him slide out from under my arm, though not without effort. His shoes crunched over the cracked pavement as he slowly approached Hallie.

"I didn't bring enough for five of you—"

"That's okay," Faust said, holding his hands out. "I'll carry that for you."

Hallie clung to the dishes. "I've got 'em," she said stiffly.

Smart woman must've seen the gleam of hunger in Faust's eye. I didn't blame him. It had taken Jazz's arrival just for me to buy groceries. We hadn't had a home-cooked meal—by someone with even an inkling of skill—in years.

"Jazz, take Hallie inside to the meeting room next to the

kitchen." If we sat down to eat, which we didn't do often, we sat in that room. Mostly because it was closest to the kitchen, but it had also remained a little more preserved than the other rooms, and cleaning it out hadn't required as much demolition.

Hallie's eyes slid from Faust to me and then Jazz, her gaze only softening at the end. She looked me dead in the eye. "People know where I am."

Jazz took her inside, leaving Faust and me to watch them go.

"She invited herself here today, right?" Faust asked.

"Damn near demanded it." I figured Jazz could handle the woman for a few seconds. "What was that before? Did you find something?"

Faust grimaced. "It's why I have Dog inside." Faust turned, staring into the forest. "Weird things have been happening."

I didn't have any room on my plate for more bullshit, but Faust wasn't an easily spooked sort of guy. "What kind of things?"

"Read this."

He handed me a small bit of paper. The edges were torn from what I assumed was a journal or bound notebook. One side was blank, and the other said in elegant, sloping letters, "Green...so much green."

It wasn't exactly a cry for help. Or a cry for anything. More statement of fact.

"It is green around here."

Faust snatched it back, shoving the slip in his pocket. "A squirrel gave me this fucking note. Hopped right down a branch and set it in my damn hand. Got something smart to say about that?"

"I got no fucking clue what to say to that, Faust. Are we

in immediate danger from your squirrel messenger? Have you gotten any other cryptic messages?"

"No. I do keep finding bits of paper, though."

"I thought that was mice?"

Faust shrugged. "I don't know, okay? It might be nothing; it might be the end of the goddamned world—again." I knew what he meant—our world had been the only one that ended the first time.

I still didn't like our options and would've killed for some middle ground. "Right now, let's assume it is nothing. When it becomes something, then we'll tackle it."

He followed me in, saying something about needing to wash his hands and check on Dog. I wasn't fooled. He just wanted at those cinnamon rolls.

He took the stairs to his room while I took the left toward the kitchen. The back of my neck itched, the feeling strengthening the longer I remained separated from Jazz.

His voice carried to me from the meeting room, and I hurried to get to him but paused at Hallie's whisper.

"You aren't tied up today."

I frowned and quickly continued forward.

"No, I...um...I'm a klepto. Knox does that to save me from myself."

I didn't enjoy hearing Jazz lie, even if I understood the reason. Hallie's intervention had only highlighted my own shame. I'd tied him up, took away the use of his hands, and left him that way for days. He should have run when I gave him the chance—bolted out the crumbling front door.

But he'd stayed. He'd offered himself to me. Giving Jazz the chance to go the first time had been difficult enough; my alpha nature wouldn't allow me to again.

"You certainly have a lot of pictures together," Hallie said absently. "Lots of happy memories. You went to Italy?"

Pictures? Italy?

I growled, rounding the corner finally as Jazz yanked something off the table. "Enough of that. Let's eat," he chirped hastily.

Jazz kept his head down, but the tips of his ears were pink. He'd been using his ability to cement our story with Hallie and relieve her suspicion. Jazz was resourceful, but, like the lie, I didn't like witnessing him fool Hallie. These were the same skills he'd use to run away.

But he isn't your prisoner.

Semantics.

I didn't want to force him to stay, but I absolutely wanted him to stay.

"He isn't a klepto." I wasn't going to defend my actions to her, but I wouldn't let her go on believing something negative about Jazz—even if he'd been the one to put the thought there.

The two dishes sat on a towel on the table. We had a few dishes, but not enough for four people to eat at the same time. "I'll go get the plates. We have to use paper ones until I can get to the store."

I expected that admission to earn me another of Hallie's suspicious stares, but she just shrugged. "I hope you have a spatula, or else one of you is going to have to use your hand."

When I returned from the kitchen, Faust sat across from Hallie and Jazz, and Dog sat next to the door with his back to the wall, his eyes on Hallie.

"Real sweet dog you have," Hallie said with a head tilt. "I especially enjoy the way he stares deep into your soul whether you want him to or not."

Jazz laughed, the sound melodic and light. "He's a good judge of character, but not a very fast one."

After Faust's third portion of lasagna, I cut him off,

wanting to save the rest for the others. I could be irritated with them without wanting them to starve. Diesel got even crankier when he was hungry.

Even Dog perked his ear up when Hallie uncovered the cinnamon rolls. "The frosting has melted a bit because of the lasagna. Should've thought of that." She'd been looking down at the tray while she spoke and looked up to four hungry stares. "Or, yeah, have at it."

Jazz attacked the sweet rolls with as much ferocity as Faust, and I made a note of his sweet tooth. He'd kept up an easy conversation with Hallie while we ate. She'd been born in Rockshell and had never left. Married her senior year in high school. I assumed there had been a child involved in that decision, but she hadn't mentioned a child yet. She had been divorced for several years, and judging by the way her hands had clenched when she spoke of him, it had been a bitter divorce.

By the end of lunch, there'd been no lingering silences, and we'd offered no additional information about ourselves, fabricated or otherwise—thanks to Jazz. She told us to keep the leftovers but that she was taking the dishes, so Faust ran them back to the kitchen to wash them for her.

"So I'll see you guys next week? Friday?"

I looked to Jazz. They'd gone inside and had been alone for a few minutes, but it hadn't been long enough for a repeat invitation.

"To teach you how to cook the lasagna, Jazz? You mentioned you wanted to learn how to cook."

He had, but I'd taken it to be more small talk than a statement of intent. When Jazz's face lit up at her suggestion, I realized I had a lot to learn about the man. "That could be fun." Jazz's eyes darted to me. "I mean, if I—we're still here next Friday?"

I didn't think he was being coy, but questioning whether what we had now would still be in a week. As if I would tire of him. Or him of me.

I couldn't say if one would happen, but I could assure him of the other. "We'll be here."

"O-kay." Hallie's eyes darted between us. "That felt a little more dramatic than the questioned warranted, but cool. I'll call you with the ingredient list. I'm too poor to be buying extra dinners in the week. Especially for a house of hungry men."

She started her car, the engine running noticeably smoother down the driveway than it had when she'd arrived.

I suspected Faust had been unable to resist the call of an engine in need.

"Thank you, Knox. That was really fun."

I gathered his hand in mine. "She's a good cook. And funny."

"Wow, I think in Knox-speak that means you love her." Jazz laughed.

I didn't want to say anything that would knock that smile off his handsome face, but we clearly needed to have a talk. "What was that about *if* you'll be here next week? Were you planning on moving along?" Try as I did to keep my question monotone, a growl slipped out at the end.

His eyes rounded briefly. "I just—I didn't—I wouldn't assume you would—"

I brought Jazz into the sitting room, tugging him to sit by my side on the sofa that faced the window to the forest. "You aren't exactly hard to keep. You eat in a day what Diesel does in a meal, and you're pretty good at entertaining yourself. Why would I mind if you stayed?"

"You guys seem to have this whole revenge thing going,

and I want to help, but you haven't seemed that open about it with me, so I assumed at some point, you'd just..." He shrugged.

I wanted to pull him into my lap and tell him he would never be leaving, but I wouldn't keep him here by force—anymore. This needed to be his choice. "It's been the five of us for so long, our days are normally silent." None of us had anything to say to each other that wasn't related to the attack. "I will attempt to speak more."

Jazz stood, his shaky movements betraying his casual tone. "Okay, okay, no need to get mushy on me. I have a favor to ask anyway."

I waited for him to find the words for what he wanted to ask. Jazz wasn't normally so formal, and this new attitude piqued my curiosity.

"If I'm going to be here a bit, at least a week, anyway..." His cheeks went red, and he spoke quickly, like he was still unsure. "I was wondering if, when you have time, you could teach me how to fight. Or, at the least, how to not freeze."

I didn't understand him at first. Teach him how to fight? When would he ever need to know how to fight? If he was ever in a situation where someone wanted to hurt him, I'd take care of the threat. And if not me, one of the others.

"I keep thinking about that guy with the knife and how my brain just blanked out. I'm usually fast on my feet, but it's like I see a weapon and..." He made sounds like a plane soaring and then crashing out of the sky. "How do I fix that?" He turned his face toward me, his eyes shining with emotion. "How do I not be helpless?"

I didn't want him to fight. He had no reason to learn. He was tricky enough to get out of most situations, and the rest...I'd take care of. But, I wouldn't have my boy feeling helpless—not in any situation.

I had Jazz change into something he could move more freely in before taking him down to the gym. Before I had Jazz to fill my hours, I spent them all in the gym. Since his arrival, I hadn't been once, but that familiar smell greeted me. Rubber from the mats, disinfectant, metal, and lingering sweat. The smell was as comforting to me as baked apple pie was to others.

"Wow," Jazz breathed, taking in the brightly lit space. "This place is..."

We were alphas accustomed to lives as mercenaries. Wild animals attempting to live in a domestic world. If the guys didn't have the weights and bags to get out their aggressions, we'd have a shitload more bruises and scrapes between us.

Still, I understood his amazement. We'd renovated some of the rooms, had made a few of them more than livable, but the gym, we'd completely redone. The wall along the entrance held windows where you could watch your form. There were free weights, bars, punching bags, an area for target practice, assault dummies, and several cardio machines, though we tended to use those less frequently.

The fluorescent lights lined the ceiling overhead, casting every inch of the room with a bright, artificial glow. The flooring was made of enforced rubber to soften things falling without a bounce. Everything was new—or had been when we'd bought it. From this room, it was easy to forget the damp, musty disrepair the rest of the place was in.

"You've been holding out, Knox. This place is awesome." His warm brown eyes took in every surface.

I preened like a peacock until I remembered what Hallie had said. If I could make one room look like this, why couldn't I do the same with the whole damn place? Then, no one would see an old haunted party spot but a—

A what? A home? My mind sneered that word with contempt. We'd had a home and had lost it. We'd failed to protect the only people in the world who had counted on us. "To get started, hop on the treadmill."

Jazz looked dubiously from me to the treadmill. "But you're supposed to be teaching me how not to freeze."

"That's an instinct thing. Everyone knows fight or flight, but in some cases, freezing is the thing that keeps you safe. It makes sense that you freeze. Animals that can hide, make themselves look like something else. Staying in one place is the thing that ensures your safety. But you can train yourself. Change your instinct."

I lifted him by the biceps and carried him to the treadmill. His curls bounced softly with each step. "Before we do any of that, you need to warm up. Five minutes, light jog. You've run from me enough times I know you can do that much."

I tapped the buttons to get the belt started, and Jazz pumped his legs to keep up. "Run? More like sauntered," he said under his breath.

He'd spent much of the previous five years running from dangerous people. And he was really good at it. It made sense that he took pride in that. What else did he have?

"Saunter for five minutes, then." I smacked his butt, and he yelped, turning his head to hide his smile. He'd must've forgotten there were nothing but mirrors in front of him.

When the five minutes were up, he joined me in the sparring square. The mats were thicker in this area, offering more impact absorption. It still hurt to get laid out on your ass, but it was better than nothing—or nursing constant concussions and broken limbs.

Immediately, Jazz brought up his fists like he was going

to fight me. His slim arms were wobbly, and when I pushed his shoulders, he tripped to the side.

"Hey, that's pushing, not fighting."

I attempted to hide my smirk.

"You're making fun of me," Jazz growled, wiggling his fingers. On anyone else, the gesture wouldn't be menacing, but on Jazz it was damn near a threat.

I eyed his fingers. I'd yet to bring up his stunt with the fake pictures. "I'm not making fun of you. You're cute, that's all."

"Oh great," he huffed, sending locks of hair flying from his forehead. "Now you're infantilizing me. Awesome."

"No to that too. You're cute, deal with it." I just barely stopped myself from ruffling his hair, and only because the way he looked at me now, I'd likely lose a finger if I tried. "Now stop trying to distract me. What's your goal in a fight?"

Jazz brought his fists up again. "To hurt the other person."

I reached out, pushing him over from the other side. "Wrong."

"Then what?" Jazz growled as he stumbled for his footing.

"To not die. That's your only goal. And you get there by removing yourself from the situation, neutralizing the threat, or staying alive until help can arrive. If you can run, Jazz, you will always run. Say that to me right now. I need to hear it."

He frowned and brought his hands up to hang on his hips. "You want me to confess to being a coward?"

I grabbed him, crushing him against my chest. Picturing Jazz in a situation where he needed to defend himself made my chest feel like a live grenade, the pin pulled, waiting to explode. He'd started as collateral, but if I was being honest, he'd turned into more than that the moment he escaped our clutches the first time. We didn't even get a good look at him the first time. His hair had been a flash of red, driving by in a car he'd maneuvered possession of. "That doesn't make you a coward. It makes you alive, which is the whole fucking point."

Forcing my arms to relax, I let him stand back on his own two feet.

"Stance a little more than shoulder width." I kicked his feet apart. "Keep your weight on the balls of your feet. You're light, you're springy. You can remain in one spot or move, but if you put your weight on your heels—" I motioned for him to do just that, pushing softly when he did. "You're unsteady. You have less control, and you will fall. Got it?"

Jazz nodded, soaking in my instruction like a sponge. "Got it. Heels bad, balls good." He inhaled sharply, finding my eyes. "You know what I mean."

We worked on Jazz's stance for thirty more minutes, practicing how to use his body weight as a weapon. With his frame, he wouldn't be the strongest man in a fight and needed to know how to use more than muscles.

He was eager to learn and took instruction well, but his body wasn't used to fighting, so when his thighs began to tremble, I put a pin in it for the day.

"I hardly learned anything," Jazz whined as I pulled him down to the mat beside me to stretch.

"You learned enough for the day." I did ruffle his hair then.

He didn't take my fingers, but he scowled, blasting a curl up off his face. "You didn't even show me a knife."

My heart stuttered. I wanted to promise Jazz he'd never see a weapon brandished towards him in violence again, that I'd be there to protect him. But I had no way of knowing where our investigation would take us, the leads we'd have to follow, and the types of places we'd have to go. With my own future so uncertain, how could I make promises to anyone else?

"This was only the first day. We can come back every day and do a little. I should be training more than I am anyway."

That pacified him enough that he sighed, letting out the air that had kept his shoulders tense. He flopped back on the mat, staring up at the lights while his hair fanned out around his head. It wasn't exactly a stretch, but I'd allow it since it had been a lighter day. "How did you learn all of this?" he asked, his eyes reflected the bulbs overhead. "Or did you come out of the womb fighting?" He laughed and rolled over to look at me. "Probably punched the doctor on the way out."

"No, brat." I slid down to lay beside him. "I am naturally athletic because I'm a shifter and an alpha—"

"What does that mean? An alpha? What is everyone else?"

I lifted my arm, and Jazz curled into my side, snuggling beneath it. There was nothing like holding Jazz after spending any length of time with him out of my arms. "Shifters. Most shifters are just that, but, every so often, an alpha is born to help protect, to nurture. Many believe alphas are meant to be the strongest man in a fight, and we are, but violence isn't our calling. We're meant to care for people. It's a shame you couldn't have met my team before. The men they are now..." I forced the rest of that air out, it tasted tainted by the memory. "We're all different. Losing Pierce was difficult, and then we lost everything else."

Jazz sighed, rolling to his side and flinging his leg over my waist.

My cock stirred, encouraged by the wayward limb.

"How did it happen?"

I inhaled his scent; the warm vanilla clung to my skin. I wanted to roll in it, cover my body with his smell. Up until this point, I'd held back from scenting him, truly scenting him, as I would if he were a pack member. But I did then, letting his essence fill me. There wasn't anything sexual about the action, despite my existing arousal.

Scenting had been a daily occurrence in our old life, an important habit to all of us alphas, likely *because* our situation was so uncommon. Intimate but not arousing, on its lowest level, scenting was about recognizing responsibility. Scenting was a claim that said *this is a person I protect*. I'd considered Jazz mine to protect from the very beginning, but I'd done so as a man. Now, I recognized him as a wolf.

"What are you sniffing up there?" Jazz asked. "Is my hair dirty?"

"No, you smell good enough to eat."

He stirred, wiggling tighter to my side, his arm and leg draped around me. "If you don't want to tell me, that's okay. I understand if we're not at the sharing traumatic things that happened to us point in our rel—friendship."

His cheeks burned bright, and he attempted to slide away, but I held him tight. "It was a mission. Nothing different about it, nothing unusual. We were in Columbia—"

"What were you doing there?"

If there had been any danger in him knowing, I wouldn't have told him, but as it was, anyone who'd been involved that day was dead now. "We'd been hired by one of the cartels. His daughter had been kidnapped by a rival, and she didn't make it. We were hired to kill the rival's son in retaliation."

Jazz gasped, and that time, I let him slide away. He didn't move to put space between us, as I'd expected. He repositioned his body, laying mostly on top of me with his hands flat on my chest. His chin rested against his knuckles. "You killed people? For money?" Despite the nature of his question, there was no fear in his eyes.

"We were mercenaries, Jazz. We didn't get hired to put on bake sales. But there are plenty of people in this world who would only improve the state of things if they no longer existed. Killing that man's son was a kindness to the people living in the local villages. The man was a menace, taking what he wanted when he wanted. We were hired by bad people to kill bad people. But that is my point. We had no reason to suspect anything was off until Pierce went in first —like always—to clear the entrance, and the entire manor went up. There could have been no survivors. The only reason myself and the others weren't killed by the blast was because we'd been tossed into the pool.

"Clearly, the rival cartel had known to suspect something, but a blast at that magnitude couldn't have been planned. It killed everyone in the mansion, Pierce included. As near as we could tell, it had been an accident—men playing with weapons they didn't understand. When we'd returned to question the man who had hired us, we found out he'd been assassinated that same day."

"I'm sorry," Jazz whispered, his face bouncing as his jaw braced the weight of his head. "That sounds horrible. You all must have been close working together for so long."

"Like brothers." Losing Pierce had been like losing a limb. I'd never known a pain so deep, until we'd returned home and I lost my heart along with everything else. "In the shifter world, it is uncommon for multiple alphas to lead at once. One is named Alpha, with a capital A, and he holds the power. But in our pack, the six of us worked together, bringing our pack prosperity and comfort it never would've had with only one of us in charge." For as long as it lasted, our situation had been perfect.

But nothing lasts forever.

Jazz's lips were warm along my jaw as he kissed me sweetly.

"What was that for?"

"You look so sad when you talk about them. I hate it. It hurts me here..." He patted his chest with his hand. "But I still want you to talk about it because that's important."

A rumble started low in my gut, like a purr. Wolves didn't purr, unless Jazz was in the area apparently. I lifted myself into a sitting position on the weight bench behind us, pulling Jazz with me so that he sat facing me, straddling my lap.

"Which stretch is this?" he joked, his laughter cut short when he met my eyes and saw the sudden desire I knew burned in my gaze.

"I like that you're here." I murmured the words I hadn't let myself say earlier. "I want you to stay, for as long as you want to. Stay, please."

"The guys will—"

"They can deal with it how they want. Our mission is the same. Once they see that nothing has changed there, they'll relax."

"Until you run out of money."

I didn't hear any bitterness as I'd expected, but there was an edge of shame that had me leaning back to see more of his face. Could he possibly feel guilt that we wouldn't be getting the money his father had promised us? The first half was ours, and we had a chunk remaining—though it didn't sit right with me to leave a job unfinished. But, when finishing the job meant never seeing Jazz again, that mattered less.

"They worry. We aren't destitute. I'll figure something out before we are." Figuring out something for them meant figuring something out for Jazz as well now, and that planted the seed of a feeling I didn't think I'd ever experience again.

Jazz's brows dipped, forming a straight line. "I'll earn my keep. I can bring in money. I have a few ongoing cons I can—"

"No." I shook my head. "I don't want you using your power on the outside. I might not want to return you to your father, but that doesn't mean he doesn't want you. Until I know why, you need to lay low."

"We live in an abandoned hotel on the outskirts of a tiny town. How much lower can I lay?" His tone dipped, the nature of his words having the same effect on him as they did on me.

I'd been pushing down my desire, tamping it back, but when he sounded like *that*? Impossible. My grip tightened on his waist. "I'm going to kiss you," I warned him, knowing that once I claimed his mouth, there would be no restraint.

Thinking about him being harmed, asking him to stay, I was already on edge, wrangling my nature to something a little more manageable.

"I want you too," Jazz sighed.

My mouth covered his, my tongue surging forward to get that first taste. His moan mixed with my growl, and I cupped his head, threading my fingers through his silky strands. Kissing Jazz felt like traveling back in time to a world that could be happy and good.

His hips wiggled, desperate for friction, and I gripped him tightly, holding him in place as I ground him against me. My cock strained against the fabric of my pants, sliding between Jazz's clothed ass. The fabric refused to give, preventing me from getting as deep as I wanted. And with Jazz, I wouldn't be happy until he'd taken all of me.

Jazz's fingers dug into my shoulders. "Wait, wait," he gasped. "If you don't stop, I'm going to come in my pants."

As gratifying as that would be to my ego, if he came in his pants, I wouldn't get to watch his cock exploding with pleasure. I wouldn't be able to taste his sweet release. "I'll buy you new pants," I said before my nails sharpened and I sliced along the seam of his sweats. They fell from him like ribbons, his shirt following immediately after.

My breath hitched as I stared at his beautiful body. Soft where I was hard, rounded where I was sharp, he complimented me in every way. My dick was no exception. His body relaxed on my fingers, aided along by the pack of lube in my pocket.

He rested his cheek against my shoulder, mewling as my fingers slid, one, two, three, then four fingers deep. I looked up, catching our reflection in the mirrors ahead. I was clothed, save for my pants being open in the front for my dick.

Jazz's naked body trembled on top of mine, his back muscles rippling as he strained to drive more than my fingers inside him.

I cupped his cheek with my free hand. The pad of my thumb rubbed over his glistening lips, swollen from my kisses. "I fuck you, and you're mine."

Delicacy wasn't my strong suit, but I had to trust that my message was clear. I'd held back the first time, needing to be inside of him more than I'd needed anything else. That was still the case now, but it was what would happen after that I needed to warn him about.

"I'm already yours," he groaned, wiggling his hips in a desperate attempt to get me to move.

How was I supposed to resist that? I didn't.

I lifted my boy so his ass hung over my cock before plunging him down. His keening cry echoed over my shoulder as he buried his face into the crook of my neck, gasping and moaning when I began to move.

I stayed stationary, lifting and lowering Jazz as I wanted him.

"You're so fucking big," he wailed. "I can't breathe without feeling your dick in me."

My groaning growl shook the bench, and I let Jazz's weight fall, impaling him on my cock. Fully seated, I rolled my hips. My thrusts no longer brought me in and out of him, but the head of my cock rubbed against his secret spot, prodding the cluster over and over.

"I'm going to—" He threw his head back and screamed out his orgasm.

I opened my mouth and stuck out my tongue to catch his sweet cream.

He slumped against me. A kinder man might've given him a moment to come down, for his sensitivity to wane. But I was not a kinder man. With the taste of his pleasure on my tongue, I took control of his hips again, plowing into him with a force that made the bench creak and lift from its legs.

Jazz moaned, his body shaking when my balls tightened and my orgasm shot out of me, enthusiastically filling Jazz with my seed.

I groaned, drawing the last of both our orgasms out while I continued to pump.

He sighed moments later, collapsing against me in a manner that could only be described as boneless.

"That was a good lesson," he mumbled as if in a daze. "We definitely should repeat that lesson every day."

I smiled, tucking Jazz against me as I looked around for something to cover him during the trip back to my room. I found a few towels that would do, as long as he stayed in my arms. He didn't seem to mind that aspect and lay sweetly while I carried him back to the room.

By the time I had the shower running, the water heating up so it wouldn't shock him, I realized Jazz had never done what I asked. The sneaky imp. He'd never promised to run.

9

JAZZ

A SEAGULL FLEW BY, giving the wall of windows a double look. Could he see through to us inside? Or did he see his only his own reflection, and he was checking himself out?

The ocean brought a fresh breeze that blew in through the cracks in the boards whether the guys wanted it to or not. When the breeze was strong enough, it lifted the papers and photos the guys had spread out over every horizontal surface. Normally, they caught whatever had been blown before it got too far; they all had crazy fast reflexes. They didn't trip or bump into things. Other than that time I scared Huntley, I hadn't seen a one of them move in a way they hadn't absolutely intended.

Sometimes, when the hours would stretch and I'd been staring at the same three lines of the same police report, I'd take a break and watch the men. They didn't talk a lot, but they communicated just fine without words. The four of them—Diesel was still protesting my presence—grunted and gestured their points across. At times, it felt like they had entire conversations without saying a word. I never knew what they spoke about, but the air changed when it happened, shimmering with unspoken words.

I wasn't entirely sure Huntley and Jagger didn't share the same brain. They weren't identical, as I'd originally thought. They weren't even blood brothers, but their blood was the only different thing about them. Their blood and Jagger's scar. I wanted to know more about it, but that seemed like the sort of story you waited for, not asked for.

Knox silently held out his hand. Faust handed him a folder labeled Perimeter Report, and Knox grunted his thank you. All they had left of their home were these photos, reports, and the evidence they'd collected. The police had been called—destruction of that magnitude would've been impossible to conceal from authorities—but the attack was so far outside of the local police's investigating abilities, they hadn't been a lot of help. It had taken five years to get anyone to tell them what their biggest clue, the matter left over from the explosive itself, was *most* like.

To add insult to injury, the explosion had released some sort of chemical into the ground that had killed everything that had survived the blasts. No trees or bushes would grow in the once-fertile land they'd called home. Knox described the gardens they'd kept—supplying fresh food to a pack the size of a small village, but after the blast, it was all just rot and decay.

The wind whistled, lifting a single sheet from the stack in front of Faust.

"I got it." I jumped to my feet, eager for something more to do. I wanted to feel like I was helping, but so far, I was just staring. We all were. The only difference was, this was my first time seeing this; the others could probably sketch every crime scene photo from memory.

The sheet fell near the door, and I bent to pick it up. I

brought it back to the table and bent over the top, searching for something that would work as a paperweight. Faust's chair creaked as he leaned in close before inhaling softly.

I looked at him from the corner of my eye, catching his expression the moment before he blinked away the shock. "I'm sorry," he said quietly.

When I looked to Knox, he wasn't upset. He stared at us with an odd expression.

The gesture hadn't felt sexual. I didn't think Faust was making a pass, but it felt *important* in a way I couldn't put my finger on. My eyes fell to the table, dropping to a picture partially concealed. I slid it out from the pile: a picture from the aftermath, of a charred structure that might've been a home.

"I didn't think it was snowing that night."

"It wasn't," Huntley replied.

"The average temp that night was forty degrees Fahrenheit, five degrees Celsius," Jagger added without looking up.

My ears tingled. I was onto something, but I didn't know what that thing was yet. "What is all this white stuff then?"

At my tone, Knox put down the file he'd been reading, and Faust leaned in again, this time to look at the picture in my hand. "It's insulation from the building. It's made to be fire retardant. That's why some is just singed."

I saw what he meant, the bits of water-soaked fluff with charred edges, but mixed within those bits, nearly identical, was something else. With my ability, where the devil was in the details, I knew how having just one element out of whack could bring an entire illusion down.

Faust reached for the photo as Jagger handed him a handheld magnifying glass. He bent over it, moving the glass over the picture as he muttered, "Is there another from this same set?"

The four of us searched the table, but Faust found the rest and thumbed through them. His movements sharpened, the intensity in his arms increasing the longer he looked.

I wasn't the only one of us waiting and watching silently. Even Dog watched his owner, his eyes never blinking.

"How did we...?" He looked up sharply, finding Knox first and then Huntley and Jagger. "He's fucking right. There is insulation that you can see in this photo."

He'd cleared everything from the surface and slapped the picture against the tabletop.

"Here and here, this is all insulation we used when constructing the buildings. But this one, *just* this one, the white stuff is slightly different, and none of it is charred."

"But what is it?" Huntley asked as Jagger searched his own files for similar photos.

Faust didn't answer.

My heart pounded, but I couldn't believe we'd found a clue so quickly.

"Did you gather any?" Knox asked Faust.

He was already on his feet heading for the door, Dog following after. "I have some of everything left over from the site and all of most that was left over."

I didn't concentrate too hard on what he said because I thought if I did, my head would just hurt, but I got the gist. If they had some of this white stuff stored away, they could identify it and figure out where it came from. If it came from the bomb, then they were one step closer to figuring out who had made it.

"Where do we take it if he has a sample?" Huntley asked.

Both twins looked to Knox, waiting for his answer. His eyebrows were in full-brood mode, but his lips were set in only a half glower. This was his thinking face. "The university up north. They were the most helpful last time around. And if they can identify it, that would mean the shortest wait time for us."

"Diesel should be here," Jagger commented quietly. His voice almost a whine, but it didn't sound petulant. More lost.

Huntley growled sharply, dropping his hand to Jagger's shoulder and squeezing. "If he wanted to be, brother, he would be. We can't force him."

Diesel was built like a redwood and a mountain came together and had a biker lumber-baby. They couldn't force him, and he wouldn't come around. Not as long as I was there. I frowned, hugging myself as I let the unhappy thought roll around in my head.

On the one hand, the guys seemed a little more vibrant these days. The twins had hung around the kitchen the entire time Hallie had been here teaching me how to cook lasagna. They were the first in line with plates when it was done too. Later, I'd gone into the kitchen expecting the mess I'd left behind, but after the twins had thanked me quietly for the food, they'd slipped into the kitchen to clean it.

I'd met the men as mercenaries. Once things had settled and it became clear I wasn't leaving, I began to see their other sides. They were hurting, every single one of them, but I hoped my presence was helping. It was a selfish thought and one I couldn't believe when it became clear that I was the thing keeping them apart.

"I've got some." Faust brandished two small plastic bags. One had what looked like insulation. The charred edges had crumbled some, leaving black bits to shake in the corner of the bag. The other looked almost exactly the same, except there were no blackened edges. It almost looked new. "And I found a lurker."

Diesel stomped in after. Either he had amazing timing, or he'd been listening after all. "There's been a development?" he asked from behind his thick strands.

"Jazz pointed it out," Huntley said.

"It could be nothing!" I piped up because there was starting to feel like too much hope in the room than I was comfortable with. Especially since this hope hinged on my idea, my observation. What if the insulation was just in a different spot of the structure related to the blast? That could also explain the difference in appearance.

"We've had nothing for five years," Diesel grunted. "This is something. Thank you."

Uncomfortable with his gratitude, I looked to Knox and found him already staring at me, his forehead lined with thought. He held his hand out, and I went to him, squeezing his fingers tightly as he pulled me closer to his side. His nose buried in my hair, and he inhaled. Unlike when Faust had leaned in to sniff, this felt romantic. My stomach fluttered at the sound of his quiet inhale. "If it's nothing, it's nothing," he said, his voice thick with contentment. "But at least now we have something to do. Huntley and Jagger will go to the university up north while we go through the photos and gather any with pictures of this stuff. Faust, how much had we ended up taking as a sample?"

"A fair amount. Judging for this picture, likely most that was present."

Knox nodded. "We'll sort that out too. Gather all that you can from the evidence room and bring it here."

With their orders, the team sprung into action. The twins prepared to leave, while Diesel took their spot, thumbing through the papers in front of him for more of the pictures. Faust went back to the evidence room, returning with a large box of similar small bags. I helped him sort through the samples.

About an hour later, we'd organized and categorized the evidence into normal insulation and mystery insulation. We wouldn't hear from the twins until at least tomorrow afternoon, so there was nothing to do but wait and hope I hadn't sent everyone on a wild goose chase.

"Don't be so nervous," Knox said after Diesel retreated again to his portion of the hotel. "They need things to do. Even things that don't amount to anything. We were away, sometimes, for long stretches of time, but when we were home, we were able to care for and protect our people in other ways. They miss it."

He glanced at my hands, and I followed his gaze. I had a paper clip between my hands and had been idly conjuring illusions. It was a flower, then a leaf, then a sample bag of that mystery insulation. The motion was comforting more than anything else, but Knox's face always pinched when I used my powers in front of him, so I stopped, letting the paper clip fall to the table with a clatter.

Knox picked up the paper clip, worrying it between his fingers. "I want you to call your friend, Hollister. You two have more in common than you might know."

My heart pounded, and my hands went sweaty. He was done with me. We'd had our fun, and now he needed to get back to the mission. All that *mine* stuff had been bogus, and—

"Jazz." Knox growled out my name, his eyes once again on my hands.

I gasped at the squirming, many-legged *creature* in my palm. It looked like a spider with the legs of a centipede, and I didn't remember conjuring it, or picking up the paper-clip, but there it was in my hand. Until I dropped it and the paper clip fell to the ground. "Sorry."

More emotions than I could keep track of passed through his gaze. He grabbed my hand; the warmth of his fingers helped cut through my sudden anxiety. "I'll make us something to eat while you call your friend. You're...it's too similar for me to be comfortable."

Despite the comfort of his touch, his vague hesitation poured gasoline on my frayed, burning nerves. I had no reason to be afraid right now. Even if Knox did send me on my way, he'd told me he wouldn't hand me over to my father. I'd be free to return to the life I'd known. I wouldn't stay where I wasn't wanted. That had always been my one rule. But thinking about what that meant just made my heart pound harder. That life hadn't always been horrible, but it didn't have Knox.

These thoughts occupied my brain on the walk to the kitchen. Knox sat me down in the chair at the small table, handing me my phone. My eyes widened. I hadn't seen my phone since I'd been taken, and after a while, I'd stopped caring about it. Seeing it now was like returning to an old hobby, one that had once meant so much but now felt foreign.

"I should've given it back to you a while ago," Knox said, his voice as clear when he was confessing his regrets as it was at any other time. He went to the fridge, leaving me to thumb through my contacts to Hollister's number.

"Jazz?" Hollister's answer sounded out of breath. "Aver, wait...it's Jazz."

There was a low rumble from somewhere on Hollister's end. "If this is a bad time..."

"It isn't!" Hollister replied. "How are you? I've been

worried, especially after you stopped texting. What's going on? Where are you right now?"

As the questions flooded in, my lips turned up in the corners. Of all my city-specific friends, Hollister was by far my favorite. Whenever I'd come into town, he'd asked no questions and had been ready for wherever the night took us. "I'm fine. Who's Aver?"

There was a louder growl from the other end, and Knox looked back sharply.

Hollister just laughed. "Babe, I didn't...it just didn't come up." Hollister's voice sounded muffled, like he was talking to someone in the room instead of into the phone.

I assumed that was Aver taking issue with the fact that I didn't know who he was. The last time I'd seen Hollister... "Oh! That hot guy at the club!"

That time, Knox's growl was sharp.

"The same," Hollister said. "So what happened? Did Knox catch up?"

Catch up, like he'd had homework or a note to give me. I pictured that afternoon we'd spent in the gym. "We caught up."

"So? And? Tell me everything!"

Under Hollister's words was a quiet coo, a gurgling, and then a stream of unmistakable babble. *Did he have a baby?* Clearly, my life wasn't the only one going through some changes. "Okay, I'll start, but you're going right after."

An hour later, Knox had made dinner, ate—while making sure I continued to eat during talking breaks—and hung around while Hollister told me everything that had happened to him. About meeting Aver, learning he wasn't the only person with abilities, and then everything that had happened after. Including his impossible pregnancy.

"Pregnant?" I balked. "Like 'child growing inside of you' pregnant?"

"Exactly like that."

My nose wrinkled at the thought. "Where did it grow? How? You don't have...the parts." There was likely a more delicate way for me to have asked that.

"It's a blessed thing," Hollister said like that explained anything. "But it really doesn't sound like what happened to me and the rest of us is happening to you. You might just have your own brand of uniqueness going on."

I told him about my journey to the Hotel Royal Paynes, the running, the chasing. I was vague on where we were now, though Hollister seemed to have some idea because he asked if I was enjoying the coast. My mind reeled at the knowledge that one of my closest friends was now a wolf shifter and that he'd had a baby. My story felt boring in comparison.

When I got to the part where I told Hollister what I could do, he interrupted me with a sharp, "All those nights you said you were paying?"

I grimaced. We'd always gone to bars somehow related to my father, but that didn't make it completely better. Especially when the bar owners went to count the till at the end of the night and found only paper. "I've been keeping track," I lied, earning another sharp growl from Knox. The man was a human lie detector.

Vaguely, in the same way I thought it would be nice to see the Northern Lights some time, I'd planned on paying back for everything I'd taken. When I'd been younger, I'd kept track in a notebook of all the things I'd stolen or places I'd stayed with bogus credit cards or letters from some imaginary important person.

"Okay, I haven't been keeping track, but I have a vague idea."

"But your dad is alive?" Hollister asked, the question coming from left field.

"Yes?" Unfortunately.

"He's your real dad?"

I scoffed. Of that, I was completely sure. There was no way my father, the great Mr. Walter Whitten, would've spent one penny on my care if he weren't sure of his parentage.

"Why are you asking if he's dead?"

Hollister didn't say anything for a moment. "The four of us all have certain things in common. All of our biological parents died early. Does the name Patrick Walker mean anything to you?"

Surprisingly, I did feel an inkling of awareness when he mentioned the name, but not enough to speak on it. "No, sorry."

"And our birthdays aren't the same," Hollister said as if what he said meant anything.

"No, remember? I came down for your party that year, and we got into the Jell-O pit with the strippers, and you kept trying to get me to eat Jell-O from their—"

The snarls came in surround sound, from my side of the phone and on Hollister's.

Hollister burst out laughing. "I do remember that." He caught his breath. "Seriously, though, this is strange. The things we had in common, the things we believe explain what's been going on in our lives, it doesn't match your life. I think this is something else, but...I don't know what. How do you feel? Are you...wait...you and Knox, are you..."

Hollister's questions started coming faster and faster, pouring from his mouth the moment the words hit his mind.

My gaze darted to Knox, who stood in front of the sink, running the washed dinner dishes under water. I knew what I wanted us to be. *I fuck you, and you're mine.* Those had been his exact words. While direct, the scope of the statement wasn't clear enough for me to answer any questions regarding our status. "I feel fine. Great actually." There, I could answer one of the questions. I could still feel the emptiness in the universe where my answer would've nestled. Were Knox and I...sleeping together? Yes. I didn't know how to answer anything beyond that.

"That's a relief, then. If anything changes, I want you to call me right away, okay Jazz? I'm going to have Nana and some of the others help me figure out how you might be connected to us. Maybe it's the same thing! But there are no more Walker cousins, so I don't know why Patrick would..." It sounded more like he was arguing with himself than talking to me.

"I will. I'll call. You too, though. I need to hear all about this baby. I expect at least a million more pictures sent to my phone by the time we talk again, got it?" As family went, Hollister was as good as a brother. That he could be so important to me and yet I saw him so infrequently was just a sad commentary on how little I needed to feel connected.

When I hung up, I expected a thousand questions from Knox, but he asked nothing. He'd been in and out during the call, mostly doing his own thing but staying nearby. I was happy after talking to Hollister but also alarmed. He said his ability was somehow related to him becoming pregnant. Would that happen to me? Was that why Knox wanted me to call? To warn me? Or to scare me away?

He'd explain it. He'd say what he thought in that crisp, clear way of his, and I'd understand everything better.

He didn't explain it, though. Had he known? Was he

worried I was pregnant? Should I be? *How was I even asking that question?*

I met Knox's gaze, waiting for him to say the perfect thing. It would be rough, and he'd bark it out, but I'd feel comforted just like all the other times. Except, when our eyes met, he didn't say anything.

Neither of us did.

10

KNOX

I LEFT Jazz sleeping on his side in my bed. Our bed. He'd had a fitful night's sleep, but I was the one causing his anxiety, so I wasn't qualified to comfort him. That only irritated me. I didn't like thinking there was something that Jazz needed that I couldn't provide.

I'd known talking to his friends would cause a disturbance, if only because now he looked at me like he thought my dick shot poison.

On my way to the kitchen, I recognized the sound of an engine coming down the driveway. The twins couldn't have been back yet; they'd only left the day before. Except, when I looked out the front window, it was the Hummer pulling up the driveway with the twins inside.

They had to have driven all night to get here so soon. That either meant they had good news or bad news. I put the coffee on.

Huntley glided inside the kitchen without making a sound. Jagger stood beside him, an equally silent shadow. "We got an ID," Huntley said.

I made myself pour my cup slowly; *keep calm, stay in control.* "And?"

"The samples weren't the same." Jagger sat down at the table while Huntley got them both mugs. "The burnt pieces were fiberglass insulation, the same we used when we built the home."

Huntley sat down, sliding Jagger's mug to him. "The second sample is mineral wool, a common material for insulation, but not a kind that we utilized."

The six of us alphas, along with the pack, had built every inch of that place. We knew best what had gone into the construction. "So that must've come in from an outside source."

An outside source. Those three words sounded so innocent, but really, this outside source could be our culprit. This was our first real lead in...ever. All of our other attempts had led to dead ends. "How did you find out so fast?"

"The chief science officer recognized Huntley. She wanted to bone him."

Huntley growled. "No, she remembered us from last time. She'd wanted us to leave the almost sulfur behind the first time so her team could study it more. She was disappointed when she realized she knew exactly what this was."

If we sent the piece to the same lab who had nearly given us an answer before, they would be able to tell if any of that same substance was present on the mineral wool, and then we would know for sure, but I didn't need to wait for those results to be certain. This was a clue, a step in the right direction, and we were going to follow it until whoever was running at the other end realized there was no place for them to go.

"Good job. You two should get some sleep."

The cups of coffee in front of them were clue enough that sleep wasn't in their near future, but I suggested it all the same.

Huntley stretched his arms over his head. "We will. I'm all keyed up after so long in the car, though. I need a run."

"More than a run," Jagger added, though his words were heavy with desire.

I turned away as they did whatever it was they did. I didn't pay too much attention to the twins' relationship. They were a unit, had been since they'd joined our pack as children. Both alphas, they'd been silent about their situation when they'd arrived, and it wasn't until many years later that they shared the circumstances of their joining us.

I opened the fridge, my eyes landing first on the leftover lasagna Jazz had made. Hallie had patiently explained the steps, answering any questions he had, though there hadn't been many. There was one piece left, and I assumed the guys were trying to be polite and let Jazz have it.

He'd been quieter last night than I'd ever seen him. The call with Hollister had obviously scared him. I hated it but had no idea how to stop it. What I was able to do.

He was mine. But he wasn't.

Fuck that. Jazz was mine.

The phone call had been too much. Too much information, too much uncertainty, but, as Jazz continued to burrow himself into our broken pack, I couldn't keep any of it from him. He needed to know what had happened.

What could happen.

What might have already happened.

If Jazz were pregnant, I would know. Or one of the others. It was a part of our pack bond. Faust scenting Jazz yesterday was proof of how the others saw him.

"Where's Jazz?" Huntley asked somewhat wistfully. His

interest wasn't sexual but protective. Faust had scented Jazz, but I could tell the others wanted to as well.

Not Diesel—my hunch was that his prolonged absence was his attempt at stopping the effect Jazz had on the others —but Huntley and Jagger were on the fence. They wanted what we all did: someone to take care of again.

But that was something none of us thought we ever deserved a second chance at.

"Sleeping," I replied. Jazz was my...mine, but he'd become someone for all of them to protect, provide for, and guard.

Was that all he was to me? A person I'd claimed owner-ship over? I snagged the milk and brought it to the counter where I had a jar of protein powder.

I wasn't like Diesel; I didn't know what it meant to have an omega. I'd loved my pack, every single member, but none of them had made my body react the way Jazz did. I didn't wish to claim any of them the way I wanted to brand Jazz. It wasn't just a pack-alpha thing for me, but did that mean he was my mate? My omega? Any shifter could claim a mate, but only an alpha could claim an omega. Omegas weren't anything someone was born as. It was a dedication, a title bestowed upon them that offered them greater protection and security, and there was some lore that claimed an omega was strengthened by their alpha.

Could I still claim an omega? When I buried the last of our people, I'd sworn I would find who had killed them and bring vengeance. I carried that anger for years. There'd been no room in me for something as soft as what I felt for Jazz.

When I looked at him I felt stronger, more worthy of being a leader. Was that love? The emotion hadn't been something I'd spent any of my life pondering. I had needs. I knew how to satisfy those needs. Sometimes, I'd satisfied those needs with the same person on a regular basis, but there hadn't been romantic emotions involved. I used to watch Diesel with Quinlan and had been baffled by his easy expression of love.

"He's coming down." Jagger set his mug on the table.

We listened, ears inclined toward the floor above where Jazz shuffled around the room.

Huntley frowned. "Did you make him mad?"

His footsteps were louder than his normal patter, and he hadn't slammed every door but had closed them with more force than usual.

"He spoke with his friends from that pack in Walker County yesterday." But he'd enjoyed the call. Or had made it look like he enjoyed the call. It wasn't until after the call that he'd seemed upset. When the fear likely set in. I didn't have any idea what the exact cause was, and Jazz hadn't wanted to tell me.

"He's not happy now." Huntley shook his head slowly. His worried frown clashed with the amusement in his gaze. "I'm going in for a second cup."

Jagger thrust his out for Huntley.

Jazz's footsteps didn't lighten as he took the hallway to the stairs. His scent charged ahead, bringing his distinct flavor of lemon, rosemary, and warm vanilla. When he walked through the doorway, Huntley and Jagger stared in rapt attention, their eyes gliding up and down his body to check for injuries.

The worry I'd noticed in Huntley faded, having seen Jazz well and whole. Now he was just amused.

I set a cup of coffee in front of an empty chair along with cream and sugar. "Did you sleep well?"

"You guys are back early," Jazz said, his voice brighter than I would have expected.

Of course, he ignored my question in the process. I bit my tongue as my alpha clamored for his submission. This wasn't anything like what I'd felt for the pack. I'd needed their obedience, but that was for their safety. I'd never wanted their submission. But everything was different with Jazz.

Huntley stretched, sliding away from the table as his legs lengthened. "Didn't take us very long, and we got an answer right away. No reason to stay overnight."

"You found out?" Jazz's eyes widened, and he reached for his coffee, finally noticing I'd set it in front of him.

"It's insulation, but a different kind then what we used," Jagger said.

"But...is it a clue?" His leg tapped nervously under the table while his brow wrinkled.

Likely noting his distress, Jagger stretched over and ruffled Jazz's red curls. "It's a clue, Jazz Hands."

One corner of Jazz's mouth lifted. "Jazz Hands?"

"You know, because of your name and what you can do," Huntley supplied.

Jazz just shrugged and turned back to his coffee. He'd been nearly smiling, glad that he'd assisted us in finding a clue. When he turned his face to me, his smile dropped, and that same pinched irritation returned.

What the fuck did I do to him?

I had no idea, but clearly, I'd done something.

Faust came into the kitchen with Dog. Faust's hair stuck up. He hadn't even run his hands through it yet, but I assumed he'd heard Huntley and Jagger and had wanted to find out what they'd discovered.

One minute later, Diesel stalked through the same doorway. He kept to the walls, preferring the corners of the kitchen, but he got a cup of coffee and lingered as Huntley and Jagger told them about their journey.

During this, Jazz took the pepper shaker off the table and pressed it between his hand. He made a stack of bills, a pile of diamonds, idly pushing his hands together and letting his creations spring forth before closing his hands again.

"Not at the table," I snarled, and Jazz stiffened. *Fuck.*

Every face swung my way, none of them friendly. At least Diesel only looked confused.

I'd been on edge already. Jazz had been scared or mad at me since yesterday and refused to tell me what it was.

He was mine, but not so much that he'd tell me what was wrong. Maybe I didn't deserve to claim him, but my alpha wouldn't allow me to let him just walk out of my life. And watching him use his abilities was too much like watching the skills he'd used to leave.

While I may have had reasons to explain why I'd snarled, none of those reasons were an excuse.

Jazz met my gaze dead-on. Unblinking, he kept his eyes on me as he pressed his hands together, letting the shaker roll out of his hands. Now it looked like a huge spider, as large as a shoebox, skittering over the table toward me.

His anger I could take. But when he looked at me again, pain was all I saw. *Had Hollister told him something? Said something I hadn't heard?* I'd remained near him during the call, both out of preference and preservation. I needed to know what Hollister had to say if it was going to affect Jazz's health. "Want to let me know what that was about?" I asked evenly, gesturing with my forehead to the shaker laying on its side in its original form on the floor.

"You said you would teach me to fight and not freeze.

You *promised*. I'm beginning to think you don't know what that word means either." His eyes narrowed, and his lips clenched, flinging each word out into the world.

I crossed my arms, needing to do something with my body that wasn't yank Jazz flush against me and kiss him senseless. His defiance and anger were an affront to my alpha nature. "Is that what's been bothering you? Training?"

All at once, every muscle in Jazz's face worked in harmony to give me the most withering stare. A lesser man would've shied from it.

My chest swelled, my biceps tingling. This was a challenge, one I wanted to meet. Jazz's anger didn't burn brighter than my concern, and if we had to go head to head to figure out what was wrong with my boy, then we would.

"I'm. Fine." Jazz downed the coffee in front of him, and I winced. He hadn't eaten a lot last night, and he hadn't eaten anything this morning. Like before, the second he looked away from me and to one of the others, his expression softened. "One of you needs to eat the last of that lasagna before it goes bad. Hallie's going to teach me stir fry next."

I let out a silent exhale of relief. I remembered he'd made plans with Hallie. That meant he wasn't planning on running the moment I took my eyes off him. I still wouldn't be able to relax until I knew what had him all wound up.

I picked up the shaker, placing it in its original spot in front of Jazz. "Meet me in the gym after breakfast."

Jazz nodded and pushed back from the table. "I'll be there." He swept from the room, leaving a huge question mark in his chair.

"What did you do to him?" Faust asked, his voice full of awe.

I looked to Diesel standing in the corner. His clumpy hair hung in front of his face. These days the only time he wasn't scowling was when he got to blow something up. But right then, he was attempting to hide his smirk. Bastard.

My head swiveled back to the doorway. "I didn't do anything. Not on purpose."

"Purposeful or not..." Huntley said.

"...Jazz is pissed," Jagger finished. "But just at you, so—" He lifted his left shoulder sharply, letting it fall.

"Ready for that run?" Huntley asked him.

The two left together, and Faust moved around the kitchen, gathering breakfast for him and Dog. "I'll start researching that mineral wool. See if I can't narrow down a supplier."

Diesel plopped down at the now-empty table. "I'll help." His scowl turned my way. "Remember basic needs," he grunted.

Caring for a pack as large as ours hadn't been a seamless process. Especially toward the beginning when they were led by six—technically, five as Pierce had been a few years older—new adults. The twins were the youngest among us but we all had more muscle than brains. *Basic needs* was the phrase we used when attempting to determine why a person was acting the way they were and what we needed to do to fix that. Were they fed, had they hydrated recently, were they rested, and when had they last showered? Answering those questions normally led to a cause for the behavior and a solution.

Jazz hadn't eaten. He'd chugged coffee. He'd tossed and turned all night, but he smelled amazing. I could eliminate one possibility, then. His anger had begun yesterday. It obviously had something to do with the phone call.

Jazz must've finished changing because I heard his angry steps plod down the stairs, turning the corner to go down into the gym. I grabbed a protein bar and a banana. If

I planned on us actually exercising, I'd insist he eat more beforehand, but today, I wanted answers more than sweat.

"Good luck," Faust called out after my backside.

Diesel mumbled quietly, "He's gonna need it."

———

I FOUND Jazz in the gym, sitting on a mat and stretching his top half over his legs. He'd pulled his curls back off his face and scowled when I entered. His brow lifted at the food, but he quickly shuttered the expression to one of disinterest.

Hungry. There was one need I could meet.

I sat down on the mat, leaving a few feet between us. I set the protein bar and banana down nearer to him, hoping that was all the encouragement he would need to start eating. He grabbed the banana and angrily peeled it open while I set a water bottle in its place in front of him. He reached for the bottle.

Hydrated. Another need met.

I couldn't do anything about his poor sleep. Not at this moment.

While he ate, I retrieved my pouch. I waited for him to swallow the last of his protein bar before rolling the pouch out, revealing my set of throwing knives. They gleamed under the bright fluorescent lighting, and though Jazz hadn't made a sound when he saw them, his spine stiffened, and he leaned away.

"No treadmill first this time?" Jazz asked warily.

"Walk with me instead." I got to my feet, lowering a hand to Jazz. He ignored it, hauling himself up on his own. My chest rumbled, my alpha unhappy with his refusal to accept my help. A few laps around the gym would be good for us both, but I didn't want Jazz pushing himself too hard so soon after eating.

We took to the walls of the room, keeping to a relaxed pace, walking the circumference of the space twice before I broke the silence. "Do you want to call Hollister again today?"

Jazz shook his head. "He told me what he knows."

Inwardly, I scowled. But now I knew him missing Hollister wasn't a reason for his anger. Figuring out the reason for his mood would take forever if I only attempted to eliminate options.

I wasn't one to beat around the bush because when you were done, the result was the same, but now you had a fucked-up bush. Spare the bush, spoil the brat? Was that how it went? "Why are you mad at me?"

I watched his face and the way his lips pursed, the sad crinkle as his eyes slanted. Seeing him like this without knowing the cause was torture, and my alpha snarled. If he'd been honest, we could've figured this out in the kitchen. He wasn't being dishonest; he just didn't want to talk to me.

"I'm not mad."

Now he was lying. I let out a low, rumbling warning growl.

"Can we just train? This is important, Knox. It could mean my life or death." On the surface, he sounded reasonable. If I hadn't caught up with him when he'd been attacked the first time, he would've been killed. Him learning how to keep his head in a dangerous situation was important. I didn't doubt that.

It was the currents running beneath his words, the lines of tension and worry. Did he think danger was coming soon? That he would recently be in a place where he needed to defend himself? Alone?

We'd lapped around the gym for long enough. Jazz had relaxed since first seeing the knives. He didn't stand quite so stiffly, and his eyes didn't dart to the pouch every other second as if afraid it would move closer when he wasn't looking.

I broke from the wall, swerving back and lifting the knives from the floor to the workout bench. Jazz followed me, a silent, wary sentry.

The collection of throwing knives I kept in the gym was my practice set. When the six of us had decided to support our pack together, we'd trained, naturally taking to different weapon styles. Faust knew Dog wouldn't stay behind, so he'd worked on preparing him for the field. The twins had their swords, and Diesel had his explosive.

After my first throw, I'd been hooked. Countless hours of training later, and the knives felt like an extension of my body. I slid one of the blades from its sheath, letting it balance on the pad of my finger. "What is this?"

Jazz frowned. "I'm not doing some wax-on, wax-off bullshit."

The snarl that rumbled out of me was all alpha. "Answer the question, Jazz."

"It's a knife!" he shouted. "A sharp, pointy thing that can kill you when inserted."

Leading him to the opposite wall of the gym, we stood about ten feet from a circular target. Normally, I trained from farther back, but today wasn't about improving my skill. I sent the knife soaring, and Jazz jumped. My alpha was just glad he jumped toward me and not away. I was still a source of safety for him, and that knowledge let me breathe just a little easier.

The knife hit the center of the target with a thud. "You described what a knife can do, not what it is. It's a tool, Jazz.

Just like a fork or a hairbrush or a screwdriver. On its own, a knife is just a tool."

"Like you," he whispered.

His quiet disrespect was the straw that broke my alpha's back. With firm but gentle hands, I grabbed his wrists, bringing him against my chest, against my heart.

Jazz went rigid before he sighed softly, his cheek nestling against my beating heart, but then it was like he remembered he was angry and pushed away. Or made an attempt to. His pushes weren't very hard, and his fingers curled into my shirt, grabbing me even as he urged me back.

"You can be mad at me, Jazz. But I still deserve your respect. The same respect I give you."

Jazz pushed again, and that time, I let him go. "Fine. I'm sorry. That was rude." He didn't sound like he meant a word of that, but I needed to choose my battles.

I continued. "A knife is a tool. It can be a weapon. It can cut flesh, or it can cut an apple. It's the intent behind the use that you should be concerned with."

"What do I do with that advice?" Jazz slid a hand up his side to cling to his hip. "Should I say, *excuse me, sir, do you plan on killing me with that knife or providing a snack?*"

My lips twitched, and I fought the smile. Smartass. "No, but becoming more familiar with the tool will help you keep your head when you spot the next. I want you to pick up a knife and throw it. And then another and another, and when you finish, we'll gather them up and you'll throw again."

"Until when?"

"Until I say so."

Jazz huffed at that. "I won't be able to reach the target," he whined.

"That's fine."

He scowled but turned toward the knives. His hand shook as he reached for the first handle.

"To start off, you'll want to hold it with a hammer grip. That will be the easiest grip while you're learning." I demonstrated what I meant, and Jazz adjusted his hold, with his four fingers bent toward his palm and his thumb clenched at the top.

"Good. Now inhale. Aim. Slow exhale. Throw."

Jazz sucked in a sharp breath, closed his eyes, and flung the knife forward. It reached the wall, about three feet from the target. The handle hit the plaster and then landed with a muffled clatter against the mat.

"Good, again. This time, keep your eyes open and don't hold your breath."

Though angry at me, Jazz took instruction well. He sent a second knife through the air. It hit the wall on the other side, but at least that time, he'd kept his eyes open.

"Good. Again."

That instruction earned me a rude look from over Jazz's shoulder that went directly to my dick. If he was hoping his attitude would upset me, he'd be disappointed. It affected me, but not with anger. I longed to coax out his submission, to show him that I could not only protect him, but that I was a source of comfort. I wanted him to turn toward me, not away.

I shoved back my arousal for the moment and watched Jazz throw the remaining knives. Each throw was a little better. His hand shook a little less, and his eyes weren't quite so wide and fearful every time he grabbed a handle. When he'd emptied the pouch, we gathered the knives from the ground, and he went again.

After cycling through the knives twice more, his face was red, and his arm shook, but for different reasons than before. He didn't flinch when he reached for the handles. And he didn't fling the knife from him like he was desperate to get space between them.

He had the last in his hand and hurtled it forward, hitting the edge of the target with a vibrating *twang*. He looked back at me, his shoulders heaving as his breaths came more quickly.

I stood several feet back and to the left, with my hands clasped behind my back. "Again."

His jaw tightened, along with the fingers on his right hand. With the look on his face, I was lucky he'd thrown the last of the blades.

I kept my tone even but firm. "Do you have a problem with that?"

Jazz's shoulders hunched forward, and he turned away, but he couldn't hold it back as easily as he had. His ears were red, and I imagined I could see steam coming from the top of his head just before he spun around, flinging a finger at my chest. "Yeah, I do!"

Finally.

"You aren't teaching me anything! You're just toying with me!" His anger exploded from him similar to the way he'd been flinging those knives. He pushed off me and headed for the door. "I don't have to stay here for this."

I advanced forward, quickly passing him to stand between him and the door. I watched his face and body language, searching for signs that this was going too far, that he was too riled up—or worse, scared—to be reasonable.

He was angry still, but it was a righteous sort that made his eyes shine. Jazz narrowed his flashing eyes. "I thought you said I was free to go," he snarled.

My hands clenched into fists. Whatever Jazz saw in my face was enough to dampen the edge off his anger.

"You said you didn't want to go." Keeping my voice even was the most difficult thing I'd had to do this morning. I had to let him leave. If he wanted to leave, I had to let him.

He stomped forward, chest to chest. "I don't want to!"

His move brought our faces close together. His vanilla breath whispered over my cheek, electrifying my nerve endings. I wanted inside of him. I wanted to stamp him with my cock, brand him with my cum, and mark him as mine. My omega. The only thing stopping me was the pain in his gaze. His anger had come and gone, as had his worry, but the pain remained.

He acted as if I had personally hurt him. "What did I do, Jazz? Tell me and I'll fix it."

He stood stock-still. I'd neared as close to begging as I ever had, but I didn't care. Not as long as Jazz continued to stand there, swallowing hard, his head lowering between his shoulders. "I won't be your distraction," he bit out, refusing to look at me.

My... distraction?

The pieces fell into place, slowly, but they eventually settled into a picture. "I already told you that you were mine." That had been all I thought I needed to say on the matter. I wanted him here, but I wouldn't make him stay. And I wouldn't trick or manipulate him into staying either. That seemed pretty clear.

"For how long?" Jazz shot back, looking at me long enough for me to see the hurt. "I know you don't want the same thing to happen to me that happened to the others. To Hollister and his friends. I don't think it has. I'm not special or blessed like they were. My parents didn't die tragically. My mom left me, and my dad despised me. For no reason. I was a little kid, and he couldn't look at me. Wouldn't let me out of the house."

Jazz sucked in a deep breath, and it took all I was to not fold him into my arms. But he needed space to talk, and I wouldn't risk silencing him after he'd finally started speaking.

"I don't stay where I'm not wanted. Not anymore. But I also won't stay with a ticking clock over my head. You want me now, but what about when you get bored? Or when the guys get more annoyed with me, or when you run out of money and realize what a mistake you made in not turning me in?"

My poor Jazz. I'd been so blind wondering what it was I did wrong, and while I had failed at comforting him the night before, much of what was troubling Jazz had nothing to do with me. He thought history would repeat itself. Abandoned and despised. He couldn't see Faust, Huntley, and Jagger already considered him more than a stranger or hostage.

"I'm sorry, Jazz. I didn't know that part was yet unclear for you. I want you with me. So much that it is difficult not to attempt to persuade you every moment of the day to stay. But it needs to be your choice, and what do I have to offer you? A broken-down hotel and a pack of broken men. I want you to stay, but why would you?"

"You always say exactly what you want. You don't hide things. Why start now, with this?"

By not assuring Jazz when he'd needed it last night, I'd inadvertently sent him a message that I'd never intended. "Because I can't make that choice for you."

"I already made it," Jazz replied, somewhat exasperated. "I'm here, Knox. I want to be around you. I want to be around the others—in a different way." He blushed.

I'd known Jazz didn't want the others like he did me—

his body gave him away—but my alpha appreciated that he'd clarified.

"I want to help you guys solve this case, and when we find the culprit, I want to help in taking him down. Then after, I want to help with what comes next. I'm in. All in."

I kissed him, a soft, sweet kiss that slowly melted away both our fears. We'd already claimed each other, but we'd both spent the time since expecting the other to want to leave. Jazz wrapped his arms around me, and my heart soared. We weren't broken in the same way, but neither of us had escaped life without so much damage that even when we were both eager and willing, we couldn't see it.

"Stay with me," I whispered against his mouth. "Always. From now on until forever."

"Knox?" Jazz pulled back. Tears filled the corners of his eyes. "You can't...we've only known each other..."

"I don't care. You're special, Jazz, and I *want* you in my life. In my home. In my *pack*. You are welcome. In the hotel. In my room. In my pants."

"Knox!" Jazz hit me with an open palm. It hardly made a sound. He dropped his face, balancing his forehead against my chest with a heavy sigh. "I want you in my pants too."

I'd been doing an excellent job of restraining my baser urges, until that moment. I gripped Jazz's thighs, spreading his legs and holding him against me. His limbs twined around my waist, hooking at the ankles as I explored his mouth and massaged the handfuls of flesh in my grip. But even as my alpha roared his approval, I had to slow down. Restrain myself. "I need a condom, baby. We can't keep risking this." I didn't know the rules. I didn't know if having a special ability automatically meant he would get pregnant, but I knew what had happened to the Walkers. At the very least, I couldn't pretend to be ignorant to the possibility.

Anymore.

"You think I'll..." He didn't need to finish the question. I understood why it would be difficult for him to.

"I don't know. This doesn't seem the same, like Hollister said. But if it happened. I could never do that to you."

"Do it to me?" Jazz repeated, clearly taking offense. "I'd be there too. It takes two to impregnate a man." He tilted his head to the side, thinking. "That doesn't have the same ring to it."

He couldn't be saying what I thought he was saying. I was ready for forever, to bind him to me in every way possible, but how could he be ready? "A baby, Jazz..."

As I spoke, I pictured a child with Jazz's soft curls. His beautiful eyes. A *child*. How long had it been since any of us had even spoken to a child?

Since before we'd picked through the rubble that had once been our pack's school building.

"No, I can't tell you right now with one hundred percent certainty that I want to be pregnant or have a child. Because that's a crazy question. Why would I ever spend any time wondering about that? It wasn't like I was in a place to assume care of another person while I was on the run. I'm not an idiot. I have concerns. I don't want it to hurt. I don't want something to happen to me or the child. I'm scared, but not so much that I don't want this. You. Maybe nothing will happen, and this is all a fluke, coincidence. Unrelated." He didn't sound like he believed that entirely. His mouth went slack as his pupils dilated wide. He cleared his throat and, in a firmer voice, said, "Whatever it is, if it includes you, I want it."

The urge to argue rose. I needed to tell him he couldn't know what he wanted because just wanting me was proof of his bad decision-making. I recognized the thought now for what it was: my own misgivings. I didn't feel like enough. I hadn't protected my pack. I hadn't protected Pierce. I'd let my brothers dwindle to shadows of themselves, and we were still stuck on the same road, spinning our tires on the same stretch of asphalt that we were five years ago.

While my qualities as a leader were questionable, I wasn't a stupid man or alpha. I wanted Jazz too much to doubt what he said was true. I covered his mouth with mine, attempting to tell him what his trust meant to me, that with him, I wouldn't fail. But, I was a man of action, not great with words. I'd tell him best by showing him.

And right now, I needed to show him he was loved.

I locked the door and brought him to the far corner, setting him down on a stack of mats. I didn't want the chill in the air getting anywhere near him, as sweltering as he felt against me, and covered him quickly with my body. Cradling his head between my arms, I nestled his body between my legs, wanting to hold him in that moment more than I wanted inside him.

He stared up at me with huge doe-like eyes, and I was blown away by trust in his gaze. I didn't deserve him. That was a fact as clear as any. But I would work to deserve him. I'd work to be the Alpha I'd once been, and I would work to deserve the title of our team's leader.

"Never doubt this," I said gently, intending to reassure more than I scolded. "You're mine, Jazz."

"You've said that before," he grumped, his cheeks pink with desire.

"I was trying to give you an out, my boy."

He clung around my neck, trembling. "I don't want an out. I want you *in*."

Smirking, I took control of his mouth. "My sweet,

naughty boy," I murmured between kisses. "I'm going to fill you up."

He moaned, deep and needy. His bottom half wiggled, searching for a firmer contact at his center. "Please, Knox. I'm burning for you." His gaze smoldered as he ground his hips up in a circular motion.

I growled, gripping the side of his waist to keep him still. "I know what you need, sweet. I know just what you need." I reclined beside him, removing his clothes so that every inch of his body was open and waiting for me. As I revealed his skin, I kissed it, rubbed my face into him, marking his body with my scent.

His face flushed; the redness crept down his neck to his chest. Suddenly, his breath hitched, and his eyes swarmed with tears.

My alpha went on alert. Some thing was making my boy sad. That was unacceptable. But I sensed no other presence. "What is it, Jazz? Don't cry, baby." I kissed his tears as they fell silently.

"I just. If you mean it..."

I growled at his use of *if*. "I mean it."

He blinked several times, waiting to speak until his lip stopped trembling. "Then this is the first time I've... the first... I've never been home before."

I understood what he meant. Not that he'd never lived someplace, but that he'd never had a place he called home. My chest tightened as a possessive wave washed over me.

This place wasn't a home yet. But it would be. I'd make it that way for Jazz. And until then, his home would be wherever I was.

I propped up on my side, hovering over Jazz's smaller form. "This is your home. This is where you are wanted. In my arms. By my side as my omega." These weren't the types of words I was accustomed to speaking. Gentle, comforting. They were outside of my normal scope, but each word felt right. I didn't search for something to say because I was explaining fact. Simple as that.

"I want that. I want you." He moaned into my mouth, and I let my hands explore his body, tickling over where my lips had been. I wanted to take my time, kiss over his body at least once more, but the whiny tenor of his moans told me my boy needed my dick, now.

I reached on the shelf to our right for the coconut oil the twins used. I pumped the bottle, filling my hand with the slick liquid as Jazz watched, his breaths rasping through parted lips.

"Why is that down here?" he squeaked. "You use a rock to wash. How do you have anything remotely close to a beauty product?" He smiled wide.

"The twins use it." I frowned, not wanting to think on this for too long. "Let's just be glad it's here."

My hand gripped his dick, erect and pointing straight up. He thrust up into the slick circle of my fingers. "Fuck, I love your hands. Big, strong." His bottom half lifted from the mat and stayed lifted as his moans became wails.

The sight was too pretty to stop, so I let him continue chasing his release. His eyes squeezed shut, opening whenever he gasped. When his cries reached a fevered pitch, I relaxed my hand, smirking at his shout of displeasure.

"We have time, Jazz. You don't need to rush."

He hmphed. "Yes I do," he whined, punctuating each word with a dramatic pelvic flex.

I tightened my grip at the base of his cock, squeezing to get his attention. "No, we don't. I'm not rushing just so I can get my dick in you faster. You're too precious for that."

He frowned, but I knew deep down he would appreciate the restraint. He may have been ready to go balls to the wall, but I wouldn't let him be hurt. Not in that way.

I stroked him a few more times, whipping him into a frenzy before diving my hand down where I found his sweet hole.

He grabbed my wrist, attempting to push it further, deeper. He was impatient, and I loved it. My boy couldn't wait to feel me. With excruciating patience, I fingered him, waiting for his cries to level before adding a second. He was so tight; I couldn't risk it. Two became three. I scissored my fingers testing that he was ready for a fourth. While stretching him in every direction, he twitched against the mat, his body spasming out of his control.

By the time I was certain I wouldn't split him open, Jazz was a whimpering, leaking mess. The spastic movements settled until he was still, making tiny whimpering sounds, each one an electric jolt that electrified my spine. I rolled him over gently, rubbing down the rounded lumps of his spine. After the morning we'd both had, this wasn't a time for a rushed fuck against the wall. I massaged down his ribs, telling him with my hands what I hadn't said the night before. *I want you here. I want you to be mine. I want you to be my omega.*

When holding back no longer became an option, I lifted Jazz to his knees. My dick was so hard I'd never be rid of it.

The change of position aroused Jazz from his haze, bringing anticipation of what was to come. He popped his ass back, bending his back and lifting his head in a beautiful expression of submission and desire. He probably didn't realize what exposing so much vulnerable flesh did to me, the trust it showed that he had in me.

I cupped his neck, feeling his gasp tickle my palm.

"Now?"

I felt the word in my hand.

"I can have you now, Knox?" Greedy hands reached behind himself to tug at my hips. "Please. I want to be yours. I want everything."

I gripped my dick, lining it up with his hole. "It's yours."

His body gave way, allowing me to carve a spot inside him that belonged to me. This was what the prep was for, why the care was necessary. When I got in him, when that sweet heat enveloped my length, I teetered on that edge where animal met man. I flexed, sinking several more inches inside, following the motion until I was fully seated.

"Yes, Knox!" Jazz screamed, his top half lifting off the mat.

I wound my arm around his chest, keeping his top half up while I rolled into him. My strokes started slow and deep. As my beast took over, I thrust faster. Jazz's back plastered to my front, and I kissed his shoulder, feeling his tongue on my cheek.

I found his mouth. His lips were desperate on mine, his mewls needy. I pounded faster, harder, making sure there wasn't an inch of him that didn't know what it felt like to have his alpha inside him. Skin slapped against skin as I thrust with animalistic enthusiasm.

Jazz grabbed himself and stroked his dick furiously. I watched him in the mirror, marveling at the fact that this gorgeous, sexual being was *mine*.

"Yes." The guttural word sounded like a hiss. "You are so tight for me, so hot. Your ass is hugging my dick, baby."

"Knox!" His eyes squeezed shut.

My balls tightened at his reflection. Jazz's dick erupted, bowing his back as he screamed with pleasure. Arching ropes of cum splattered against the mat. As he came, his inner muscles rippled, sending me hurtling toward my climax. My cock pulsed once, a warning before I lifted my face and howled. I held his body tight to mine, kissing and licking the back of his neck while my orgasm ebbed. "So good. So sweet. You are perfect, Jazz. You're perfection." I kissed the shell of his ear and down his jawline.

Jazz's eyes fluttered open once before shutting again. Then he stilled. His eyes flew open and found my reflection in the mirror. "I just realized..."

He didn't finish the sentence. I didn't need him to. We knew what this might mean. Or rather, what it had the possibility of meaning.

I met his gaze without blinking. "I love you."

That wasn't all that I'd meant to say. It didn't have the comforting words I thought the moment required, but Jazz's expression cleared all the same. There was no worry or anticipation. And no pain either. Just happiness. "I love you too."

11

JAZZ

When I woke up, I knew without opening my eyes that Knox wasn't in bed with me. Not only did I not feel his comforting weight compressing the mattress; I just knew. The room was warmer when Knox was present. I fidgeted less, not only because I curbed my ability when he was around, but because he made me calm. His presence. His dependability.

And then there were all the little things that I'd never known to expect from a person. Like how he was always concerned with when I ate or drank, if I got good sleep.

If I let it show I was sore or aching in the slightest, he'd fuss until I could convince him every step wasn't the excruciating pain he imagined. Though still a brooder, he never looked annoyed or upset to see me—the opposite. The moment our eyes met every morning, his steel-gray irises flashed like pools of diamonds.

Even though I knew he wasn't there, I rolled over to check all the same, frowning when the empty space confirmed his absence. His pillow was still warm, so he couldn't have gotten up that long ago.

Some mornings, Knox went out to run. I wasn't much of a jogger, and I was even less equipped to run with Knox and the others when they tore through the forest. Sometimes, they took the winding trail from the hotel down to the sand, and I would spot them sprinting down the beach from the operations room. Their morning runs were the only time I got to see the men cut loose. Knox, Faust, Huntley, Jagger, and Diesel would gather wordlessly in the entranceway, heading out as a unit and returning sweaty messes.

If Knox was going to return a sweaty mess, then I could plan ahead and meet him in the shower.

I threw off the covers, my momentary sadness at Knox's absence gone now that I had a plan to see him naked soon.

I got the water going, waiting for the spray to steam as I undressed. Every morning, I studied myself in the mirror, checking to see if I could notice any changes. A baby bump. A mysterious glow.

It had been a week, and though I was pretty sure these sorts of things took more time, each day I looked the same, I became more confident that what had happened to Hollister and his family was not what was happening to me. There were similarities, but my situation didn't match theirs, and Knox wasn't a whole lot like the Walkers either. Other than that they were all shifters. Knox was an alpha, like they were. But Knox and his team had *all* been Alphas of their former pack. There'd been no in-fighting.

Each Alpha had a representative who'd acted under their orders when missions took the alpha team off pack-lands. Diesel's representative had been Quinlan, his mate and betrothed omega. I didn't know who the others had been.

Shucking off the rest of my clothes, I stepped under the spray, inclining my head toward the warm water, enjoying the heat while the water washed away the remnants of sleep.

Life in the hotel had settled to a new sort of normal. Knox shut down and dismantled the cell he'd been using to contact my father. Without it, the great Walter Whitten had no way of communicating with them. He didn't know where we were or that we were still even on the west coast. I didn't know why he suddenly was so obsessed with imprisoning me at home again after so long on the lam. With any luck, I'd never know.

I shook the shampoo bottle, feeling the contents slosh around. It was half empty. I smiled as I squeezed a small dollop in my palm. An emptying bottle of shampoo shouldn't make me so happy. I smiled anyway, humming as I worked my hair into a lather.

I should've waited a little longer to get into the shower. I preferred it when Knox washed my hair. His fingers were gentler than I thought possible from a man with his size and experience. Each washing, he slowly worked through my easily tangled hair, never tearing or yanking, as I was prone to do. Knox was always silent during, focusing every ounce of his attention on his task while looking at me with so much love and devotion I couldn't keep the contact for long.

It was stupid to be this happy this soon. To be this confident. But Knox knew everything about me. It helped that there wasn't much to know. I'd lived a pretty inconsequential life before Knox. I'd moved from town to town, meeting up with friends when I could, moving on when things started to smell fishy.

I'd stayed longer at the Hotel Royal Paynes than I had anywhere—other than my father's house before I'd turned thirteen. But that had never been home—and though I sometimes got that panicked feeling like I needed to move on or danger would get me, Knox always sensed my distress and sat a little closer. He seemed to understand the power of his touch. His presence. But he didn't wield that power like a weapon. He offered it in bountiful amounts.

And the sex...well, there had been a sore few days after we'd cleared the air when my body got used to his lovemaking. He was the type of man who gave his everything, every time, and somehow, he still got better. At some point, his expertise would have to peak, but he never failed to play my body like an instrument he'd personally made.

My dick twitched just from thinking about him. The night before, we'd trekked down to the beach and watched the sun set. When it had gotten cold, he'd shifted, curling his large wolf body around me so we could stay out a little longer and see the stars.

After rinsing the soap from my body, I had no other reason to stay in the shower. No hygienic reason anyway. My hand fluttered over my chub, and I hissed. That felt so good I could see no reason not to reach down and stroke myself a few times. If I came before Knox got back, it would serve him right for taking so long.

I didn't really mean that, but I smirked and stroked my dick anyway. I didn't need to picture porn or a dirty fantasy —just my memories. The fast, brutal way Knox had taken me in this very room; the slow, contented lovemaking sessions in the gym where he'd hold me against him while his wet heat blossomed inside me.

I angled out of the spray so I could gather my precum, swiping it down my dick. I scooped a bead of precum on my fingertip and swirled it around the head, groaning softly. More leaked, and I used it like lube, slathering my hand before continuing to stroke. My forehead fell forward, braced against the wall of the shower. The steam billowed, filling the shower and bathroom with a white haze. I moaned as my balls tingled.

"Naughty boy." Knox's deep voice made me gasp. That, and the cold blast of air that rushed in when the shower door opened. "Playing with what's mine. Wasting that sweet cream."

He grabbed my wrist, pausing my strokes before he gently tugged the hand away and brought my palm to his face. Holy shit, he was going to make me explode looking at me like that, saying words like he was.

He searched my palm and frowned.

"What's wrong—"

Knox licked from wrist to fingertip, concentrating in the crevices between my fingers. His chest vibrated, making that purring sound that made me want to fling myself over the closest surface and demand that he take me. His eyes were hooded but his grip firm, his expression one of utter contentment. Knox was doing exactly as he wanted exactly when he wanted.

Like always.

The moment his tongue touched my skin, my dick started to throb. The feeling increased, driving all my blood downward. I licked my lips, tasting water and sweat. "Knox," I whimpered, jerking my hips pathetically.

His responding growl urged me back. My shoulders hit the cool tile. The spray hit the back of Knox, splashing off him in shimmering droplets. As broad and tall as he was, he could keep the spray from my body if he wanted. I shivered against the tile, and he stepped to the side, bringing me against his chest as he stepped us directly under the warm water. "You're up early. I thought last night's activities would make you want to sleep in longer," he murmured against my cheek.

I probably would have if I'd woken and found Knox beside me. "You weren't there. The bed isn't as comfortable without you."

He made a pleased sound in his chest, but his eyes crinkled with concern.

"It's okay," I laughed, trying to relieve his worry. "I slept long enough anyway." I lifted my face toward his so he could see my arrogant smirk. "I'm building sexual endurance."

"Are you now?" he asked with a wicked gleam. His hand dipped between our bodies, and he grabbed my cock, smoothly spinning me around until my face was to the tile. With his dick nestled between my cheeks, he stroked me, never going quite as fast or hard as I needed to orgasm. His hardness pressed against me like an iron rod dipped in satin. His head brushed against my hole, and I yelped, but he didn't push forward. He grazed over my pucker again, and again, but only ever that much. A gentle caress. A whisper of sensation.

Not enough.

With a sudden burst of sexual frenzy, I growled and pushed off the wall, dropping to my knees before Knox could catch me. My lips found his round head immediately, and I sucked him deep.

Knox cursed. "Fuck yes, swallow that cock. You are so fucking amazing. So good, keeping your throat open for me."

His words had the intended effect, spurring me to bob faster, deeper.

Knox filled my mouth as surely as he did every other part of my body. The heavy weight of his member sliding in my mouth sent ribbons of pleasure that wrapped around my body and made Knox rumble with appreciation.

I loved it when he looked at me like he couldn't keep his

hands off me. I was pretty sure that was the exact way I looked at him. And experiencing that look while on my knees pleasing him gave me a satisfaction that had nothing to do with how my body felt and everything to do with my heart and mind. I pleased him. I made him happy. Not just his dick. All of him.

I might not have been a shifter, but I still longed to make my alpha proud of me. I hummed at his pulse of precum against my tongue. Peeking up the wide expanse of his body, I found his loving gaze. His eyes were soft like his mouth. Was it ironic that when he was at his hardest, he was also at his softest? Maybe, but I didn't have a lot of time to care, not when his thick fingers fisted in my hair and he urged me deeper.

His hands trembled, revealing just how much he still held back. I never wanted him to hide parts of himself from me, but at the moment, I appreciated the restraint. As cocky as I'd been, I was still getting used to the size of him. Wildly ramming his dick down my throat would probably be my last memory in this world. But at least I would die happy, with my alpha's dick in my mouth.

"I need in your head," Knox snarled. "What makes you look like that? What are you thinking of, love?"

Dying with your dick in my mouth.

I couldn't tell him that. I still had some dignity. Instead of answering, I brought my right hand up to cup his balls. He growled, and I squeezed, rewarded with the first shot of his release down my throat. He held my head firmly, his fingers loose but very much there, cradling my face. He watched me, and I him. Our eyes locked as he released his pleasure. My mind danced, greedy for the taste of him. For *all* of him.

Knox panted several seconds longer. He didn't let me

stay on my knees, easing me up and draping me against his chest instead.

"Mine," he rumbled contentedly.

I rubbed my face against his chest, letting my teeth rake against his nipple. For as tough and hard as the team of mercenaries seemed, Knox was a big fan of touching. He'd rub his chin over me like a cat. He said it was to keep his scent fresh, that it calmed him when I smelled as much like him as possible. And he always looked so very pleased when I did the same. Though I didn't benefit from the whole scent thing, rubbing against him had became a habit.

He reached for my erection, and I slapped his hand. "No way. That's your punishment for teasing me."

He blinked. "My punishment is an amazing blowjob? Baby, I don't know who taught you about punishments—"

"No. Your punishment is not being able to give me one."

He lifted me so our faces were even and arched a challenging brow. "That's diabolical."

I smiled and hugged him tightly. "What took you so long?" I mumbled against his neck.

Knox sighed loudly, and I pulled back. Often, he looked like he held the weight of the world on his face. Right now, he held the weight of this world and all the rest of them.

I smoothed the wrinkles at his forehead. "What happened?"

Adjusting me more securely against him, he turned off the water and carried me out of the shower. He draped a towel over my shoulders. By this point, I knew better than to try to help dry. When I did, he'd let me, but he'd get this pinched look, almost like it was hurting him to watch me care for myself.

"Nothing happened," Knox said, concentrating on my arm as he ran the towel down the limb. "Faust hasn't been able to narrow down the mineral wool to a single distributer. It's too common of a substance."

"And the guys are restless?" I asked.

His face betrayed each emotion as he felt it. Worry, uncertainty, and then finally, resignation. "They need more to do."

He grabbed my lotion, pumping some in his palm and rubbing his hands together before smoothing it over my body. He spared no inch, moisturizing me from head to toe. When finished, he washed his hands and carried me back to the bedroom.

"We have more remodeling to do today," I said brightly.

He nodded. "We do. They are fine. I'll take care of everything, Jazz. I don't want you to worry."

I understood his concern, but what about what I wanted? "I'll worry if I like. I care about what happens to them too."

Knox's lips twitched, and he kissed my forehead. "Yes you do." His nose nuzzled the delicate skin just under my earlobe and inhaled deeply.

Once I was dressed and Knox had no reasonable excuse for keeping me in the bedroom, we headed out. The others were already moving around. I must've grown more accustomed to their sounds because I knew the twins were in the kitchen and Faust was outside. Diesel's room was farthest from the common spaces, but, somehow, I knew he was there too.

Knox put a pot of water on to boil before rummaging around in the fridge for oatmeal toppings. He grabbed milk and then raisins, cinnamon, and brown sugar from the cupboard. His face was serene as he set the dishes out in front of me. Knox couldn't cook any better than I could, but he still tried, every day, to make food that was healthy and tasted good. Before I'd come along, they'd lived on fast food and raw meat they hunted themselves.

"I'm going to ask Hallie to teach me some breakfast things next time she comes over." Hallie visited every Friday, staying for longer and chatting more each time. I realized after the second visit that Hallie's worry had been what brought her to me, but her loneliness was what kept her coming back.

She'd lived her whole life in Rockshell. She knew every person who came and went, but she never spoke about friends. The only person she spoke about on a semi-regular basis was her ex-husband. I liked the man less and less the more I heard about him.

"I don't mind making you breakfast."

"Take the hint," Jagger said, coming into the kitchen with Huntley right behind him. "He's sick of oatmeal."

Jagger veered my way, taking the path behind my chair. He paused directly behind me, his face looming overhead. When I looked up at him, his eyes darted away.

"It's okay," I said. "The smelling thing you do. I don't mind it. You don't have to hide it or...smell me in secret." I looked sharply at Knox. "Unless...?"

Knox had the same expression he would have if he were corralling a frightened animal that he was afraid would spook at any moment. "If you don't mind." His eyes gleamed. This was more important than he was letting on. His face told me that much. Maybe I didn't get the sniff thing, but I could indulge it, and besides, I liked feeling accepted. And that was what it felt like when the others did it, an acceptance.

Jagger leaned in, his nose actually grazing the corner of my ear. It felt nice, but not arousing like it would if Knox were the one doing the nuzzling. He moved from behind me, and Huntley took his spot, doing the same but on the other side. When they sat down, both looked pleased and maybe also a little calmer.

"I know my skills in the kitchen aren't ideal." Knox pulled the oatmeal from the stovetop and stirred it before scooping some into a bowl. "If you want to take over a few breakfasts."

"I don't want to take over. I just want to help." I turned to the twins, searching for some backup. "I should help, right? Earn my keep."

Jagger frowned while Huntley shook his head softly. "Jazz Hands, you do your job by being around and keeping *this guy* off our ass." Jagger gestured rudely to Knox.

"Once you find something you really enjoy," Huntley added with more reason in his tone. "Then you can do that. But there's no reason for you to tackle a job you don't enjoy, Jazz. It isn't like we don't have the time."

I didn't know if Huntley meant the double meaning, but the atmosphere in the kitchen grew thick with tension.

I ate steadily and silently, finishing nearly at the same time as Knox—which never happened. The man could open his mouth and inhale food whole.

I got up to soak the dish, and on the way back, Huntley snagged my wrist, his expression troubled. "I didn't mean it like that, Jazz Hands."

"I know."

He still looked upset so I leaned forward, inhaling slowly at his forehead like how they had done. The motion made me feel silly. I couldn't claim intimacy as I could with Knox. But scenting Knox made him happy; maybe the same thing would make Huntley happy.

At first, there was only shock when I studied his expression. Slowly, the shock melted into something that looked more like satisfaction.

"We'll figure it out," I whispered, stealing a line from Knox's script. I turned to Knox. "What's on the agenda for today?"

Knox's face was unreadable, like he was purposefully trying to remain impassive, blank. Then he blinked, and the empty slate cleared away, replaced by a smirking, confident alpha. "Demolition."

———

KNOX ASSURED me I didn't need to help, but he'd gathered two pairs of goggles, two scrapers, and two sanders. In the days previous, Knox repaired the outside half of the entryway. The week before had been spent tearing out rotting boards, replacing what he could and doing a total rebuild in the spots where he couldn't. The eave no longer sagged on one end, and once we sanded the old paint away and put on a fresh coat, the entrance would look as good as new.

Originally, I'd thought it had been Hallie's comments that had sparked Knox's increased motivation to fix the place up. I'd watched his face while she'd spoken about the hotel. The five men had moved in and done just enough to make the place livable. But now, they worked for pride, not just survival.

After an hour of grueling labor, Knox called for a break. My body screamed its thanks. Scraping the layers of grime and paint made my arms hurt and my body sweaty, and I didn't want to imagine what my face looked like.

I sat on the ledge of the fountain and looked back at the mess—work we'd done. The fountain, path and steps up were cracked and crumbling, but scraping wouldn't fix that damage. "When do you think we'll be able to paint?" Along with my cooking skills, my construction and repair skills also lacked. But Knox and the others knew enough to make up for my deficit.

"Coming days. We'll need to check the weather." He wiped sweat and dust from his brow.

The weather changed quickly at the coast, going from bright blue skies to dark clouds without warning. Today, the sky was partly cloudy. When the sun lurked behind white pillowy clouds, it wasn't so bad. But when the clouds passed, the rays beat down on my neck and shoulders.

A rustling bush was my only warning before Faust stepped out of the forest with Dog beside him. "Another note," he growled to Knox. "*Tall tower*. A bat swooped over my head and dropped it in my damn hands."

I hadn't the foggiest what that meant, but Knox's eyebrows knitted together.

Faust hissed sharply, the sound coming from closer than I'd expected. "His neck is burnt," he said accusingly to Knox. "You need sunscreen."

He ran inside with Dog at his heels while Knox neared to inspect my neck with a low, unhappy hum.

"I don't get it," I whispered as he traced the edges of my red skin. It probably was burnt—my skin fried just from looking at the sun—but no one in the history of my life had ever cared about such a thing. "You guys are scary. Or you can be. When you were chasing me, at first, I didn't think you were real. You were focused, determined, and smart. I imagined you were monsters. One hundred percent. But you guys are also so…" I couldn't find a word that didn't sound demeaning. "How can you be mercenaries *and* caretakers?"

Knox pulled me in his lap, I assumed partly to block my

neck from the sun, but mostly because if he wasn't working, he preferred to be touching me. "It was Pierce's idea," he said softly. I twisted my neck to look at him, needing to watch his face in case this was too much. He wouldn't admit to as much on his own. While the sorrow was thick, it was no more than usual.

"Pierce was a few years older than me and Faust. Had grown up close with Alpha Carrier and the Elders—the Elders are appointed by the Alpha to act as financiers, or investors, for a pack. The money they provide helps the pack operate with limited outside contact," he explained after seeing my confusion. "Though, at that time, there were only two Elders remaining. We lived in relative peace. Our isolation kept most packs out of our territory, and if anyone did try to attack, we were ready to defend our land. Alpha Carrier lived a long, peaceful life, as did the Elders, and when they died, we were left with a pack terrified of change and six alphas to fight for Alpha Carrier's position. Faust, Diesel, and I were barely old enough to lead, the twins were even younger, and none of us knew how to be an Alpha. Pierce was the obvious choice, but he didn't have Elders. Knowing the pack needed to be supported in some way, we came together and decided to share Alpha leader status. We took on jobs, the more lucrative the better, and quickly realized the process could work. It likely helped that the six of us spent a limited amount of time actually on pack lands. And when we did, there wasn't tension. Being born an alpha gives a shifter more strength and capacity for skill, but being a chosen leader, an Alpha, wasn't about strength or power. It was recognizing a responsibility to provide and protect your people." He made a sharp, choking, growling sound, and I assumed he was imagining what had happened to that pack he'd cared so much for.

My heart broke for him. For all of them.

"Here we go," Faust announced, returning with a bandanna and sunscreen.

Knox stood, lifting me with him. The moment my feet hit the ground, my stomach turned, and my head felt light. I worried I'd stood up too quickly and reached back to grab Knox's arm when my stomach rolled. The next thing I knew, my mouth opened, and I projectile-vomited all over Knox's chest.

Once spent, I hunched over, grabbing my knees. Knox's rushed questions sounded muffled as my head pounded.

"Jazz?" Worry made my name a rumble.

I sucked in a deep breath. My mouth didn't taste like it should've after throwing up, but my body felt worn out and achy. I wiped my face, stood up, and peeked at the mess I'd made.

My mouth fell open, but this time in shock. The liquid that covered Knox's chest and stomach looked nothing like vomit. It wasn't murky or lumpy. My puke was...beautiful. Like oil in water, the ribbons of color didn't mix or blend together. Streams of red, orange, yellow, green—the entire rainbow—dripped slowly down Knox's front.

"I threw up a rainbow. How come I threw up a rainbow?" I sounded dazed even to my ears.

Knox pulled his shirt up over his head, using the backside to clean his face. He lightly circled his arm around me, checking my forehead with the back of his hand. "You aren't hot."

"Is there *glitter* in it?" Faust sat on his haunches, staring at the vomit on the stone, while Dog sat next to him, staring at the puke with clear disdain. "It smells like...bubblegum."

Huntley, Jagger, and Diesel bounded out the front door, coming to an abrupt stop at the strange sight.

"We felt—what is that?" Huntley asked over Jagger's shoulder after slamming into his backside.

"What did he eat?" Diesel asked from the entryway, his lip turned up. His dark hair looked less maintained than the last time, a fact I would've worried about if I hadn't just made my life into a Skittles commercial.

Knox's face loomed over mine. I could see only him as he searched my face, touching my cheeks and forehead. If his frown got any deeper, his eyebrows would touch his chin.

"It's probably nothing," I said quietly. My throat felt tight. After today, Knox wouldn't ever let me help again. "It *is* nothing," I said with more confidence. "Maybe I ate a bath bomb in my sleep." There weren't any bath bombs in the hotel, but I would've said anything to stop the concerned looks.

"Don't move too quickly, Jazz Hands," Huntley warned as I pushed gently away from Knox in an attempt to prove I didn't need his help to stand.

The moment I stood straight, my stomach heaved, and I unleashed an ungodly amount of rainbow, glittery, bubblegum-scented vomit over the shoes of anyone who was unfortunate enough to be standing too close.

The next thing I knew, Knox had me in his arms, unconcerned with the muck I'd gotten and was getting all over him. The others flanked him, bringing me inside as a unit.

Knox set me down on the sofa in the sitting room, sliding to kneel on the floor next to me. Faust handed him a cool rag that he folded and set on my forehead. "Breathe in and out. Deeply. If you feel it again, we have a bucket."

"I'm okay," I said, realizing as I spoke that I truly felt fine. "It's passed, I think. Whatever it was."

No one looked convinced. In fact, the men stood scattered around me, staring at one another in one of their silent conversations. If it had to do with me, the least they could do was speak out loud.

I reached for Knox's sleeve, intending on tugging it to get his attention, but he dropped down, caressing my cheek gently. His expression was shuttered. "I'm calling the Walkers."

12

KNOX

I OPENED the door before the woman on the other side could knock. She had a narrow face, a bright smile and shiny, straight black hair pulled up in a ponytail. Her fist was up, in the process of beginning to knock when I'd opened the door.

"You're fast," she said brightly. "I'm Dr. Tiffany Lewelyn, but everyone calls me Dr. Tiff."

When I'd called the Walkers the day before, they said they were sending their pack doctor immediately. I appreciated the haste, but Dr. Tiff was a shifter and, as such, dangerous.

It didn't matter that I'd asked for her to come or that Nash and the other Walker alphas had vouched for her. She was a stranger capable of violence who I was letting into my home, near my omega. "Are you trained? How long have you been a doctor?"

Dr. Tiff's eye brows rounded. "Huh. Normally I get a *hi* back, but okay. I completed my bachelor's in Sexual and Reproductive Health from the University of Washington and graduated medical school from Pacific Northwest

174

University-Health Sciences. After that, I completed a four-year residency at the largest all-shifter hospital in the US—Los Angeles Center of Shifter Medicine. Following that, I completed an additional two year fellowship on pack lands working under Nana Walker. I've been secondary pack doctor for a little over four years now and primary pack doctor for one. Is that sufficient?"

I regarded her carefully, narrowing my eyes at the cheeky glint in her dark gaze. "It's a good start."

She rolled her eyes, and I couldn't be mad at the disrespect. Right then, I deserved it. Dr. Tiff stepped past me into the entryway, where she looked around with wide eyes. "This place is half amazing, half soggy," she said, tightening her ponytail. "Where is the patient?" She wandered toward the stairs. "I assume this way?"

A low growl vibrated from the next floor. Dog stood in the center of the landing, his teeth bared at the stranger attempting to gain entry. "Is this the doctor?" Faust asked, walking out from the shadows.

"I'm Dr. Tiff. Hey there." She gave a small wave. She cupped her hand while looking back at me. "This isn't the blessed one, right?"

Blessed sounded like a fancy way of saying unexplainable. "We don't know that."

She frowned, dark eyes darting between us.

"Faust is not the one you are here to see. You're here for my omega, Jazz. He's upstairs."

"Your omega? Should I be reporting in with an Alpha?"

It should've stung that she didn't just assume I was the Alpha, but my behavior toward her so far had been more barking guard dog than it had been a wise leader. "No. We—no."

By then I heard the twin's heartbeats, down the hall,

always half a beat faster than everyone else. They remained hidden, lurking, while doing just as I, Faust, and Dog had done, protecting Jazz.

"Let the doctor through," Diesel grumbled . He joined us from the kitchen. "You called her here. Now you're treating her like a spy. Something is wrong with Jazz. Rainbow puke isn't normal. Let her see if she can find out."

My immediate urge was to ignore him. Out of all of the men, he'd accepted Jazz the least. His version of Jazz acceptance was avoidance. He wouldn't care if Jazz was sick or if Dr. Tiff meant him harm. Or if this even was Dr. Tiff and the true doctor had been intercepted and murdered.

"Did anyone get a sample?" Dr. Tiff asked, her mood as chipper as when she walked in. If she noticed our overprotective behavior, she didn't let on. Or she was used to it. "I'm very eager to get a look at that."

"I did," Faust said. "I'll bring it to Jazz's room."

"And Jazz's room would be... ?" She pointed her finger in one direction and then the other.

Diesel stepped close to my side. "My opinion once meant something to you, Knox. As the only one of us who has any experience with having an omega and mate, listen to me. The suspicion will never fade. Neither will the doubt. Welcome to having an omega."

"Oh, there's more than one omega here?" Dr. Tiff asked brightly.

Diesel's face closed down, like watching the door to a bank vault slam shut. "No." He stomped down the hallway toward the gym.

Diesel's pain was so thick in the air. There was no avoiding the burnt taste of his sorrow. We'd been tasting Diesel's grief for years, and I knew by now, there was nothing I could do to soothe his pain. I took the first step up the stairs. "I'll take you."

At the door, I knocked. "Jazz, I'm coming in with the doctor. Are you decent?"

"Will it matter?" Jazz shouted back. His voice rang clear and strong. "The doctor is going to see me naked anyway."

"I like him," Dr. Tiff whispered.

I shook my head before pushing open the door and letting her pass. "It's hard not to."

———

Dr. Tiff pulled off her latex gloves, tucked one inside the other, and tossed the bundle in the trash can. "What about any former doctors, Jazz?" she asked. "In an ideal world, I would have records to compare to today." She picked up her clipboard, scratching her pen over the paper as she made notes.

Jazz shook his head. His curls bounced, no longer plastered to his forehead by sweat. "I've never seen a doctor."

Dr. Tiff paused, her pen frozen against the paper. "Never? Not once?"

"Not that I can remember. I don't really get sick a lot."

That was true. When he wasn't vomiting rainbows, Jazz was in good health, especially considering the junk he used to eat.

"Can you remember experiencing any medical emergency?"

"I almost drowned when I was little, but I don't remember going to the doctor's after."

"But no flu? Ear infections? Broken bones?"

"Not yet. Why? Is that weird?"

Dr. Tiff scrunched her nose in what I guessed was her

177

thinking face. "No. Not average, but not weird. Do you feel comfortable enough to tell me more about the near drowning?"

I'd already stopped my pacing right around the time Jazz admitted to *almost dying*. It had happened when he was young, long before I'd known the young man existed. I still felt as if I'd failed him. He'd nearly *died*. That was unacceptable.

Is that any worse than what you've done to him?

I shoved the thought down. Paying attention to Jazz was more important than my shame.

"I don't remember a whole lot. I was so young. I was at a park, back when my father still took me places, so I couldn't have been older than four, if that. I'd fallen into a creek or something. I just remember breaking through the water and seeing the sky overhead and having this clear idea that my father would finally be happy once I was gone.

"But then someone grabbed me, I think? He patted my back as I coughed and held me while I cried. I remember that part clearly, being held. And then he sent me back to my father, still sitting on a bench screaming at his assistant until he saw me, and then he yelled at me for getting wet."

I was going to kill that bastard. His own son had nearly drowned, and the man never knew.

"I'm sorry that happened." Dr. Tiff squeezed Jazz's hand. "Records would've been lucky, but we don't need them. I would like to take another look at your stomach if you don't mind."

I tensed. In the beginning of the examination, watching her push and poke at Jazz without getting between them whenever he made a noise of discomfort had been difficult. She touched him for medical reasons, but he'd still winced, and it had taken all I was not to pick the woman up and remove her from the room.

Jazz, however, didn't look worried in the slightest. He yanked his shirt up, eager to get cleared by the doctor so he could get out of bed. I wouldn't let him before.

"Hm..."

"Hm?" Jazz repeated. "Are doctors supposed to make sounds like that?"

Dr. Tiff laughed. "Maybe not. It isn't a bad hm. I just didn't notice this before. Do you use bronzer or body makeup?"

Jazz's forehead wrinkled. "Not at the moment?" He lifted his shirt higher and looked down his body. "Why?"

I stepped close enough that I could peer over the top of both of them and the three of us stared silently at Jazz's stomach. He'd had a soft, flat tummy before, and it was still soft, but not quite as flat.

It had only been a night since he threw up. I'd looked him over from head to toe the evening before. Jazz had spent every hour the evening in bed with me or alone with me nearby. This didn't make sense.

In addition to the small swell, Jazz's skin directly around his belly button *shimmered*. The shade of his skin circling his belly button was darker than his normal skin tone. It looked tan at first glance, but when I looked closer, the ring was clearly golden.

"There was glitter in his vomit, could that—are the two things related?" That had sounded like a reasonable thing to ask while the words had been in my head. Spoken out loud, I sounded insane.

Dr. Tiff sighed and straightened. "I've certainly got my work cut out for me. And I haven't gotten my hands on that sample yet. Don't worry. I enjoy a mystery. Your vitals are good. Blood pressure well within range, and your temperature, oxygen, and respiratory rate are all within normal ranges. So we have a mystery, but we do not have a problem."

I didn't know how the woman sounded so chipper all the time. I wasn't accustomed to such bright, sustained happiness. Jazz was happy, but he was other emotions too.

I'd known her a few hours, but so far, Dr. Tiff moved around like a big ball of sunshine.

"But do you know what's wrong?" I asked.

"Wrong? Jazz is pregnant, but there's nothing wrong. I'll give him a test to confirm, but I'm going to use my powers of deduction. If you aren't, you will be. That seems to be how these things work."

"What things?" Jazz squeaked.

Dr. Tiff looked from Jazz to me, the first wrinkle of concern forming between her eyebrows. "Blessed births."

"Hollister mentioned that term..." Jazz whispered. Without looking my way, he stretched out his hand, and I grabbed it, rubbing the knuckles against the thin skin of my wrist.

I watched the gears turn in Dr. Tiff's brain as she looked between us. She was bright and happy, but not dumb.

All those times I'd been with Jazz without protection, despite knowing what had happened to the Walkers... If anything happened to him—

I wouldn't let anything happen. But if anything did...it would be my fault.

"With your alpha's permission, I'd like to stay for the next couple of weeks at least. There are some differences. Your size, for one. The rate of growth seems a little wonky to me right now, and I'd like to figure out why that is before too long."

Both looked to me.

"Of course. I'll have the guys set you up a room and take you into town for any supplies you might need."

"That would be great," Dr. Tiff replied. "I'll get the supplements I want you to start taking while I'm here. For now, I'd say take it easy, but you don't have to stay in bed—unless you start to feel worse." Her tone deepened to one with more authority. "I mean it. Tell me if you feel anything strange or unusual."

I called down the hallway for the twins and almost immediately heard their steps approaching. As I'd suspected, they'd been eavesdropping down the hallway.

"We're on it," Huntley said.

Jagger had started cleaning out a room the moment the doctor arrived, so it was ready by the time she finished her exam.

Dr. Tiff stepped out, shutting the door softly behind her. Her dark gaze burned a hole in my chest, and I met it, bracing for the lashings I deserved. "He's asking for you," she said, but instead of moving out of the way, she remained, worrying her bottom lip between her teeth. "What is happening to these men—Jazz, Hollister, and the others—it is magic, Knox. More so than people who can turn into wolves. At least with shifters, we have years of decades, experimentation to pull from. Before the Walkers, blessed births happened so infrequently, the only literature about the phenomenon is ancient by medical standards. I'll do my best to fuse magic with medicine, and one thing all the blessed births have had in common was that when the time came, the body knew what to do. It's important you realize there was no reason for you to expect this to happen to Jazz. He needs you clearheaded and *there* for him. Okay?"

Huntley's gaze held new respect for the doctor. "She's

right, Knox. Stop kicking yourself in the balls for what's happened, and we'll focus on what will happen."

Dr. Tiff beamed, all the seriousness from moments before vanished. "Exactly. And *this time*, I'm going to be in the right place to help."

It sounded like there was more to that story, but I needed to get to Jazz. I found him in bed with the blankets thrown off.

"She said I could," he piped when he saw me.

"I know. I was there." My steps slowed as Jazz neared.

His face twisted, eyes dropping to the floor between our bodies. "Is everything okay?"

I'd been silent once when Jazz had needed me to speak. I wouldn't make the same mistake, even if I had no idea how to say how sorry I was. How ashamed. "Jazz, I—" My voice sounded like gravel, not soothing and supportive like it should have been. "I don't know how to tell you..."

Jazz lifted his finger to my lips. "Then don't," he said with a frantic edge. He clung to my shoulder. "I know it's strange. But it doesn't feel bad. Unless..." He pulled away, fresh horror making his eyes round. "Unless you aren't happy?"

"Oh, baby." He fit against my chest like I'd been carved to match him. "Happy isn't the problem here." My chin bounced against the top of his head. "I'm always happy with you."

Jazz turned his face to my chest and pressed. "But not with a baby?" In a sudden burst of energy, he ripped himself from my arms, pacing nervously toward the other side of the room. "Of course you wouldn't want a baby. You have your investigation. We're just now starting to piece things together. It isn't like you need more to deal with. I'm sorry—"

My sharp growl made him jump and warily look over

his shoulder at me. "Don't apologize. Not ever. You're my omega, right?" I tried counteracting my rough movements with a gentle nuzzle.

His lips parted as I ran my nose up his jawline, and he sighed, relaxing into my hold. "Yes. Your omega."

"That makes you my—"

"Responsibility," he interjected sharply. His shoulders were tense again, sticking out from under his t-shirt.

"It makes you mine. I take care of what is mine. Anything that happens to you happens because I allowed it or failed you. I should be apologizing, Jazz. You did nothing wrong. You are perfect, the things you do are perfect, you smell perfect, and you feel perfect." My hands couldn't help trailing lazily down Jazz's spine, cupping his ass softy.

"You trying to make another baby?" Jazz pushed his ass back into my hands.

I groaned, giving his cheeks a few meaty squeezes. A man had only so much control.

He used my hands as a brace and leaned back, bringing his face up. "I think it's a one-at-a-time sort of thing," he joked.

I kissed his forehead. That felt so good I continued down to his nose, chin, and then lips. "How are *you* handling this so well?"

"It could be worse. I could be in pain. Or Dr. Tiff could've told me I was having an alien baby. Or you could be angry. Since none of those things are true, I'm counting this whole experience as a win."

I kissed down his face once more, scenting him with my nose just under the curve of his ear. "You have a shockingly low standard for what you consider a win."

Jazz only grinned, the expression taking my breath

away. He was, without a doubt, the most appealing thing that existed in this world.

And look what you've done to him.

———

WHEN DR. TIFF returned with the twins a few hours later, we were in the operations room. Faust had his laptop out, his fingers softy clacking against the keyboard.

Dog lay at his feet, sleeping with one eye open.

"That looks cozy," she said to Jazz.

He looked up, inhaling like she'd caught him napping. Which she had.

Faust had the chair made before we got there, the seat and sides lined with blankets and pillows. He'd used a box, draping it with blankets as well so Jazz could prop his feet up.

Jazz had made a fuss when he'd seen the chair the first time, but after Faust asked him to just give it a try for his sake, he sat down and, as of twenty minutes ago, had started to doze off.

Jazz stretched two fists over his head and yawned.

"It's good to see you in a different room," Dr. Tiff said warmly. "And one with such a view." She walked to the battered wall of windows.

The sea was calm today, pristine.

"I'm going to go check in with Alpha Tyson and then probably take a nap as well."

The twins went with her to make sure she didn't get lost before they returned, taking their usual spots at the table.

"Do any of these companies mean anything to you?" Faust asked, slipping a sheet of paper under my nose.

I scanned the list of names, recognizing a few but not

from any personal attachment. "No. None of those do. Diesel needs to get down here. He and Pierce handled most of the building supplies."

"I'll take it to him. This is too important to wait."

Faust left with Dog silently trotting at his heels.

Jazz had a newspaper clipping from the day after the attack on his lap, his head lolling as he fought sleep.

"That's our sign." I scooped Jazz up bridal-style.

"No, I want to help," Jazz mumbled like a kid who didn't want to miss any of the party.

"You do help," I murmured, but Jazz was already asleep.

———

I washed my hands with plans of returning to the bed and not leaving for at least several more hours. In the three days since Dr. Tiff had come, Jazz had grown tired. But not weak.

Dr. Tiff had emphasized there was a difference.

She was likely at her wit's end. Between myself, the twins, and Faust, she had to deal with daily barrages whenever Jazz winced or groaned or sighed a little too loudly.

Even now, as I turned the bathroom light off so it wouldn't shine in the room and wake Jazz up, I listened to his heartbeat, sure that it was just a little bit too fast.

I returned to the bed, my neck tight with dread. My teeth clamped together as if they were gates that could hold back whatever it was that I sensed but didn't want to know.

Jazz stirred. His eyes fluttered opened, and he spotted me, smiling after. "Hey you," he murmured.

Relief flooded my burnt edges. Jazz was fine. He was awake. Smiling. His voice thick with sleep but also satisfaction. He was happy.

He pushed the blanket back, swinging his legs to the side.

My eyes dropped to his stomach. His shirt lifted just enough for me to see that the small swell Jazz had gone to bed with was now a solid bump. The skin shimmered, a second ring having formed around the widest part of Jazz's stomach. This one was silver.

"Knox?" Jazz asked, seeing my face. He followed my gaze, his hands moving to cup his tummy at the same moment he noticed his sudden growth. He whispered, his words catching in the air between us, "Oh shit."

13

JAZZ

I EXPECTED Knox back soon and quickly buttoned up my jacket, stuffing one of Knox's baseball hats over my frizzy hair. I'd convinced him to let me go with the team into Rockshell to get baby supplies. If he knew I'd woken that morning with a third ring around my tummy, he'd never let me go.

"They're showing up steadily," Dr. Tiff had murmured, hunched over as she slid her stethoscope over my stomach. "I'm going to contact the clinic in Rockshell and see if they have any imaging equipment. I won't feel comfortable until we can take a look in your oven."

Dr. Tiff had a soothing habit of always sounding like we were talking about something completely ordinary. Our plans for the weekend. What she had for breakfast. When really we were discussing an unknown entity growing inside me. Sure, it was probably a baby, but the rainbow puke wasn't normal. Neither was a spontaneous, unexplained pregnancy. She kept using the same word to describe it: blessed.

Maybe I felt blessed in finding Knox—or them finding

me. Their companionship, however prickly, was leagues better than my mostly solitary, nomadic life.

Dr. Tiff was still staring at my belly when she made another concerned hum. "What if...?" She cocked her head to the side.

"What if? Dr. Tiff? Ha. I rhymed."

Dr. Tiff's lips tweaked into a fast smile. The woman couldn't ignore a bad joke. "This is a very silly idea. One I want to research a little more before I start spouting it around. Your alpha is already suspicious of me. I don't need to give him a good reason to be."

"Knox is just..." It wasn't my job to make excuses for Knox, but that wasn't what I was trying to do anyway. There'd been a time when Knox and the others had a clear purpose in life. They'd been leaders, mentors, and guardians. I knew they wanted that again, even if they were afraid to admit it. "Knox is intense at times. Especially at first. Bark back. That works best. Or tell me, and I'll bark."

She smiled and rummaged through her medical bag, pulling out a coiled measuring tape. Her hands were warm, but the tape was cool against my tummy. I had three rings now: the center golden one that had first appeared; the silver ring that circled around the larger part of my stomach; and now, a third gold ring, nestled just inside the silver one.

It wasn't scary for me to look at them as it was for Knox. His eyes pinched, and he'd rub my stomach like he was trying to wipe the rings away. I thought they were pretty. I didn't know what they meant, but I wasn't afraid when I looked at them. I was comforted, like watching a train arrive on time to the station.

"What if the rings indicate stages?" Dr. Tiff wondered aloud. "Like growth rings of a tree. The rings themselves are not the same width, but if another appears, we can start tracking the rate and maybe even get us a more accurate due date."

Anything would be more accurate than what we had now. No due date.

"Can I guess that since you came into my room without your alpha shadow, he doesn't know about this?"

I sighed. "He will. He might right now. He's very nosy. If he doesn't, I'll tell him. But after...after..."

"After you finally get to leave the house?" she offered kindly.

"Yes," I breathed. I loved the hotel. I felt safe there, both because the guys were always around and because I knew the hotel well enough so I'd be able to at least hide if there was ever danger. But the last time and only time I'd left had been to get hygiene supplies during that first trip to town. I needed out, if only for the afternoon.

Which was why it was so lucky that Knox and the others had been out on a training exercise when I spoke to Dr. Tiff. They'd left Dog, who I met in the hallway outside of the doctor's room.

He'd looked me once up and down, disapproving as ever, before grunting and heading down the hallway toward my room. He stopped a few paces down and looked over his shoulder, clearly waiting.

The dog was as bossy as the rest of them.

Dog stood in the hallway while I changed. He turned his head at the exact moment the others stomped up the hallway. I hadn't been expecting all five of them, even Diesel, dressed in combat-black from head to toe.

"I thought we were going baby shopping? You look ready to start a coup," I said.

Knox gave me shifty eyes.

This was going to be an experience.

————

THE CLOTHES WERE my first clue. Knox parking furthest from the Rockshell Food and Drug store entrance and unfolding a battle plan over the dash was my second.

"Like we practiced," Knox barked to the others.

Practiced?

Diesel sat in the front passenger seat, I was sandwiched between the twins, and Faust had the back row to himself. He'd left Dog with Dr. Tiff, though neither had looked thrilled by that.

"You guys, we're just here for diapers and a crib, if they have that sort of stuff here."

"A crib?" Faust croaked. "Why would you buy a crib?"

Did shifters sleep with their children? Like wolves in a den? That was a cute image, but not very practical. "For the baby?"

"Psh, I'll make you a crib before we buy one."

I searched for Knox's eyes, finding them in the rearview mirror. He just shrugged, agreeing with Faust. "Any of us could make a crib. A bed, a rocking chair, most furniture." He smoothed out the large sheet of what looked like blueprint paper. There were already marks, X's and dotted lines that reminded me of a football play. "Luckily, the baby items are all centered here." He pointed at the map where the majority of the X's were. "We'll concentrate our security to this section. If worse comes to worse, it's a straight shot to the exit, and we can fight our way—"

"Fight our way?" I squeaked, my heart pounding. "Guys, we're baby shopping. Not assassinating a foreign dictator."

Knox rotated in the seat, but only so he could shoot me a disapproving glare. "You are much more important than some asshole foreign dictator. If we take that sort of care killing him, imagine how much we should take protecting you."

I didn't understand why that meant we had to Navy SEAL our way through the drug store, but if we ended the trip with some bottles, diapers, and formula, I'd feel a little better about this glowworm in my stomach.

He unlocked the doors, the sharp click filling the men with determined vigilance.

The twins opened their doors on either side of me, sliding out of the Hummer in a synchronized motion.

"Stop!" I lunged for Huntley's wrist, pulling him back in. It wasn't until they'd gotten out that I noticed they were armed, their matching dual sword handles stuck up over their shoulders. "You can't go into the store armed like that. You'll cause a riot. You're both scary enough without the swords."

The twins' eyes flitted to Knox, whose face had dropped into full-brood mode. He sighed. "Leave the swords."

With matching sour faces, the twins removed the weapons from their backsides, grumbling all the while that if they ended up needing them, they wouldn't hesitate to say *I told you so*.

That was a risk I was willing to take.

Minutes later, the twins announced via the earpiece that it was clear for entry. Walking across the parking lot felt like being transported over a war zone, but we finally made it inside. The soft background music tinkling over the speakers set a backdrop that only made the guys' actions all the more ridiculous.

While over the top, their decisive military movements meant in less than thirty minutes we had nearly everything on our list.

Knox pushed the cart while I trailed ahead, Faust a few

steps in front of me. I stopped suddenly, realizing too late that I was about to get a shopping cart to my ankles, but Knox had a tight grip on the handle.

"What is it?" His words were sharp as his eyes flitted in every direction.

"Nothing. I just thought ice cream sounded really good. And peanut butter."

Knox's eyebrows softened from the angry accent marks that they'd been.

"I'll get it," Faust said, like he could sense Knox's weakening resolve.

He swiftly took off toward the wall of freezer doors while the twins came out of nowhere, sliding into his spot.

"I thought I recognized those shoulders," Hallie said happily. I couldn't see her yet—she was too far away from the mouth of the aisle—but I heard her and witnessed the twins' covert glances toward Knox.

"Silently menacing as ever, good to see. If you're here, does that mean..."

The twins tensed, but short of blocking her way or carrying her out, there was nothing they could do to stop Hallie from walking down the aisle. "Hey, Jazz! I was wondering when I'd come over again to..." The word dropped like a rock falling down a well. She'd walked half an aisle's length to get to me. Plenty of time to look me over. Maybe a stranger wouldn't have noticed the change, but Hallie had seen me recently.

She stopped a few feet away. Knox stood flush by my side.

"Do I need to know something?" she asked quietly.

Knox held my hand, his forearm coiled with trepidation. "Hallie, this isn't the place," he said in a low voice.

I watched Hallie's face at Knox's unsurprising reply.

Her eyes, round with worry, hardly paid Knox any attention. Her mouth was soft, turned down in a look that was so caring and motherly that I couldn't help the tears that burst forth.

My face crumpled, and I tried to say I was fine, but what came out just sounded like a garbled whine.

"What did she do?" Diesel barked angrily from the mouth of the aisle.

Hallie stiffened. "I didn't do anything. Stop it. You're upsetting him more." She gestured at my face, where I couldn't get the tears to stop. "C'mere, baby," she soothed, dropping a warm arm over my shoulders.

I didn't look at Knox, couldn't see him through the tears, but knew he'd stepped back to give Hallie space. Either that, or Hallie had just pushed him back. Her arm didn't feel at all like Knox's did. When he held me like that, I felt cherished, safe, and turned on. With Hallie, it felt like a hug from a mother I'd never known.

I broke down, unsure where the emotions were coming from—this couldn't all be me and my subconscious. She squeezed my shoulders tightly. "You all get that stuff through the line. I'll wait with whichever of you wants to come cause I know one of you will want to." She led me away, toward the exit, and stopped to see all five of the men stalking silently. "One of you," she repeated. "We'll wait in the car."

She led me to the Hummer. Knox hurried ahead and opened the door. I wasn't even sure why I was crying anymore. Just that Hallie had looked like a mom, and I was going to be a parent, and that fact hadn't seemed so strange in the safety of the hotel. Out here, faced with marketing and packaging, pictures of babies sleeping soundly on blue fluffy clouds, parents smiling down—the whole situation felt impossible.

"Jazz, what's wrong?" Knox asked in the muted quiet of the Hummer.

"Nothing's wrong with him," Hallie snapped, her arms circling around me like protective bars. She had to know that something was going on with me. She'd noticed the change in my size, hadn't blinked an eye at my emotional outburst. Though no one had come out and said what had happened, she didn't need it to be. "Have one of the guys drive my car to the hotel." Hallie dug in her pocket and tossed Knox her keys.

Like Knox, Hallie didn't ask; she told.

But this time, Knox listened. I thought it had something to do with how I'd stopped crying in Hallie's embrace, my breath hitching instead as I leaned into her warm shoulder.

"I'm sorry," I mumbled, my voice thick and goopy. We were nearly back to the hotel. Faust trailed behind in Hallie's car.

"You have nothing to apologize for. Hormones are a bitch." Hallie twisted her upper half, looking at where the twins had filled the back with bags. "I see a pint of peanut butter ripple in that bag. Come on. I'll show you how it's done."

She led me out and toward the hotel, never once looking back to make sure the others were there or that they'd brought the bags. They were, and they did.

Dr. Tiff met us at the bottom of the stairs. Her straight black hair was still wet but pulled up in a ponytail—I was beginning to see it as her signature look. "Oh my, what happened?" she asked when she saw my face.

Hallie and Dr. Tiff faced off. I suddenly wasn't sure

what to expect and was reminded of those old Godzilla vs. Mothra monster movies.

"Nothing ice cream won't fix," Hallie said suddenly with a smile after staring at the woman for several seconds. I didn't know what factors she'd taken into account to make her decision, but she'd clearly decided Dr. Tiff was a friend.

The two hurried into the sitting room that looked out onto the forest. Blankets, pillows, and bowls of ice cream appeared as if by magic, and an hour later, I was warm, my face was dry, and my stomach happily digesting too much sugar. The two women kept up a steady stream of easy conversation talking about everything from their favorite microbrews to how to get blood stains out of clothes. I knew why Dr. Tiff needed to know that, not why Hallie did.

Meanwhile, Knox and the others lingered back, periodically walking by the entranceway with wistful, uncertain expressions.

Hallie let out a loud sigh. "You seem sufficiently ice creamed. I should get going." She got up and stretched her arms over her head.

I hadn't expected her to stay the night, but how could she leave before she'd even asked about what was going on? "Don't you have questions?" I asked. After her first question had gone unanswered in the store, she hadn't asked another about my condition. How could she not be curious? Clearly, she knew *something* was up.

"Not at the moment." She brushed off her arms. "I'll be back in a few days with some peppermint foot cream. That was the only thing that helped me when I was preg—practicing for a marathon. My feet always ached."

After a round of hugs, Hallie stepped out, yelling at Faust to stop messing with her passenger door. There wasn't any anger in the demand; she likely knew he'd been the one fixing her car little by little when she came over. Faust never asked, though, choosing to act more like a mechanical ninja.

The smooth rumble of her engine faded, and Knox dropped by my side with no small amount of relief. Staying away while she'd visited had been difficult, especially with how upset I'd been when we got home. I understood now much of my emotional reaction was just hormones, but some had been me letting out the stress and worry I'd kept bottled inside.

I rested my head on his shoulder, watching the trees dance outside. *Practicing* hadn't been the word Hallie had meant to say, but if she wasn't going to ask me questions that I would have a difficult time answering, then the least I could do was return the favor. For now.

14

KNOX

THINGS WERE quiet for a few days after the baby supply excursion, until a fourth ring appeared, shimmering around Jazz's stomach, his bulge noticeably larger. My chest clenched when I saw it. I battled contradicting emotions. Jazz was breathtaking pregnant. He didn't so much glow as he shone, his light impossible to miss. But there was too much uncertainty for me to be sure nothing bad was about to happen.

Dr. Tiff was ecstatic when I told her.

"Now we'll be able to get some answers," she announced, running for her bag she'd left in her room. She had a habit of running to places in the hotel. I didn't know if she was scared or if all that happy just ran a little faster than the rest of us.

The sharp patter of her feet quieted before growing loud again.

Jazz lay quietly as she stretched the measuring tape over his stomach, measuring the distance between the rings, the width of the rings, and how much space remained before the outer rings met his belly button.

"I mean, it's a crazy idea," she muttered. She turned her face around to me. "Do you mind if I call Nana Walker?"

I'd met the older woman briefly at the Walkers' home. I remembered her calming force. "If you think she'll have answers."

"Nana never has answers," Dr. Tiff replied with a secret smile. "But she always has suggestions."

Dr. Tiff gathered her measurements while I gathered Jazz.

"Knox, I can—" He looked into my face and stopped, curling into my body instead.

I kept my growls quiet enough to not be heard, but Jazz could feel them vibrating in my chest. I'd been an idiot. A horny fool. Getting Jazz under me had been more important than making sure he was safe, and now he had to endure days of us staring at his body like it was a science experiment, all the while none of us knowing what would happen to him next.

"Knox," Jazz whispered, smoothing the wrinkles from my forehead as I carried him. "It's gonna be fine. I know it."

I wanted to tell him he couldn't know that. No one knew that. But that would only bring him down to my level of barely restrained panic, which wouldn't help anyone. "Of course it will be." I kissed his cheek. "All these other people around to help you. I just like carrying you now and again."

He wasn't fooled, but he let it drop. We were in the meeting room by the kitchen, and I settled him in a chair, disappearing into the kitchen to gather a quick breakfast as Dr. Tiff got ready to call.

Her cell phone sat in the middle of the table when I returned, ringing through the external speaker.

"Tiffany," Nana answered. Her voice was rich and

warm, reminding me of a garden on a sunny day. "How is the blessed one?"

I felt the wrinkle form at the upper ridge of my nose. Without a clear definition, the term felt more like a catch-all for things they didn't understand. We'd already established the details that had linked the others, making it possible for them to produce life, weren't consistent in Jazz.

Nothing about Jazz's pregnancy had mimicked anything like what had happened to the others.

"Is the blessed one there?" Nana asked like she already knew the answer.

Jazz leaned over the table closer to the phone. "I'm here."

"Hello, dear one, and your alpha? Is he there?" she asked with such an edge, I was only glad I *was* there.

"I'm here...ma'am."

"Elder Walker is fine," Nana replied.

My lips flexed into a near smile. "Of course, Elder Walker."

Dr. Tiff leaned forward. "Nana, another ring has appeared, this one gold. They are appearing in alternating colors, as I thought. And besides the first ring, which appeared around his belly button, the others have started from the outer circumference of his stomach and have appeared going inward." She rattled off a series of numbers that I realized were measurements. Each ring was the same width with the same distance between the outer ring and the two that had grown inside of it.

While Nana listened, other voices floated through. She either had company or was at someone's house and had stepped out when she got the call. "It's an interesting theory. But tree rings tell us how a tree grew, not how it will grow. Still, the timing is too consistent to be ignored. Since the rings have been appearing so steadily, how long before the outer rings reach the inner?"

Dr. Tiff frowned, but it was a clever sort of expression instead of a frustrated one. She did say she liked mysteries. "Let me do the math." She bent over the paper, the very tip of her tongue sticking out the corner of her mouth as her pen scratched. Then her pen stopped. She exhaled sharply.

"What?" Nana, Jazz, and I asked simultaneously.

"The rings should reach the center...I mean...if my math is right..." Dr. Tiff's face was flushed. She kept looking down at her math like she was trying to make the numbers change. "One more week. Two weeks in total from the first ring to when the last should form."

"Two weeks?" Nana breathed. If something had shocked this woman, it seemed like a pretty good fucking cause for concern. I didn't know her well, but I knew shifters as old as Nana didn't live that long out of stupidity. Left to natural causes, a shifter's lifespan was near double that of a human —but that meant a shifter had to leave it up to natural causes, which didn't happen as often as one might think.

"That's impossible," Jazz breathed, but even as he spoke, I watched his wheels turn.

All of this was impossible. Turning into wolves, making illusions with just your hands, a body transforming without notice to support life...

Which meant a two-week gestation may have been impossible, but that didn't mean it wasn't what would happen.

One more week wasn't enough time. Jazz was still very much a human. I would know; I scented him from head to toe every morning. His individual smell had changed since arriving. The manic, sharp flavor he'd carried had dissipated, leaving only mellow lemon, rosemary, and vanilla.

Potent and pure, that was what Jazz smelled like when he was happiest, with nothing bothering him. But there was nothing animal about his smell.

I'd been relying on at least a month to get the nursery ready. I'd started clearing out the adjoining room next to ours, but it still needed repairs, paint, and all the supplies moved in. We needed to decorate, get a shit-ton more of diapers and formula. I had the emergency protocols and drills to update so they included the child, not to mention baby-proofing an entire hotel. Shifters didn't go crazy locking every cabinet, door, or window in their house. Shifter children had more senses to detect danger with, after all. But we lived in a hotel that had been teetering on the brink of ruin when we got it. In that time, we'd managed to make it teeter less, but it was a work in progress. Most importantly, while I was rushing to prepare, *Jazz would have a baby after two weeks.*

"Maybe I'm wrong," Dr. Tiff suggested hopefully. "I know my math is correct, but maybe the rings will slow or double up. The only thing we know for sure is that we should prepare for this possible outcome." Her voice cut out, but she coughed, clearing the uncertainty. "And we will be, Jazz. I promise. We might not know exactly what is going to happen, but we will be there, ready to intervene when it does." She reached over the table for Jazz's hand.

"And I will hurry the care package plans," Nana said serenely.

My initial instinct was to growl at her peacefulness. At first glance it looked too much like indifference. Then I caught Jazz's face, the slight change in his tense jaw. He didn't need me to prove how worried I could become. He especially didn't need me letting it show. I'd never been this scared before. I'd rather face a heavily armed guerrilla army naked than sit idly by while my omega suffered.

"And I'll get the others started on the baby's room," I said, fashioning my voice to sound more like Nana.

On cue, the hammers started pounding upstairs. The others were listening. The snippets of sound I heard over the hammers told me it was the twins upstairs, their already rapid heartbeats going in double time now. They were worried.

"And I'll..." Jazz looked around himself, absently searching for the thing he would do to make himself feel better in an otherwise uncontrollable situation. "I'll... read up on how to care for a baby, I guess." He shrugged, since there really wasn't a lot he could do at that moment in addition to what he was already doing.

With a ticking—or, rather, shimmering—clock over our heads, no one could just sit and wait. No matter if it was a week, six more weeks, or longer, this baby *would* come, and when it did, we would be ready.

———

ON THE EVE of the two-week mark, all eight of us—Dog included—eventually found ourselves in the operations room.

Dinner had been a subdued affair. The twins and Diesel had gone out to hunt, too keyed up to stay inside while we ate and watched Jazz for the slightest sign of discomfort. The remainder of the rings had formed around his tummy, just as Dr. Tiff had hypothesized. Jazz hadn't grown nearly as large as other pregnant women I'd seen—I'd never actually seen a pregnant man, just the aftermath of children—which was the only example I had to go off.

After dinner, no one wanted to separate. Jazz said he wanted to do research before bed, so I took him in the operations room and watched as the others slowly joined us.

The clock on the table said it was eleven fifty-five, nearly midnight and past time for pregnant omegas to be in bed. Jazz had fallen asleep about an hour ago in his daybed. Dr. Tiff sat in a chair next to him reading a medical journal. Her mug of tea had long since stopped steaming, but that didn't stop her from taking small sips.

We didn't know what would happen, what to expect. Jazz wasn't a wolf. His scent was nothing like a shifter, and other than an unerringly accurate ability to pinpoint where the others were while in the hotel, he didn't have the enhanced senses of a shifter either. But while none of us knew what would happen next, we knew something might happen and weren't willing to part. I sensed distress in the others but didn't really need my senses to see it. The guys got up several times, drifting Jazz's direction so they could discreetly scent him. The action soothed the men more than it did anything else, and Jazz had already said he didn't mind it.

I more than *didn't mind* it. Each time I spotted one of the twins, Faust, or Dog wandering Jazz's way, lifting their nose to his hair, my chest warmed in a way that emphasized how cold it had been before. I'd known the attack and loss had changed me, but I hadn't realized how empty I'd become..

Dr. Tiff watched it happen with professional curiosity. Not every pack scented—it would be difficult for a single Alpha to track the scents of every one of his pack members —but scenting had always been our habit. There were enough of us that we could care for our people on a level that other pack Alphas couldn't.

None of us were great with words, Pierce had been the most eloquent of us. But by scenting, we could monitor our people, recognize when things changed, and have a foundation to base how best to help.

"Most of these companies get their insulation from one supplier, American Insulation and Supply." Faust made several notes on the sheet of paper between him and Diesel. They'd pulled out Faust's company list, trying to link the mineral wool to a supplier which would hopefully set us on the next leg of discovering who had killed our pack family.

"Not this one," Diesel rumbled. "*Portal Ventures*. What do they do?"

Faust tapped on his laptop keyboard. "They're primarily an investment company. What would an investment company need with insulation?" His fingers bounced off the keys as he set forth to answer his own question.

His voice warbled with near excitement, enough that I looked away from obsessively staring at Jazz while he slept to look at the two of them.

Diesel's glower was almost light enough to be called a scowl. He was excited too.

"Portal receives all of their building supplies from a supply company called BrimNet." There was more keyboard clacking, a few clicks. "This is interesting. BrimNet is—"

The clock turned over, marking the end of the hour and officially bringing us into the new day. Like reminding your body to wake up at a certain time after a nap, my subconscious had been doing nothing but track the time, so much so that I felt the new day as it came. I looked sharply to Jazz, the others doing the same.

None of us breathed, Dr. Tiff included. We watched Jazz, waiting for...something.

Jazz murmured in his sleep. He pushed his curls off his forehead and turned to the side, bringing his blanket tighter under his chin.

I sighed, and Jazz wrinkled his nose, the lines creasing up the adorable slope. His eyelids fluttered open before opening fully to a group of people staring at him. "Hey, I must've fallen asleep. What's..." His voice faded like he'd picked up on the tension in the room. He frowned, wiggling his lower half while he pulled the blanket out so he no longer resembled a cute burrito.

"What is it?" I asked, standing.

"Nothing, I just feel..." Jazz pushed the blanket off, raising his shirt to look at his tummy. He giggled. "Look at that. I'm like a turkey." His chin hit his chest as he peered down at his belly button. His adorable innie had become an equally adorable outie. "I wonder what that me—"

He hissed sharply, and every person who wasn't him rose to their feet. The twins jumped into action, clearing a space on the floor as we'd planned. Without more to go off of, we'd drafted a procedure for each room in the case that Jazz went into labor and couldn't be moved.

They had the area ready by the time Dr. Tiff and I helped Jazz, moaning and holding the roundest part of his stomach, to the ground. He lay back, his head resting against a pillow. The skin over his stomach rippled, each gentle undulation as terrifying as it was mesmerizing.

He screwed his eyes closed. Dr. Tiff placed her stethoscope over his elbow before sliding it to his stomach.

Jazz's lips moved, quietly repeating the same phrase over and over. "Please don't come out alien-style. Please don't come out alien-style." The whispered plea should've been ridiculous. Instead, I silently chanted with him.

Please don't come out alien-style. I can't lose him. I can't be the reason he is lost.

He groaned, but the sound wasn't laced with pain as I expected. "I've never felt the little guy move so much," he gasped. The truth of that was easy to see. The skin over his tummy rolled like water brought to a boil. "I think he's looking for a way out—" Jazz's head flew back, hitting the pillow hard. If it hadn't been there to catch him, he would've injured himself.

His entire body flexed, holding tight as his back bowed, his weight balanced on his feet and the top of his head.

He screamed, a long, unwavering single note that I wasn't sure was even coming from his mouth. A beam of golden light shot down from the ceiling, enveloping Jazz's entire body while forcefully blasting the rest of us away.

I scrambled for my footing. Dr. Tiff rushed forward with me, her hands outstretched. She dropped them when we reached him. The beam of light still had him surrounded, and he looked frozen in that same awful back-bend. His spine couldn't take much more. Bodies weren't meant to bend that direction.

"I don't...I don't..." Dr. Tiff licked her lips. Closed her eyes. When she opened them, her gaze was clear. "The body knows what to do," she said resolutely. "We're just here to help if it looks like he needs it."

Could she not see my omega? He absolutely looked like he needed help. I stomped forward, and she threw her arm out. "The body knows what to do." Her voice was sharp, as close to an order as she'd ever given me.

I nodded, turning back to Jazz the moment a second pulse of light burst from him. This one felt more like a flash bomb, meant to momentarily disorient and blind its victim. I blinked through the bright spots in my vision, careful not to move too far forward in fear of traipsing over my omega.

My sight returned, and I dropped to my knees. Jazz's body was gone, and in his place, a tawny wolf lay curled up in sleep. Two huge white wings rested against his back, looking like they'd shot out from his shoulder blades. Nestled in the safe pocket of his curled limbs was a calico puppy, with two small matching white wings folded over his back. The puppy was tawny like his father, with spots of dark black and brown like my wolf.

"Am I seeing wings? Are any of you seeing wings?" Faust asked, the first of us to recover.

"We're seeing wings," Huntley replied. "Doc, have you seen anything like this?"

Dr. Tiff shook her head. Her signature ponytail sagged lower than normal at the end of such a long day. A day that had just gotten longer.

Both father and baby slept soundly. I leaned in, relieved to realize Jazz smelled mostly the same, and the child carried his scent. My body folded with relief, shifting into my wolf form before I'd consciously instructed it to do so.

I sniffed Jazz's face, licking his muzzle. Jazz's face moved, sniffing softly with his eyes closed, searching for me even while asleep. As I watched over my mate and child, a certainty settled into me, lining my bones, fortifying my muscles. My pack. My omega. My *son*.

Dr. Tiff leaned back. "From everything I can see and measure, they're fine. The Walker omegas all shifted at birth, so I was expecting that, but they didn't have wings. And they were relatively conscious after." She flattened her feet, no longer balancing her weight on her heels. Faust dropped his hand to help her stand. "I'm going to get what I might need for the night and then set up a bed somewhere."

She looked around the room, clearly staking out a place to sleep.

Diesel grunted something about a cot and left behind her.

I looked to the others and cocked my head. Faust shrugged and shifted, padding to the foot of Jazz's makeshift nest, where he curled up in a matching position and set his head down. Dog followed him but did not lay down. He stared at Jazz and the baby like he was memorizing their features.

The twins shifted as well, choosing the corner near the door to sleep in. I didn't think they were rejecting us but offering to cover the room from a different angle. I nodded, laying my head over the top of Jazz's wings.

Wings.

They were softer than I'd expected. Part of me thought I'd touch them and they'd fall off like parts of a costume. They certainly looked picturesque. Layered with shimmering feathers, they'd likely stretch three feet out on either side.

Dr. Tiff's sharp steps heralded her return. She'd changed—into pajamas, not into her wolf form—and tightened her ponytail. "I'm not too worried about either sleeping a bit longer. We've let Jazz's body do what it needed to do, and I don't see any reason to stop that now. I'll do what research I can on the wings, but honestly, I don't know where to start with that one. Probably Nana. I need take his vitals at least once an hour until he wakes up, so make sure I have a clear path so I don't have to bother you every time." As she spoke, she fumbled with her phone. I assumed she was setting up alarms to get her through the early predawn hours.

Diesel returned with her cot. He set it up before

awkwardly standing a few feet from where Faust and I lay with Jazz. Our eyes met, his human to my wolf. Was this too much for him? Was seeing new life, my omega, and everything else too much of a reminder of what he'd once had? I didn't want to hate him if he chose to leave, but a part of me would. Still, I kept my face clear—an easier feat when there were fewer muscles to control.

Diesel stepped toward the door, his legs seizing at the knees like he was fighting an inner battle. He spun around, shifting as he rotated so that he fell on all four facing us. His wolf was solid black and rigid with uncertainty.

He didn't look at me, but at Jazz and our child—*who still needed a name*. With everything else to prepare, we hadn't spoken about what to call our child. I wouldn't make that choice without my omega's input, so the little pup would have to remain nameless a bit longer.

Diesel tracked the sleeping pair as if expecting their eyes to fling open at any minute. They didn't, and he got close enough to lean his muzzle in, nearly touching the tips of Jazz's ears, and inhaled to scent him.

I chuffed proudly, both for my new family my pack brothers had all accepted and of Diesel's strength. Quinlan had never technically been his omega, since Diesel had insisted on waiting until the gap between their ages didn't mean as much. But Quinlan had *always* been Diesel's. Anyone with eyes could see that.

If our places were reversed and I was forced to watch a pack brother find what had been stolen from me, I didn't know that I could do as Diesel had done.

He exhaled, inhaling a second and third deep breath before directing his attention to the child and doing the same. When he was confident he had their scents, he padded to the opposite corner, across the room from the twins, where he could watch the room from yet another angle.

I wouldn't sleep much this night, but I would feel comforted knowing my pack, no matter how small or troubled, was there with me.

———

No one slept well that night. Dawn came, bringing uncertainty rather than promise. Father and son were both sleeping soundly. Dr. Tiff checked them every hour, but as we faced a second night with them still asleep, I had Dr. Tiff teach the rest of us how to give Jazz his hourly check-ups.

I thought about transferring Jazz to the bed in our room, but the system worked so well with him in the operations room, I decided against it. The others liked having them near while they went about their day, and I couldn't expect everyone to huddle in our room for long hours.

When evening came for a second time, everyone resumed their positions from the first night.

"I'll take first watch," Faust murmured, still at the table where he mumbled at his laptop. "You and Dr. Tiff should both get some sleep."

We were all tired, Faust needed sleep as much as the rest of us, but I wouldn't disrespect him by claiming to know more about what his body could handle than he did.

Dr. Tiff was asleep before she'd rolled all the way over. I took my preferred spot where I could shield and hold my omega and son at the same time. My fingers carded through Jazz's thick tawny hair. As I toyed with it, I saw bits of his red curls shining through.

He was shaped like a wolf but still smelled the same.

Even his wings, foreign and shocking as they were to witness, smelled of him. They were as much a part of him as his leg or tail.

I'd take comfort in what I could smell, not what I saw. I'd never heard of a winged shifter. Dr. Tiff hadn't either. She'd called Nana Walker, and when the matronly shifter said she'd never heard of a thing either, that was when my concern skyrocketed. Somehow, Nana Walker not having any suggestions was more of a statement than anything else had been.

I imagined that was partly the reason Faust offered to stay up first. He and Diesel had uncovered enough that they were sure *something* suspicious was happening between Portal and their insulation supplier, but he didn't know *what* that suspicion was.

I closed my eyes. The ocean was louder tonight than normal. That always happened when the tide came in far enough the echoing crashing sounds had nowhere to go but up the craggy stone cliff, filtering into the hotel. The waves seemed an apt representation for how I felt inside. Churning with uncertainty. My guts turned, frothing with fear. Jazz and my son were here, by my side, breathing, hearts beating.

At what point was *sleeping* medically called something else? We hadn't tried waking either up, which Dr. Tiff had described as an important deciding factor. I had to believe my omega would wake up, that they would both be fine. I had to believe that, or I wouldn't be able to live with myself.

I SHUDDERED awake with a ragged gasp. Rapidly gathering my wits, I recalled where we were and why. I wasn't in my nightmare; those things *hadn't* actually happened. My racing heart dredged up old feelings of failure, of not being strong enough or smart enough to prevent what had happened from happening.

"Knox?" Faust asked, just loud enough to be heard across the room.

"I'm fine," I grunted, delicately removing myself from Jazz's close proximity. A glance at the clock told me Faust had stayed up longer than his shift was supposed to be. "Get some shut-eye. I'll watch until morning."

Faust didn't complain. He shifted, turning three times before settling in a spot next to Dog—out in minutes.

Rain pattered gently against the windows. The cloudy sky meant there wasn't as much moonlight to illuminate the room. The hallway lights were always kept on since Jazz joined us. I stared at the chunk of light in the doorway, unable to stop the worst parts of my nightmare from resurfacing. The team had been in a helicopter flying home. We'd breached over the last of the mountains to a clearing in the trees. The clearing itself was only a handful of acres and housed every pack member we had. I'd smiled, excited to get home, when the clearing suddenly exploded with a mushroom cloud to rival a nuclear bomb. The helicopter banked sharply, spilling my brothers out and sending them sailing to their deaths. I shouted, though the sound was silent. Believing somehow that I could save them, I leaped from the helicopter.

If it hadn't been dreamland, a jump like that would've killed me. Instead, I landed hard on a mound of dirt located directly outside the charred ring of our former home.

Here lies Jazz Whitten.

It wasn't a mound of dirt. It was Jazz's grave.

You did this.

None of the others could be blamed for putting Jazz's life in danger. That had been me and my dick.

I'd known what could happen, that it was a possibility. I'd known and decided I wouldn't protect him.

No wonder the guys didn't always see me as their leader.

What qualities did I have that qualified me to tell anyone else what to do?

"Knox." Diesel's low rumble came from the other direction. His voice was soft and low-toned, like dragging heavy wooden furniture over a smooth floor. "Remember what the doctor said."

She'd told me this wasn't my fault, that I couldn't have known. But I had known. I had known this had happened before.

"Jazz isn't dead. Don't put him in the ground before he belongs there." Diesel spoke with a hard edge, each word dipped in a thin candy-coating of bitterness. "You've failed your omega when he's hurt or dead. Not before. Don't pretend there isn't a difference."

His anger couldn't be ignored. Suffocating in its intensity, I wanted to claw my way out of it, but his anger was deserved. I was being a poor leader, a poor alpha, by pitying myself. Maybe I had made a mistake, but the time to wonder and agonize was later, when there wasn't a task at hand.

I understood what Diesel meant. *Take care of Jazz now. Always. Even if you doubt your ability.*

"Thank you."

Diesel's reply was a single wolfy grunt.

· · ·

I watched the ocean light up. As the sun rose in the east, it illuminate the dark west coast waves. Up here, the water wasn't turquoise and clear. It was an enraged type of dark-blue, turning grayer or greener depending on the conditions. This ocean didn't entice you with tropical dreams of coconuts in the sand. It dared you to challenge it.

I preferred these sorts of beaches. Our work took us around the world, in plenty of picturesque locales. But nothing in nature was as awe-inspiring as endless miles of taunting seas all crashing right outside your doorstep.

The small hairs at my nape stood up, and I looked around the room for the cause. Dr. Tiff was still asleep. I'd taken over checking Jazz's vitals after Faust went to sleep. The twins were in the other corner in their wolf forms, their legs twisted around one another. Diesel remained in his corner, asleep as well. And Faust and Dog were both laying down with their eyes closed.

Only Jazz was awake, and I smiled at his warm gaze before getting to my feet when my brain caught up with what I was seeing.

"You're awake." My throat was tight as the weight of failure—the absolute knowledge that I had killed my omega —sloughed off me like old skin. I hadn't failed. He was here. He was awake and in his human form. They both were, though only Father was currently awake.

Before I made it all the way to him—a journey that consisted of an entire four steps—the others woke. The twins bounded in, able to be playful in their wolf forms in a way they didn't feel as humans. Faust and Dog rolled over to face him, and Dr. Tiff got to her feet, hands automatically to her ponytail as she unleashed her hair before restraining it once more.

"Look what I found. A baby," Jazz joked. His eyes shone

with tears and pride. He yawned suddenly, lifting his free fist above his head in a stretch. "What happened? It is not the same time I remember it being."

Dr. Tiff took over filling Jazz in as well as examining both father and child now that they were awake—mostly. My son had Jazz's button nose, his oval face. I already knew he took after us both in his wolf form and wouldn't mind if he'd taken only Jazz's human traits. The kid would be luckier that way.

My gaze never wavered as the others pressed in, scenting my omega and pup now they were in their human forms. Huntley lifted Jazz's hand with his muzzle, flopping it back until Jazz's palm rested between Huntley's ears. Jazz scratched him, seeming to understand how Huntley needed the contact.

I'd do my own examining and reassuring once the others had their fill and I could take Jazz and our son into our room. I'd inspect every inch of both of them—likely more than once. I could be generous now since I knew I'd have both to myself later. For the moment, I hung back, simply enjoying the rare peaceful moment.

15

JAZZ

WHEN KNOX TOLD me I'd sprouted wings, I'd started laughing. It sounded like a joke.

You were surrounded by this bright light, and then the light exploded, and you were a wolf...with wings.

That was ridiculous. And yet it was exactly what Knox and the others claimed had happened.

I craned my head over my shoulder, trying to look at my back in the mirror after an afternoon nap. No wings. Not even spaces for wings.

I'd been too exhausted—despite being told I'd slept for more than two days—to try shifting the day before. Even so, this morning, Dr. Tiff said she had to get back to the Walker County pack now that I'd given birth and we were both doing well. She'd come back for our checkups every couple of weeks, and I'd spent the morning helping her pack up. That only meant I'd spent the morning directing the twins on how to help her pack up since I was still too fragile in all of their minds to lift a dainty finger.

I wasn't stupid enough to complain. Unlike before, now, I felt fragile. I hadn't gone through labor in the normal sense. There hadn't been hours of panting and threats, but I'd still gone through a transformation. One that I was still trying to catch up with.

I had a child. I was a wolf. Neither felt very true yet. I'd only been pregnant for two weeks. By the time I came to terms with the fact that I was pregnant, it had been time to have the baby. And I hadn't felt all that involved. Hearing the story told, I hadn't been that involved. I'd screamed silently and then slept. And I was still exhausted.

Knox mentioned something about taking me down to the beach to stretch my legs. I didn't think he meant my human legs.

Lifting my nose to the air, I waited for the bouquet of scents to reach me. I was a shifter now. That meant being able to see, smell, and hear much better. Except I smelled my lotion, the fabric softener in my shirt, a faint whiff of peppermint from the cream Hallie had left—I didn't know how to break the latest development to her and was pretty sure our silent agreement to not ask questions would end about the time she spotted the baby outside my body.

I couldn't detect anything outside of what I'd already been able.

I pulled my shirt over my head. I could stare in the mirror all day and wonder why everything had happened the way it had, or I could make my way downstairs and find my son and alpha.

It wasn't a very difficult choice.

I sensed Knox downstairs. At least that quirk was still the same. My feet must've sprouted wings as well because I zoomed down the hallway and flew—not literally—down the stairs toward the kitchen.

I heard Huntley's voice first. "Samuel is a good name. You have it backwards."

"No, the kitten is on the front. That's what the picture looks like. You don't think we should choose Pierce?" Knox asked.

They knew I was outside the kitchen. I wasn't sneaking, but I still lingered. We hadn't talked about baby names. My father hadn't named me. I'd arrived on his doorstep with a pack of diapers, a can of formula and a birth certificate with the name Jazz Whitten already supplied. I wouldn't name my child after either of my parents. And though I had no real reason to not want to name my son Pierce, I still found my nose wrinkling at the suggestion.

"It's a fine gesture, but you need your child to represent the future. Not our past. The stretchy part goes in the back. The tabs pull over the front."

I'd never heard Diesel sound so reasonable. It wasn't that he sounded unreasonable all the time; he just didn't *sound* for more than a few grunts. He had a good point, and not just because I didn't want to name my baby Pierce.

"Jazz, what do you think your baby should be called?" Faust called out.

My head hunched between my shoulders like I'd been caught doing something naughty. I wasn't, though, so I strode forward with my head high. "I agree with Diesel... what are you guys doing?"

I knew *what* they were doing. Changing the baby's diaper. But they had the kitchen table cleaned off and covered with a sheet, making it resemble an operating table more than a changing table. Ignoring the fact that the table wasn't the best place to change a baby, they had more than one diaper out, several ripped primarily along the tag portions, and enough baby powder sprinkled everywhere to put on a convincing *Scarface* reenactment.

Which would make the gently wiggling bundle on the

table my little friend. He didn't have a lot of hair, but what he did have was coppery. "Why not Angus?"

The others looked from me to the child, clearly testing the name in their heads.

"Yes," Jagger responded first. "I like Angus."

"Hold on. What's your last name?" My face twisted with horror. I was pregnant and attached to a man whose last name I didn't know. How scandalous.

"It's Hart," Knox rumbled with a smirk.

Diesel, Faust, and Huntley all nodded. I wished Dr. Tiff could've stayed a little longer, not for any medical reason, but because I liked her. She was always chipper and had a way of looking at every problem, no matter how big, like it was nothing more than a mystery to be solved. She was the Walker County pack's doctor, though, and they had far more people who depended on her.

"Knox? What do you think?" I leaned my head against his shoulder.

Knox wrapped the baby—I'd have to trust they had the diaper on correctly—and handed him to me. While my baby nestled in my hold, my alpha embraced us both.

"Angus is perfect. It's new, but strong."

"Just like our baby."

I felt something settle, a notch clicking into place as the name was decided. Angus. My little angel baby had a name. "Does he need anything?" I asked.

All the books had said the baby would appreciate a regular schedule, naps at the same time, meals at the same time. But while this was my first experience with a baby and I only knew what I did from the parenting books I'd read, it wasn't Knox's first baby or any of the others.

Their old pack had members from birth to those in their silver years—a fact that never failed to make me tear up. When I thought about how much these men had lost...

"Jazz?" Knox said my name softly.

I shook my head. "I'm fine. Should I make him a bottle...or?"

Knox nodded. "A bottle is a great idea. Do you want to feed him and then go down to the beach? Or go to the beach so he can eat while we figure out your wings?"

Figure out your wings. That sounded faintly ominous, but mostly because of the ambiguity. Maybe my wings were a one-time thing, and when I shifted again, I wouldn't have any.

But now I had a difficult choice. Spend precious moments with my son? Or explore my new and unusual wolf side? It was an impossible decision, and I expressed that fact with obvious wavering.

Knox laughed, turning me by my shoulders so I face the door out. "I'll make the bottle, you bundle yourselves up, and we'll decide when we get down there, how about that?"

The suggestion was perfect, just like my alpha.

———

THE SKY MIGHT HAVE BEEN blue and clear, but a fierce wind made bundling up a necessity. I wasn't sure what would happen to my jacket when I shifted. Faust had tried to explain how our wolf forms assumed our clothing with very little outward change, but the concept was too mind-blowing to think about for long.

Knox insisted on carrying me down the narrow path that wound down the stone cliff leading from the hotel to the beach below. I carried Angus and was appreciative of Knox's concern. My biggest fear was tripping and falling with Angus in my arms. It was funny how falling on the walk hadn't been something I was afraid of hours before, but now it was the only thing I could think about.

Knox carrying me relieved that worry. He didn't trip or stumble, never placed a foot anywhere than exactly where he wanted.

The others tagged along. None of them had seen a winged wolf before either.

When we got down to the sand, I retreated to a bleached-out log where I could feed Angus while the others messed around. They were often so serious in their human forms. I thought maybe their emotions were different—or if not different, they were able to handle them differently—in their wolf forms. They hopped, yelped, and frolicked. There simply wasn't a better word for the loping gait of the twins as they spurred each other on.

Angus finished his bottle, his little lips parted in an O even though I'd pulled the bottle nipple out. He hadn't had very many awake hours. But I would have time to gaze into his eyes. My impatience wouldn't last forever.

A shadow blocked the sun on our log, and I looked up to Diesel's glowing silhouette. "I can hold him, if you want to go...figure things out."

My breath hitched, even though I was trying so hard to not make this moment seem like a big deal. Diesel's dodgy expression told me he was uncomfortable, but he was still trying. I got to my feet, leaning into Diesel's chest to transfer the baby. I hadn't quite worked out how to hand him over without it looking like I was transporting a bomb that would go off at the slightest jostle.

Diesel didn't strain away from my closeness, though. He leaned in, his nose nearly touching the spot behind my ear where they all enjoyed to sniff.

"Thanks. I'm gonna go try not to...I don't know, fly away?"

Could I actually fly? What else were wings for? I met Knox and the others on the hard sand.

Faust shifted and grabbed his phone from where he'd left it with his shoes. "I told Nash I would record this. They haven't stopped talking about you over there."

My nerves hit then. My thoughts reduced to a molecular level, painfully aware of the way I was made of atoms, and though I seemed sturdy, I was actually a collection of very fast moving things. That hadn't seemed like an important point until right then.

What if I got things wrong in the scramble?

"You've already done this," Knox reminded me. "It was natural then, and it will be again. That's all I want you to think about right now. You don't coerce your body into a wolf. You allow your body to exist in the form it prefers."

What form did I prefer? I was excited to be a wolf, but scared as well. Which was silly because I wasn't afraid of Knox when he was a wolf. He didn't seem any different—not on a level that mattered.

My head turned away from the waves and toward Angus and Diesel, knowing they were still there but needing to check anyway. My baby was a wolf, and whether I understood how to shift or not, he would still be a wolf. I couldn't miss out on this bonding opportunity.

I nodded resolutely. *Okay, I'm ready.* That had been what I was about to say, but when I attempted to speak, I had a wolf's muzzle and a wolf's lolling tongue.

A fresh wave rolled in, getting my paws wet. I shook off the cold, shooting forward before I remembered to check if I still had wings. A gust of wind ruffled my hair, bringing new scents—I could smell a little better in this form, but not as well as Knox and the others could even in their human forms.

My body moved and stretched, unfurling as if for the first time. I wasn't sure how I was doing it, but I could manipulate my wings—yep, still there—stretching them far out on either side.

With both wings deployed, the next gust of air lifted me off my feet. I gave an experimental flap. My paws didn't lift any higher than a few inches, but the force propelled me forward, my claws skimming over the sand instead of digging into it.

I skidded to a stop—moving forward had been easier than stopping moving forward—and turned around, racing back towards where the others waited. The head-on wind had lifted me to a hover, but the tailwind propelled me a half foot in the air and forward at a speed much faster than what I could've managed on only four legs. I came to another sliding halt, coughing on the sand I kicked up.

I really needed to get a hold of this whole stopping thing.

When the dust and sand settled, I spotted Knox's face, eyes wide and unguarded. Beside him, Faust's mouth hung open. But the twins weren't looking at me. They were looking at *Angus*. He was a puppy again.

"He shifts when Jazz shifts?" Diesel asked.

I took his tone to mean that wasn't a normal thing. Knox dropped a comforting hand at the back of my neck, likely sensing my sudden distress.

"Most shifters can't shift until they are older. Generally around puberty, though some earlier, some younger."

"I've never seen a baby shift," Faust said.

"Yesterday, we'd never seen wolves with wings," Jagger added. "Imagine what we'll see tomorrow."

"Can you do that hover thing again?" Huntley asked me while looking at Angus.

I obliged, flapping my wings. Without the wind, I had to flap harder and couldn't manage more than a few inches of distance from the sand, but that was enough to make Angus's wings begin to flap, though the puppy was still clearly asleep. He floated out of Diesel's arms for a second, until Diesel held him sturdy again.

"Could they be linked?" Huntley asked. "Since the baby is so defenseless, maybe he's bonded with his father. It would be interesting to see what he does when someone isn't holding him, but that is too dangerous of a thing to try today." He didn't look to Knox to confirm.

When it came to things that were dangerous, the five of them generally agreed.

After a bit more practice, everyone but Knox shifted and then the fun really started. Turned out I could run faster than any of them when I brought my wings into it. Jagger, who had previously been the fastest among them, growled, but the sound came from somewhere behind me. Far, far behind me.

I finally stopped to show him mercy, and Jagger limped over to Huntley, who licked his muzzle consolingly.

I couldn't smell or hear as well as they could, but I could run faster, and for my first conscious day as a wolf, that was pretty good.

After an afternoon on the beach, I was tired all over again, but I hated the idea of being cooped up in the room knowing everyone else was together working on the investigation—especially now that the Jazz-related problems were winding down.

I spent most of that time holding Angus and staring at his face for longer than I'd ever stared at anything in one sitting.

"Do you have the report from the Columbian police?" Huntley asked Faust.

Faust ruffled through a stack of papers to his right but must not have found what he was looking for because he jumped up, saying he would go get it from the evidence room. Things would've been easier if they'd just move all the evidence into the operations room, but I figured they had a reason for not doing that.

After Faust left the room, Diesel stood, his steps bringing him within a few feet of me. I peered up, curious, but sensed I should wait and let Diesel come to what he wanted to say rather than have me yank it from him. "I thought about your gift. Your power." He rummaged in his pocket and pulled out a small brown satchel smaller than my hand. The items inside clinked together. "You were using single items, and I didn't know if that was the extent of your ability or if something like these would be useful."

He dropped the satchel in my palm, and I adjusted Angus so I could open it, pouring the contents into my hand. There were seven marbles in total, all glass with green, blue, and silver swirls.

My lips curled, ideas coming faster than I could remember them. Marbles were small enough to hold all at once, but if I concentrated, I could transform each one separately. I'd done similar things with bits of paper.

I cupped the marbles, letting them roll out of my hands and onto the floor while making it look like I was unleashing a swarm of praying mantises toward where the others sat.

Huntley shuddered and got to his feet, stepping back from the insect army. "Thanks, Diesel, that's terrifying."

"You're afraid of a praying mantis?" I asked, shocked.

Huntley glowered. "No, I'm not afraid. They're just creepy. They bite off their mate's heads, you know," he offered like it was all the proof that was needed.

Jagger chuckled, stooping over to pick up the marbles and protect his partner. "I thought you liked it when I bite," he teased over his shoulder while depositing the marbles back in my hands.

Smirking, I closed my hands over the marbles again, laying my two palms flat when I was finished.

Diesel sucked in a sharp breath.

I'd recreated the pack. A tiny version of us each. They stood still like statues—it was too difficult to make a human mirage move realistically. There were just too many factors to try to account for them all. Animals and insects were easier because they had more predictable physical responses.

Faust returned with a cardboard box. He took one look at my hands and said, "I'm taller than Knox."

Knox growled.

Faust set the box in his arms on the table. "This is everything from Pierce's death. Columbian reports—the translations are on the back. Any security footage is going to be on the flash drives in the envelope at the bottom." He dropped the box, his eyebrows rounded in dubious curiosity like he wanted to know why Huntley had asked for the evidence but didn't think it would come to anything.

Huntley ignored his doubt and tore the lid open. He found the report he was looking for and leaned back, flipping the first page to read the translation on the back.

The others went back to their tasks, and I resumed

staring at Angus while he slept, but less than a minute later, Huntley quickly stood. "I knew it."

Jagger glanced over, not nearly as excited as his twin. "What did you know?"

"After the fire, the police took statements from everyone they knew had stepped foot on that street."

I assumed Knox and the others had not been included in that list even though they'd been on that street.

"But none of the eye witness reports had any usable information," Knox said.

"They still don't, except for this." Huntley emphasized with his finger against the paper. "This guy, Donald Seafer, he was driving by at the time of the fire."

"So?"

"So he was there as an expat for Portal Ventures."

Diesel and Faust both dropped what they were doing, stretching to read the report.

"Donald Seafer, Portal Ventures employee, states he was driving by when he witnessed a fireball large enough he saw it from over the security wall." Faust scanned the next several lines. "That's all there is about him. But...Portal Ventures. That's the second time that name has come up, in two entirely different countries."

"That's more than a coincidence," Diesel growled.

Knox scratched his chin, and I watched him. The others watched him as well. As their leader, his thoughts on this would decide what they did moving forward. "Okay, I want everyone switching gears. By the end of the week, I want to know everything about that company, particularly why their name keeps popping up. Faust, can you pull up the Columbian estate on the screen?"

Faust stood, kneeling at the end of the row of surveillance monitors and tapped at the keyboard there.

The third screen in flickered, revealing a black and white image. Four ten-foot security walls enclosed a charred, soggy expanse of land.

"Rot and decay, just like our packlands," Knox snarled. "We start now."

"What about...?" Faust didn't finish his question. Instead, his eyes flitted to me and then back to Knox.

I sat forward, adjusting Angus to sleep over my shoulder. "What about what? If it has to do with me, I want to know."

Knox shot Faust a look that clearly conveyed how much he appreciated Faust asking what he had. "Baby—" Knox started.

I got to my feet. "Don't 'baby' me. What?"

"It's something I should've handled weeks ago," Knox snarled in a way I knew wasn't directed at me but himself. "The man who attacked you outside your hotel, the man who made it possible for me to catch you. He was trying to kill you."

I thought back to that night, but the details were fuzzy. The whole night hadn't been a great look for me. Particularly when I'd been running from Knox, slipping through his fingers for the last time. So many things had happened since—terrifying, amazing, impossible, wonderful things. Why would I dwell on a man who had wanted to mug me?

I must've said as much out loud because Knox shook his head. "He wasn't ever trying to mug you. He never asked for your wallet. He clearly said *your father* before I took him out. It's another loose end. Another thing that doesn't add up, and I—"

"I know, I know. You don't like it when things don't add up." I understood why Knox was curious, just not what he thought the information would do. I wasn't going back to my father. Whatever his goal had been in trying to bring me back, he'd failed.

But, none of that would convince Knox this issue didn't need their time or attention. He hooked his hand around the other side of my hip and brought me and Angus in to sit on his lap. "I didn't want you to worry about it. That's why I didn't bring it up. But if I had found something out, I would've told you."

Knox had a need for answers that I didn't share, but I wouldn't try and stop something that so clearly made him feel better. I kissed his forehead, dropping my lips to his mouth when he grumbled.

"I understand. Thank you, Alpha." I smiled.

Someone—I was pretty sure Huntley—made a gagging sound, and Knox flicked a paper clip, sending the projectile his direction.

"You're welcome, my omega."

16

KNOX

I grabbed Jazz's wrist, pulling him to sit in my lap. His legs folded obediently, crossing at the ankles and tucking between my calves. His tempting bottom sat squarely on top of my dick, a fact that was both appreciated and intended.

Dr. Tiff didn't bat an eye at the intimacy. Since she'd returned to Walker County, she'd called every day, asking for measurements and asking questions about baby and father. Jazz's exhaustion was cause for worry, since he still slept as much as he had the days after labor.

Jazz turned his profile toward me. "He's sleeping. Like you said." Jazz's bottom lip plumped, pushing his top into a soft curve.

I tucked my face into the sloping harbor of his neck, rubbing my nose along his jaw. Jazz's face was smooth. He didn't have the same stubble as I did that left red marks on his skin. "It's okay to check."

We'd only just started laying Angus down to sleep in his nursery the day prior. His crib, crafted by Faust and me from Oregon white oak, had sat unused in his nursery for the first week of his life. During the rare moments when Angus wasn't being held by one of us, he'd slept in a bassinet next to the bed. Or, if we slept in our wolf forms, he slept in the bed with us.

I was well equipped to understand Jazz's need to check on him again and again, despite the fact we had a video monitor sitting right next to us that displayed Angus sleeping peacefully in his crib, and we were only in the next room over.

"Like I was telling Knox, I'll bring iron supplements with me when I come for Angus's well-baby exam after the weekend. You had a baby in two weeks. It's possible your body will need longer to heal after such rapid growth." The screen behind Dr. Tiff flickered with movement.

Coming from the hallway behind her, there were hushed whispers, and several times, someone loudly shushed another while their angular shadows danced against the wall behind the doctor. They were as astounded as the rest of us over Jazz's transformation. Dr. Tiff ignored the crowd that slowly grew and didn't ask about Jazz's wings.

She could've closed the door, blocking the onlookers, but their curiosity was expected and not dangerous unless the wrong person said the wrong thing.

"I'm pleased with baby's growth. Since your pregnancy was so swift, there was a concern that baby's growth would continue at that same rate. But I'm happy to say he's well within shifter infant ranges."

Jazz cocked his head to the side, the move causing his crimson curls to tickle the side of my face.

It was so easy to forget Jazz hadn't always been a shifter and only knew what he did about shifter culture because we'd taught him.

"The differences aren't substantial. Initially, shifter children grow faster than human children, but that tapers off once the child enters preschool or school age. The easiest way of framing it is to take human baby milestones and subtract a few months—though every baby is different."

"I won't have to wait as long to see him crawl or walk. That sounds good to me." Jazz wiggled when he spoke, his excitement apparent in his constant movement.

My dick also noticed how he couldn't keep still. The opportunistic prick wasted no time nestling between Jazz's cheeks, despite us both having our clothes on. My dick didn't mind the muted pressure, not when he was where he always wanted to be.

Jazz gasped softly while Dr. Tiff continued talking.

He rolled his hips back, playing a dangerous game. I gripped his hips tightly, stilling his movements. "Bad boy." My lips ghosted over his ear as I whispered.

"That's all I wanted to go over for this chat." Dr. Tiff leaned away from her computer and turned her head toward the hallway. "Would you both be willing to answer a few questions regarding Jazz's shift? My Alpha was curious, as well as some of the other pack members."

I'd been hired to bring Jazz to his father's home, a place that had once acted as Jazz's prison. At the same time, Walter Whitten's lies for wanting his son home were unfounded. I could only assume that meant Jazz's father didn't have his son's health and prosperity in mind. He wanted something else, and I needed to discover what that *something* was before Walter grew tired of waiting. All of that amounted to one very good reason to keep Jazz's status a secret. At the same time, this wasn't any pack. These were the Walkers. Faust had done work for Nash in the past. They'd developed a rapport. They were

Elders for the pack and had only ever been helpful and friendly.

"I don't mind," Jazz answered before I could voice my protests.

My desire to give Jazz exactly what he wanted to keep him happy warred with the desire to keep him safe.

Jazz's upper half rotated to face me. "Unless you mind?"

That he'd paused to ask me my opinion meant he trusted what I had to say, and that above everything else convinced me. "If we keep the questions to a minimum and the group small."

Dr. Tiff looked back again to relay the message, but the owners of the shadows were already spilling through the doorway.

The shifter at the lead couldn't have been much older than Jazz. If that. He was average height—uncommon for an alpha. His chestnut brown hair curled around his ears. Beside him stood a massive black man, his chest so wide his body wouldn't fit entirely on the screen.

"My name is Alpha Tyson, and this is my omega, Tyrone," the young Alpha said with a polite nod. He had a soft, musical voice with a soothing resonance. "I'll admit right away, I asked Hollister about you." Alpha Tyson's shy confession was further evidence toward how unlike an average Alpha this man was.

Due to our location, our old pack had been insulated from much of the shifter-to-shifter violence and conflict. We hadn't needed to bother ourselves with how other Alphas led their packs. The way they commanded their people wouldn't have worked with our situation. But it was still the shifter way, and I recognized that, my pack acted as an outlier, not the other way around.

Paul focused his gaze on me. He didn't harden his

expression or do anything else that could have been considered posturing. His lips remained in a near smile, and his blue eyes were bright, open. "I've heard less about you...*Knox?*" The light incline in his tone conveyed he was asking what I preferred or what my title was.

I bowed my head. "Knox is fine."

"It's a pleasure to meet you. I've only been Alpha here for a few months, and I haven't met too many other..." He rolled his hand in a vague reference toward the other shifters he'd met while holding the position of their leader.

His omega leaned over, pressing their arms together in silent support.

Alpha Tyson's hand calmed and settled somewhere off screen. "Anyway, wings, huh? And rainbow puke? That's crazy."

Jazz leaned closer to the computer, encouraged by Alpha Tyson's casual tone. "Thank you. That's what I've been saying this whole time. Totally crazy. I prefer the bubblegum puke to the normal kind, though."

The two shared a grin I might have been jealous of if I couldn't clearly see how well suited Alpha Tyson was with his omega. The omega had yet to say a word, but I didn't need him to speak to be able to see their connection. They reminded me of a tugboat and a freighter, both ships vital in important ways. Neither of them were what I would call a stereotypical representation of the types of shifters that generally filled the roles of pack Alpha and omega.

"Do you have any ideas about why this has happened?" Alpha Tyson asked. The more time I spent watching him, the less I thought about how he wasn't the usual shape of a leader, and the more time I concentrated on the ways he excelled. I doubted that his amiability was fabricated and recognized how his gentle approach kept Jazz calm and open.

"None. I mean, there's what happened to all those guys over there," Jazz said. "Is Hollister there with you?"

Alpha Tyson shook his head. "He's at the Walker house. He told me to tell you to call him when you can and asked why he hasn't gotten any baby pictures yet."

Jazz beamed. "I will. We're still...it's been an adjustment."

Alpha Tyson waved away Jazz's mounting regret before it could grow. "We understand. The blessed omegas had months to adjust to the idea while they were pregnant. It's life-changing and requires time to adapt and heal. I hope you'll keep us updated with any changes to you or baby. Dr. Tiff had only glowing things to say about your pack. I'd like for this friendship between our packs to last." He had a way of sounding so sincere all doubt or misgivings were obliterated.

I wouldn't be able to make my final decision on what I thought of the man until I sat in the same room with him. I needed to take in information from all of my senses to do that. But, for now, I liked him and his silent, mountainous omega.

We said our goodbyes, confirming Angus's well-baby checkup for the following Monday.

I closed the laptop, and Jazz spun around in my lap, straddling my hips. My cock lamented the loss of his warm heat but celebrated in this new position that opened so much more of Jazz to my touch.

"That wasn't so bad." He looped his arms around my neck, letting our faces rest close but not touching.

"He's an interesting Alpha."

The right side of Jazz's mouth lifted, a prelude to one of

his easy smiles. "I like him. He's not like you or the other guys."

I snorted, making Jazz bounce. My dick liked that. "Thanks a lot."

"No, I don't mean it like that. I like the way you are. It's sexy."

I appreciated that he'd left the others out of that statement.

"He just seems like a good guy. I'd be glad if we became their friends, but I'll understand if you have a point of view I haven't thought of yet."

I rubbed my lips along his chin, stealing a kiss along the way.

Jazz's motions transformed, his limbs taking on the consistency of liquid and I lifted him at the hips, setting him back down against my lap while rubbing our erections together over our clothing. My little finger slipped beneath the waistband of his sweatpants and traced his hidden hipbone. When Jazz had first come to me, that bone had been less hidden, sticking out from a waist that had needed rest and healthy food. *And putting a baby in there might have made a difference.*

I had just enough selfish male pride to be pleased by that thought.

"You may continue, Jazz." At his inquisitive brow, I clarified, "Talking about how sexy you think I am."

His cheeks flushed sweetly, and he squeezed his arms while trying to hug his yawning face against my neck. I held him back with a hand on each shoulder and studied his face.

His lazy smile and drooping eyelids told me all I needed to know. Hearing how sexy I was would have to wait. "On second thought, it's about naptime for omegas."

"What?" he protested. "But I'm the only one here!"

I smirked. "Exactly."

Jazz tried to scramble away, and I gathered his limbs, holding his wrists in one hand behind his back. The position pushed his chest out, and he whimpered, clearly thinking I'd changed my mind, and we were once again on the road to nudity. I dropped a loud, smacking kiss at the button of his nose. "You need your rest. You heard Dr. Tiff."

Jazz drooped as the fight left him; a larger yawn stretched his mouth obscenely. "I am a little tired."

Seeing his mouth gaping open weakened my resolve, but the battle was already won. I pulled the blanket back from our bed, settling Jazz on his side while tucking my pillows around him. He mentioned feeling better when he slept that way, but I also preferred surrounding him with my scent before leaving. Even if it was just to the other room.

His eyes closed before he burrowed his head into the pillow like a cat kneading a cushion. I kissed my sleeping prince and then stepped into the nursery. Peering over the side of the crib, I spotted two blue eyes staring back at me. His eyes weren't the most noticeable thing about him at that minute. The stench surrounding him like a toxic green cloud was.

I'd spent time in countries with zero sanitation services. We'd once transported a decomposing body in our trunk through the Guban Desert. We'd ended up having to torch the vehicle since nothing else would get rid of the persistent stench.

And despite all of *that*, picking up my perfect infant son brought me to tears—and not in a Hallmark type of way. I didn't want to unleash this stench so near my sleeping mate. He might suffocate on the stink cloud.

Lifting Angus from his crib revealed the problem was larger than I'd imagined.

This *problem* had leaked over his diaper, up his back, and into the tight sheet that covered his sleeping pad. No amount of wiping would clean this. There was only one solution.

Total decontamination.

———

"He doesn't like his arm like that."

"How do you know what he likes? He looks the same no matter what."

"No, there's a dip in his eyebrows."

"He doesn't have eyebrows!"

I pointed the sprayer toward the bickering twins. "He has eyebrows. They're just still light."

Huntley's gray t-shirt turned black and clung to his shoulders as he growled and lunged forward. The urge to retaliate made his fingers curl.

Jagger caught him around the middle, effectively halting his forward progress. "You'll hurt the baby."

Huntley visibly relaxed but shot me a look that said he'd get back at me when I least expected it.

"Your bickering was hurting the baby," I barked.

Huntley smiled. "No it wasn't. He likes it. See, he's smiling."

Angus lay on his back in a baby bath chair made to fit in kitchen sinks. After the initial rinse-off that had spurred tears from both sides of the skirmish, Angus had mostly surrendered, content to lay back and let what would happen happen.

The sheet and the clothes he'd been in had gone straight

into the fire. That hadn't been my most reasonable moment, and we couldn't start throwing items away when Angus pooped on them, but I knew a lost cause when I saw one.

The twins had been drawn by the smell. Like twisting your neck to stare at a crash on the highway, they'd wandered in, curious about the source of the smell. Then they'd made it their job to offer commentary.

Faust and Dog waltzed in the kitchen. Dog lifted his nose into the air and promptly turned back around.

"That means you need another rinse," I told Angus, who stared serenely.

"We got the air flow controller installed onto the existing ventilation system. Diesel went to turn it on while I told you in case something—"

The hotel started humming.

"—happened." He cocked his head to the ceiling with an expression of trepidation.

We waited for something to explode or fall apart. Repairing the ventilation in the hotel had turned into an endless list of smaller tasks. The existing ducts needed to be repaired and clean. A new system had to be delivered and installed. But once Faust got it working, we'd finally be able to tackle the largest problem the hotel had: mold.

"It sounds really goo—"

A muffled boom shook the floor just enough that we all noticed the vibration. I wrinkled my nose against the pervading scent of exhaust and burnt oil.

Faust scowled at me like I had anything to do with it. "You cursed me," he spat, turning on his heel in the same second as he strode out the door.

They'd get it figured out, I had no doubt. I'd put money on the system up and running by the next morning at the latest. Lifting Angus from the water, I turned to Huntley, who had his towel out and ready. He wrapped Angus burrito-style before handing him back.

When I brought him to the table to dry, lotion, and redress, I couldn't help my moment of smug accomplishment. The baby was clean. The hotel became more of a home every day, and with each success, my faith in my brothers strengthened. We'd been broken, but that didn't mean we couldn't mend.

"AND YOU'RE SURE the message can't be traced back?" Knox asked Faust.

Both men sat in the front of the Hummer while Angus and I sat in the back. I pulled down Angus's new onesie, smoothing the front image. The Walkers had sent their care package, and Knox had driven into town to pick it up. It included diapers, bottles, rattles, and a tablet that Angus was a long while from being able to use. He wore one of the onesies now, a mustard-yellow color with blue lettering that said, *Howlin' good time.* I assumed it was a wolf joke. Thankfully for Angus, he didn't seem to have quite as bright red hair as I did, and yellow didn't turn him into a hot dog with mustard and ketchup.

"There's nothing to trace. The worst Portal can do is not reply, but then we're in the same spot we are now."

Once the guys started learning all they could about Portal—the company whose name kept popping up in strange places—they'd been like fleas on a dog. Early on, they'd learned all they could about Portal from information readily available. Particularly how BrimNet, the company they sourced their mineral wool from was actually a business financed by Portal. I didn't know the details of the email Faust had sent, but it was meant to be exploratory, testing the waters to see how they reacted.

And Knox was worried about the danger, which meant all systems were operating normally at the Hotel Royal Paynes.

"It's the weekend, so I don't expect a response," Faust continued. "Depending on what they say, I want to take Diesel and stop by for a visit to the west coast branch."

Knox nodded, smoothly pulling the Hummer into the parking lot of Cat's Fresh Catch, or as it was known by myself, *The only restaurant in Rockshell.* That wasn't one hundred percent accurate, but it felt true enough. Cat's Fresh Catch offered more than seafood. They were a catchall type of place, opening to customers who were looking for a greasy spoon breakfast in the morning before slowly transforming into a seafood restaurant at night.

The hours in between were anyone's guess.

This was where Hallie had suggested we meet when I called. I was hoping for a place more private, but maybe it was best to introduce Hallie to Angus where she wouldn't be as likely to make a scene.

Though I wasn't sure what sort of scene Hallie would make. The woman was unflappable, which was why it was so disturbing to spot her outside standing in decorative gravel as some guy aggressively gestured at her chest.

"What the..." I opened my door before the Hummer came to a stop.

"Jazz," Knox growled. "Wait here."

He had to know I wouldn't. I hurried with Angus's buckles. Faust and Knox were out of the vehicle and eating up pavement. Neither Hallie nor the man she argued with noticed their approach. I stopped with Angus several feet away while Knox called out Hallie's name.

She glanced over once quickly and then again. Her eyes narrowed, the skin beneath them darker and baggier than I remembered. "Knox, I—"

"Who the fuck is this?" the man snarled, looking Knox up and down like he actually stood a chance if things got physical.

"Friends," Knox snarled. "Who the fuck are you?"

"Her husband."

"Ex!" Hallie shouted—that didn't sound like the first time she'd declared as much.

Hallie didn't look at any of the men; instead she searched the parking lot behind them. She spotted me, her expression tightening. "I told you I had a date with friends," she said to her ex. "This is them. So go away."

Any normal, sane person would've realized that this wasn't the time for their anger. Not her ex. His mouth twisted, reminding me of a wrinkly cat butthole. "You don't have friends in this town."

I growled.

A real growl.

I didn't get any super hearing or super smell, but I *could* growl in a way that actually sounded scary.

Angus cooed and wiggled into me. He liked my growls.

Hallie's ex turned his head, noticing me for the first time. "Who's that fucking idiot?"

I winced, but not because his question hurt me. This guy's opinion of me mattered as much as space mattered to an elephant. While I didn't love comparing myself to an elephant, Hallie's ex wouldn't love what would—

He dropped without ever seeing the punch. It came from straight in front of him, but Knox moved like he'd set his remote to fast forward. Faust yanked off his shoe—on a rare day when he wasn't wearing combat boots—and tossed it directly under the spot Hallie's ex's head would hit the pavement. Falling so hard against Faust's shoe couldn't have felt great either.

The man moaned, rolling pitifully on the asphalt with his eyes squeezed shut.

"Great, Knox, now he's going to call the cops. You'll go to jail," Faust said drolly. He leaned against the brick building, his arms crossed over his chest while his right foot propped vertically against the wall.

Without missing a beat, Knox deadpanned, "Then I guess I'll just have to kill him."

Whether or not Hallie had caught on to their little play, I didn't know, but she stepped forward. "He isn't worth it, and he won't call shit. Probably has a warrant already." Her voice was as strong as I'd heard it since I got out of the car, and I hated how that implied there was something that existed in this world that she cowed to. Especially when that something was such a clear pile of shit.

I breathed deeply. If Angus noticed when I growled, he'd notice if my heart pounded with furious rage. Faust helped Hallie walk around her ex. He'd nearly pulled himself into a sitting position, so he was probably fine—but if he wasn't, I didn't know how much I'd care.

"Are you okay?" I looked her up and down, and while she didn't have bruises, there were bags under her eyes, and her skin was pale.

"Okay? Yeah, of course. There's a reason why they're exes, am I right?" She laughed, the sound forced like a foghorn.

I couldn't laugh, not even to help her save face. This was the woman who had accosted me with her kindness. She'd worried more about me than herself and had stood up to Knox—something not many did. "Hallie, are you okay?"

She sucked her bottom lip between her teeth. "I haven't had the best time lately. Roy was staying with friends, but they kicked him out, and he's been trying to come back. It's... tiring."

"Come on back to the hotel," I suggested. "I'll introduce you to Angus in the car, and then we can have lunch or something. Think of it as a final exam for all those cooking lessons you gave me."

"I gave you like two," she grumbled.

"Then I won't make it a very good lunch."

WE GATHERED in the meeting room next to the kitchen. Hallie held Angus, cooing and making baby talk as Knox watched on. Other than Dr. Tiff, Hallie was the first non-pack member to hold Angus, and Knox was finding the moment difficult. I hoped Hallie wouldn't be too offended. Knox wouldn't have let her come back to the hotel if he hadn't trusted her. This sort of stuff was just more difficult for him.

True to my word, I made a so-so tray of cold cut sandwiches and piled enough grapes and carrots on the side to make up for the sandwiches if they turned out less than edible.

Hallie and Knox both thanked me before reaching for a sandwich. Knox took a bite and froze, and Hallie, who had been lifting her sandwich to her mouth, paused to stare.

Knox brought the sandwich away from his face. He grabbed something from the middle and pulled. "Just a wrapper."

"I'm sorry!" The only horrible thing I'd ever found out

about Knox was that he preferred American processed cheese to real cheddar. It probably looked like I'd left the wrapper on as a passive-aggressive jab, but really I just forgot.

"It's okay, baby. It's...interactive." He was such a good man.

Hallie snorted as she watched Knox unpeel his cheese and place it back inside his sandwich.

"Yours is fine," I told her. "It's real cheese."

"American is real—never mind." Knox wisely shoved food in his mouth instead of arguing.

Faust plopped down next to Knox, plucking a sandwich and pulling out the cheese before taking a bite. I figured the others were also listening in from wherever they were.

I offered to take Angus so Hallie could eat, but weirdly, she didn't seem that hungry. The food was just a trick anyway. I'd hoped eating would relax her enough to tell me what the hell had happened back in town.

She rocked in her chair, soothing herself and the baby.

I picked up a sandwich, decided against it, and grabbed handfuls of grapes and carrots instead.

When it became clear she wouldn't start it, I cleared my throat. "So...Roy."

She didn't stop rocking or look up from the baby when she answered, her voice sad and soft like she spoke from far away. "It wasn't always bad. We married in high school and *not* because I was pregnant. That didn't happen until much later, after I'd turned away from all my friends, my family, and had made my life about him." She leaned in, kissing Angus on the forehead. "We lost her, and it was horrible, but he was there at the hospital. We were going to get through it, but those false promises hadn't even lasted until we got home. I'd always known he could be mean, one of those that wouldn't bat an eye crossing a line if it got him what he wanted. But he'd never turned that meanness on me. I'd been stupid enough to think that elevated me somehow. Like I was special. From that day on, I couldn't do anything right. He sniped about my cooking, how I dressed, the way I did my hair." She handed Angus over and I settled him against my chest.

"But he was still the guy everyone in Rockshell wanted at their parties. The nicest asshole you'll ever meet. Women used to tell me how je-jealous they were. I wanted to ask them—jealous of what? Being ridiculed?

"But not all the time. Never when someone would see. Living with Roy was like being sentenced to death by a thousand cuts without anyone ever noticing a thing. They think I'm the bitch. That I ruined our perfect marriage. The man is a mean drunk, has so many DUIs there's a warrant out for him, and they *still*—" She angrily sucked in a breath like she blamed the air and being inhaled was its punishment. "He wasn't lying earlier. I don't have friends here. But I don't have friends anywhere. And I *know* here." She scoffed, the sound full of so much self-loathing it physically hurt to hear. "That sounds stupid, doesn't it? I sound stupid."

"No, Hallie. No. It doesn't sound stupid at all. It sounds like you've had a tough time." I gave Knox and Faust a sad smile. "That's something we all have in common." I bit my tongue to keep what I'd been about to say from coming out. I hated the idea of someone amazing as Hallie living in a place where she was despised.

Never stay where you're not wanted only worked if you had someplace to go and a way to get there. But I didn't want Hallie to leave Rockshell; she was my only friend.

That was selfish, but it coincided with what Hallie

wanted too. I looked to Knox. This wasn't my thing to offer, and I couldn't be positive Knox was even on the same page, but he nodded, and I hoped.

"Why don't you move in here, at the hotel?" Knox asked. He coughed and grabbed another sandwich. "Jazz would like it if you were closer..."

My old softie.

"Would you want to?" My voice trembled with enthusiasm. "Would you want to move into the hotel? You could have all your own space, and I wouldn't use you as a free babysitter, I promise."

"Hearing you promise that is giving *me* doubts," Faust said, his teasing directed at me.

I figured this had been one of those alpha wolf moments where the five of them had a conversation without ever speaking—or being in the same room.

"Stay here? With the ghosts?" Her eyes rounded, and I imagined that was how they'd looked when she'd come to the hotel as a child, daring her friends to see who could get the closest.

"Ghosts?" Faust scoffed. "That's just Diesel."

Hallie looked like she might be in shock, but I hoped it was the type of shock that faded rapidly into excitement. She didn't exactly resemble a person who was excited, but her lips were pursed. She was thinking about it.

Which meant I should get the next thing out of the way.

"Before you say yes, if you do say yes, you'll know a secret, and it's a secret you can't tell anyone, and if you do tell someone...I mean, I don't know what will happen..." I was butchering my threat. There was no way Hallie could live here and not know that everyone else who lived here could turn into a wolf. She'd taken Angus's rapid birth extremely well. It helped she'd had an adorable baby to distract her while I gave as best an explanation as I could without actually explaining. If she moved in, telling her we were shifters was an unavoidable risk, but she didn't strike me as the type of person who would blab if she decided this sort of crazy wasn't what she wanted.

"Another secret? Will this explain how you conceived and gave birth to a baby within a month?"

I beamed because Hallie was curious. Not curious and skeptical or curious and afraid, just curious. "Absolutely. This will explain everything."

18

KNOX

THE PROSPECT of leaving Jazz alone in the hotel was as appealing as shoving sand down my pants, but if he came he would try to help, and he wasn't resting enough as it was. He claimed not to be tired, but I kept catching his eyelids drooping or a surreptitious yawn breathed into a secretive elbow. Faust was leaving Dog—already standing guard next to the door—so Jazz wouldn't be left unprotected, but he still felt left out.

"Hallie gets to go," Jazz pointed out with a mutinous nod in her direction.

Hallie gawked back, clearly wondering how she'd been dragged into this argument. "You're mad because you *can't* help me move?" She shook her head letting Jazz know just how crazy that sounded to her.

Like everything else, Hallie took the news that we were shifters—and that shifters were a thing that existed—as well as she took everything else. I understood her actions better now. Hallie was lonely—the type of loneliness that took years of neglect and disdain to take hold.

Jazz's bottom lip stuck out, shiny from where he'd licked

it. The lip begged for a pair of teeth marks, a nibble or two. I couldn't decide how I liked Jazz's mouth more: when he was whispering he loved me or when his lips were wrapped around my dick.

My omega caught my gaze, heating the air between us. He knew what was on my mind, and I was fairly confident he'd just conjured up a few dirty images on his own. My dick pulsed, wanting to hear my omega's dirty fantasies, but that would have to wait until after we got Hallie's things out of her house. I'd offered to make her ex stay away instead so she didn't feel like she had no choice but to move in, but she'd waved the idea away.

The choice to tell a human our secret hadn't been a reckless spur-of-the-moment decision. I'd made the decision quickly, but in the field, we often only had seconds to make a choice. I didn't doubt my choice to offer her a place in my home, but I didn't know if that meant she had a place in the pack.

That wasn't something I could force on the others; each of them would have to decide on their own. But, until that happened, Jazz would have a friend, and Hallie would feel safe in her home—as safe as anyone could feel living with a pack of wolves.

"By the time you get Angus down, we'll be back." I led him away from the front door to the sitting room and sat him down, taking care to adjust the pillows and blankets so that he sat as comfortably as he could on the sofa.

Jazz frowned, but he didn't try to get up. He let his gaze drop to Angus, blue eyes open, taking in the world around him. "I guess I won't be here alone, anyway, will I? I have Dog and Angus." He brought his face down, pressing his nose close to Angus's head. "I get it now. The sniffing thing. I could sniff him all day."

I grinned smugly, pleased my omega hadn't remained upset for long. We wouldn't be gone more than an hour. I'd toyed with asking Hallie or one of the others to stay, but if we went all at once, we'd be able to get Hallie's things out of her house in the shortest amount of time—which would lessen the chance that we'd run into her ex again. I wasn't worried about the prospect but knew it would only cause problems.

I brushed the tip of my nose along the shell of his ear, scenting him as he did our son. He *smelled* happy, with nothing sharp or bitter to muddle his fragrance.

"When I get back and finish moving everything in, I'm going to be hot and sweaty," I whispered.

That was the guys' clue to load up. They needed to hook the trailer up to the Hummer anyway. I had time to make my omega's temperature rise.

Jazz tilted his chin, offering me more of his neck. "Yeah?" he breathed. "That sounds like a personal problem."

My sweet prince attempted to make it sound like he wasn't interested, but the hitch in his breath gave him away.

"It is a personal problem, baby. It's *very* personal."

Jazz visibly trembled. "Okay, okay, get out of here. I'll scrub your back once Hallie's all moved in." He couldn't resist his desire for long—a fact I was infinitely grateful for.

With one last kiss, I went out to join the others, glad that it wouldn't be long before I had Jazz in the shower.

The guys had the trailer attached by the time I got out there. Diesel waited in the Hummer with the twins, while Faust sat, with the engine going, in Hallie's boxy blue Volvo.

"I can't believe you got him to stay." Jagger slid into the passenger seat.

"Incentive to get this done," I grunted. I'd given us thirty minutes to load before. Now I'd push for fifteen.

I'd suffer along with my omega while we were apart.

Even if we loaded Hallie's stuff in fifteen minutes, there was the drive there and back. Thankfully, Faust had already pulled down the crumbling driveway. Diesel took the spot behind them, the trailer squeaking as it settled.

The short stretch of highway between the hotel and town followed the edge of the forest where it met the ocean cliffs. We were ten miles from city limits, and Hallie's house was another three minutes after that. I counted up the time Jazz and I would be apart while idly watching Faust push the Volvo forward. He'd done so much covert maintenance on the car. He was probably glad he could finally reap the rewards of his work.

"Sounds better than it did," Diesel grunted.

"He damn near replaced the engine by the time he—"

"What's that?" Jagger asked sharply, jerking his head toward the forest side of the highway, where something shot through the trees heading straight for Faust and Hallie.

His question was answered in the next half-second. A black truck burst from the forest, slamming into the driver's side of Hallie's Volvo and sending it into a barrel roll before it fell off the cliff.

There wasn't time for shock or fear. This wasn't an accident. Someone was waiting for us. Did that mean they'd been watching the house?

The black truck squealed to a stop, and the tires smoked as the driver spun the truck around, headlights pointing directly at us as it accelerated.

We couldn't go in reverse, not with the trailer on the back, which mean there was no place to go but forward. Diesel gunned the engine.

"Come on, motherfucker!" he snarled, spinning the

wheel at the last moment so we whipped around the other truck instead of slamming headfirst.

Whoever was attacking us had a death wish.

I blocked my concern for Faust and Hallie and grabbed the handle to keep my head from slamming against the window. The trailer swerved precariously, dragging the Hummer erratically.

Diesel cursed and spun the wheel clockwise and then the other direction as he drove into the swerve while attempting to keep us from rolling. "This fucking trailer," he spat, glancing in his rearview.

The truck had spun around and gunned toward us.

"We got this," Huntley said right before opening his door. The twins leapt out with matching growls, heads down, pulling out their swords as they ran toward the oncoming vehicle.

Huntley stopped suddenly, landing on his knee with his back rounded. Jagger never missed a beat and used Huntley's back as a springboard as the other shifter lifted, shooting Jagger in the air. He rolled gracefully before landing in the truck bed and spun, thrusting his sword through the back window.

Jagger jumped, landing in Huntley's arms, and the momentum of his movements sent both rolling before they came to a stop.

Without a driver, the truck slowed. The tires veered toward the cliff but stopped several feet before the truck could fly over the edge—like Faust and Hallie.

"Diesel—" I snarled, reaching for my knives from the glove box. This was a lighter set I kept around for moments exactly like this one. I didn't know who these people were or why they'd attacked us, but they would see how big of a mistake that was—if they hadn't already.

Diesel didn't respond. He just brought the Hummer to a stop and ran toward the cliff. I didn't imagine what it was he saw when he peered over and kept my attention on the passenger in the black truck.

The twins were on their feet, approaching the passenger side as a man fell from the cab. He spotted the twins and reached for his waist. My blade embedded in his temple before he could grab the handle of his gun. *Fuck.* I couldn't let him get his weapon, but interrogating him would be impossible now.

The twins had the better angle, and they checked the rest of the cab. "Clear," Huntley announced.

I ran for the cliff, for Diesel, for Faust and Hallie. A human couldn't have survived that fall, but maybe a human and a shifter had a chance.

"Diesel?" I shouted.

"I see them." He didn't turn his head from the water. It churned, frothing angrily against the jagged rocks below.

I searched the stone, hoping I wouldn't see evidence of them while also hoping I would.

"No, there." Diesel pointed away from where the water crashed against the rock, further out to see. A tiny black wolf with an even smaller human clutched around his neck doggy-paddled back to shore.

Diesel clenched his fists, furious at his inability to act. "The rocks will tear them apart."

"We'll get them. We'll find a—"

"Incoming!"

A second truck burst from the forest like it had been waiting there the whole time.

Because it had been waiting there the whole time. Why wait while we killed their friends? It didn't make sense.

There wasn't a lot of time to ponder the answer before

the truck slammed into the Hummer. The vehicle was empty and attached to a trailer that made it much more difficult to push into the sea.

"What are they doing?" Diesel asked.

I was more concerned with why. The first attack had been sudden but not well thought-out. Now the backup had arrived—after their friends were dead—and they weren't trying to hurt any of us, just push the Hummer into the sea.

Why would they want that? Who would want that?

"Jazz," I growled.

Diesel's head turned sharply, like he expected to see him running up the street.

The men in the second truck rolled down their windows and began firing. Rapid shots split the air. I didn't worry for my team; we'd navigated through more dangerous scenarios than this. But with Faust stuck in the middle of the ocean with Hallie and Jazz at home like a sitting duck, we couldn't waste anymore time. I ducked behind a tree as Diesel did the same. "Jazz," I said again, the name meant more as an explanation.

Diesel nodded, bullets zooming through the air between us. He reached under his jacket. "Do you want any of them to be able to talk?" he asked.

"Negative."

That was all Diesel needed to hear. With a smirk, he slipped out from behind the tree, moving faster than a man his size had any right to. He lobbed the object in his hand over the hood of the Hummer. The grenade slid on the pavement, coming to a stop directly beneath the second truck. The throw was beautiful. The fireball bloomed like a flower, enveloping the truck and the passengers inside in seconds.

"Save Faust and get rid of the wreckage before anyone

sees it," I ordered, the ticking clock pounded in my head turning my insides into rot. I needed to get to Jazz. He had Dog there, but if this was what was sent for us, I didn't want to think about what had been sent for Jazz. Or who.

The most obvious choice was Jazz's father. But he'd always claimed he wanted Jazz alive. Why track him down to hurt him? Why not just hire someone to kill him? I pulled out my phone as I ran.

"Knox." Jazz was out of breath.

"There's been—"

"Knox, my father's here. He wasn't alone, and Dog, I don't know where Dog is."

Terror threatened to close my throat, but I needed the air. I needed to breathe to save my mate. I tamped it down. "Hide. I'm coming for you."

There was a short pause, a gasp, and then, "I can't . He's coming for me and Angus. I can't let him get Angus." Jazz sounded frantic, his sharp breaths chopping his words like a blender.

"Negative. Do not engage, Jazz. Stay away. Hide." I jumped over a log, landing five feet ahead of it on the other side. "I'm almost there, Jazz—"

"There isn't enough time, Knox. I'm better now. I'm not afraid. I have my magic. I won't let him hurt my child."

His cold resolve was the scariest thing I'd ever heard. Panic made my bones brittle. I pushed my legs forward faster, barely hitting the ground before I pushed off again. If I'd ever suspected our gym sessions would lead to a moment like this, I would've put a stop to them right away. It was my pack all over again. I'd chosen to keep Jazz at home; I'd let Hallie come with us. One was clinging to life in the middle of the ocean while the other—

"Do not engage," I let my alpha's dominance leak into

my command. If he wouldn't listen to me as his mate, he'd have to listen to me as his Alpha. "Hide. That's an order. Confirm."

"Knox—" His voice trembled with regret.

Several shots fired on Jazz's end.

"Confirm, Jazz!" I roared.

The trees thinned, allowing me to spot slivers of the hotel ahead.

"I'm sorry," Jazz gasped before the line went dead.

My roar sounded in my head. I couldn't waste the oxygen I needed to get to my mate. I ran a few seconds longer before I jumped out of the trees, scrambling to gain purchase and continue forward, when I spotted Jazz through the sitting room window. His father stood ten feet in front of him, holding a gun.

No, wait, I'm almost there—

Begging wouldn't get me there faster.

Jazz's hands were clasped before he opened them, releasing the marbles that Diesel had given him. Instantly, the marbles looked like wolves—they looked like us—stalking forward with menacing intent.

I couldn't imagine the concentration it took for Jazz to project something so much larger than the source item.

The wolves charged forward, toward Jazz's father. He scrambled back a step before coming to a stop, his gaze narrowing at the approaching wolves. Walter smiled.

He wasn't buying it.

My chest went cold, my wolf aware of something I'd yet to catch up to.

The man lifted his gun a second time. He ignored the wolves, even as it looked like they were right on top of him, and fired.

I leaped through the window, shattering the glass the

moment after Jazz hit the ground, blood pooling from his head to the floor.

My knees gave out, and I dropped beside him with a sickening crunch. I yanked my hand back. It had nearly dipped into the deep-red puddle.

I had failed him. I'd failed my pack. I'd failed my omega.

19

JAZZ

Knox's kiss still tingled on my lips as he went out to join the others. I knew he didn't like leaving me and Angus, so I tried not to make too big of a deal about being ordered to stay home.

That hadn't meant I couldn't complain. Really, if I hadn't, Knox would've thought something was wrong and would've spent the whole time stressing over it.

I had no doubt they'd be back before I knew it. I smiled at Angus, nursing happily at his bottle. Dog's toenails clacked against the hardwood as he walked down the hallway. Apparently that whole standing guard by the door thing had been for show.

I'd always liked children, but in the same way I liked tigers. They were best when you just looked at them and worst when they were in the same room as you. Angus wasn't like a tiger at all. He was everything that was good in this world wrapped up in a pudgy baby's body. He didn't know that he turned into a winged wolf whenever his father shifted or that he floated when his father used his wings.

That additional bond, the unexpected connection, had

cemented over any doubt I'd had lingering about any part of the situation. He shifted when I shifted and floated when I flew because I was meant to protect him, and somewhere deep down in his baby soul, he knew that.

The sound of glass breaking down the hall wouldn't have been half as terrifying if it hadn't been accompanied by the deepest growl I'd ever heard. *Dog?*

I stood, squeezing Angus just enough that I was sure he was there still in my arms.

"Dog, what is it?"

Do you think he's going to answer? Maybe. Dog seemed more man than animal most of the time. Funny because the rest of his pack worked in reverse.

This old house was still settling, and after I didn't hear anything further from Dog, I let out a relaxed breath, assuming the sound had something to do with that.

But when I padded softy into the foyer, my skin prickled with awareness.

Someone was here.

I palmed my phone to call Knox. Before I could, Dog yelped from down the hallway.

"Dog!"

He snarled, and then a man shouted, screaming in pain. I jumped back from the echoing boom of a gunshot. Angus began to scream.

"I should've known." Walter Whitten, my father, walked out of the kitchen and through the meeting room. He carried a gun in two hands, like he'd watched one too many procedural crime shows. "If you want something done right, do it yourself."

And there's his snazzy catch phrase. Cue opening credits.

I would've rolled my eyes if I hadn't been panting my

way up the stairs. I took them two at a time, unable to risk more without possibly falling and hurting Angus. He screamed in my arms, upset by the loud bang and my frantic breaths over his cheek. "Shhh, baby. Please, shh."

My father's shout wasn't nearly far enough behind me. "Who would've thought killing a single person would be so difficult? Is that why they want you dead?"

They?

I sprinted down the hallway, passing my room while rapidly realizing how idiotic I'd been. I'd ran up the stairs.

Fucking hell. *Up* the stairs, Jazz? I was every stupid teen in every cheesy horror movie, except the thing chasing me was the one man who was supposed to care for me the most in this world.

I hadn't expected that sort of emotion from him in a long, long while, but *ignoring your existence* felt like a distinct set of steps away from *actively trying to kill*.

I'd clearly graduated.

I ran to the end of the hallway and shouted—silently— for joy. These rooms weren't utilized yet and most of the furniture was covered by a white cloth and then a thick layer of dust. I turned my head, frantically searching for a hiding spot. I yanked out one of the drawers from an old dresser and lined it with a drop cloth before setting Angus down.

"Shh, shh, baby, Angus, you have to stop crying."

Immediately, Angus's mouth closed, and he looked up at me, his breath stuttering with leftover sobs. Maybe the same force that bonded us in wolf form worked in emergencies too. I wouldn't question it. "I love you so much, baby boy, but I have to leave you here, okay? Just for a little bit." I kissed his chubby cheek and pulled quickly away so he wouldn't feel my tears.

My father's steps echoed, sounding far away. With any luck, he'd turned down the wrong hallway. As his footsteps grew closer, I remembered I was Jazz, and I had no luck. Just skill.

I patted the marbles in my pocket, glad I'd kept them on me basically every day since Diesel had give them to me. I pulled free one of the blankets wrapped around Angus. This one had been knitted and had large gaps that made it more of a decorative blanket than one used for warmth. I held it tightly in both hands. This sort of item manipulation, projecting a mask over a flat surface, had once been impossible and was still extremely difficult. I'd only managed it successfully a handful of times. Most of those times had been after I gave birth, and I had a hunch becoming a shifter had upped my skill level a little.

I concentrated on the color of the dresser, the wall and the floor, making up the descriptive details I couldn't be sure about. When I shook the blanket out, fixing it over the top of Angus like a tent, I stepped back to quickly admire my handiwork. Tugging the blanket a little to the right lined up the edges I'd missed. The tent resembled the wall and floor.

If someone was chasing their son trying to kill them, they'd pop their head in and see an empty room.

If Angus can stay quiet.

But he was only a baby. That he hadn't started crying yet was a miracle, especially now that he couldn't see me.

My father's steps were louder, maybe halfway to us. There was a loud bang, a door slamming against a wall, and I realized what was taking him so long. He truly didn't know where I was and was searching each room.

I crept toward the adjoining door that connected this room with the one next to it. The rooms were connected that way all the way down the hall—I had no assurances that they were all *unlocked*—and if I got out in front of my father, I could lead him away from Angus and maybe even outside, where my alpha was sure to come crashing in and rescue me.

I shut the first door behind me and tiptoed across the room. This one was in the same state as the one before, and it took precious seconds to maneuver around the furniture. I made it to the next door and paused, trying to see if I could hear my father.

My phone vibrated. "Knox?"

I longed for him to be here, my instincts telling me to turn to him when I was in danger. But he wasn't here. Only me.

His warm baritone was like honey in my head. "There's been—"

I didn't have time for a recap. "Knox, my father's here. He wasn't alone, and Dog…" I'd heard his growls *after* I'd heard the gunshot, right? "I don't know where Dog is."

"Hide. I'm coming for you."

A second bang told me my father was coming closer still. I cupped my hand over the phone and waited against the adjoining door. I'd already checked the handle to make sure it was unlocked. "I can't. He's coming for me and Angus. I can't let him get Angus."

Another door slammed open, this one loud enough I jumped.

"Negative. Do not engage."

I could barely hear him, the majority of my concentration on the sounds from the hallway, on my father's steps as they came closer.

Closer.

"Jazz. Stay away. Hide. I'm almost there, Jazz."

264

I shook my head, even though Knox couldn't see me. "There isn't enough time, Knox." I spoke at a level that could just barely be called sound. I hated his worry, thick even through the phone. "I'm better now. I'm not afraid. I have my magic. I won't let him hurt my child."

My father's footsteps were dull and unrushed. The arrogant bastard probably thought I was trapped, that he'd already won.

It wasn't until that moment that I considered exactly *why* Knox wasn't here, but on the phone. If he knew there was danger, nothing would keep him from me, which meant something was trying.

"Do not engage." He sounded different, his tone richer, commanding and vibrant. But there wasn't time for pleasant floaty feelings. "Hide. That's an order. Confirm."

Did he think I didn't want to confirm? The *only* thing I wanted to do was jump in his arms—with Angus—and never leave.

The small hairs all over my body stood straight up. My father's footsteps were directly in line with where I stood. The door to the room a few feet after that.

I clenched my hand on the knob, waiting. If he didn't see me, he'd just keep going. When I saw the hinges begin to spin, I yanked my door open, standing in the doorway long enough for my father to spot me and fire several shots.

Either I'd been hit and my body didn't want me to know, or the bullets had hit the plaster instead. At least my father was as bad at shooting as he was at parenting.

"Confirm, Jazz!" Knox screamed as I panted, sprinting to the next door and then the next. I knew my luck would run out, that one of these doors was bound to be locked.

I needed a plan. I couldn't run and leave Angus behind.

Hiding him was entirely different from abandoning him entirely.

The idea struck me at the same time my father yelled my name down the hallway.

If I hadn't been sprinting—and panting so hard I was sure I'd pass out—I would've cried because this time, I couldn't do anything to alleviate Knox's worry.

"I'm sorry." I let the phone fall from my hand, veering toward the entrance door. These rooms were cleaned out, indicating I'd almost made it back to the stairs.

I didn't run directly into my father, but he wasn't far behind. Anyone could aim if a target was close enough.

I banked hard to the left, taking the first step fast enough I was a single slip from breaking my neck. I tripped, stumbling down several steps before catching myself against the banister and scrambling to my feet. I couldn't shift and risk the baby floating.

My knees screamed like they were cut but I somehow kept from landing on my face and pushed off the last step. My father was too close. I wouldn't make it to the other side of the room. I needed to improvise. I skid to a stop, snagging one of Angus's receiving blankets off the sofa before I spun to face my father.

Seeing me stop made him wary, and his steps slowed as he circled around to stand in front of me. "Finally stopped running?" he panted, his face red and eyes bright with hostility.

I reached for my marbles. "Looks like it. You said someone else wants me dead. Who?"

He scoffed.

"If you're going to kill me, why does it matter if you tell me?"

My father sneered, and for some reason, the expression

reminded me of the moment I'd taunted Knox with a fake gun to my head. *Do you think you'll get paid by my father if you drop me off with a hole in my head?* It was ironic, really. Clearly, my father wouldn't have minded how many holes were in my head. Had he always intended for Knox and his team to kill me? Why not just hire them to do that?

I didn't like thinking about how my story would've been different if Knox *had* been contracted to kill me.

"It matters, *son*, because it's something you want. And I am loathe to do anything that will make you happy."

I could appreciate his brutal, gut-wrenching honesty and quickly palmed the marbles behind my back, having already tucked much of the receiving blanket into my back pocket. My hands heated, the marbles transforming to my will before I tossed them forward, pleased when wolves sprouted in their place.

I *was* getting stronger.

The wolves stalked forward with low growls and fake drool dripping from their gleaming fangs.

My father's eyes widened, but only for a moment. I took hold of the receiving blanket, watching his shoulder and waiting for him to raise his gun. He might be able to tell the wolves weren't real. They'd literally sprung from nowhere after all. But he still couldn't see *through* them. He also couldn't see me throw the blanket over my face, waiting for the crack of his gun before flinging myself backwards. I should've thought about the fall, taken precautions, but the time to do that wasn't *when you were falling,* and my head hit the floor hard. My stomach lurched as a bright light swallowed me whole.

.　.　.

I BLINKED against the light and sat up slowly. "Knox?" My eyes wouldn't stay open for long. Everything was suddenly too bright, like someone had lifted off the hotel roof and pulled the sun closer.

Had my plan worked? Was my father fooled? I'd figured if he just wanted me dead, I'd die, and then he would leave, or Knox would get there and take care of him.

I frowned, this time because the world around me had dimmed. At least I could open my eyes now.

I blinked through my confusion and rapidly came to one important conclusion.

I wasn't in the hotel anymore.

I didn't know *where* I was, but it didn't feel scary. My arms and legs felt light, filled with an effervescence that had not been there moments before. The warm air loosened my bones, allowing my muscles to relax for the first time since I heard the glass break.

I sat in a grassy field sprinkled by a heavy dusting of wild flowers. The blossoms shone brightly, pinks, blues, and purples as vibrant as a neon light. There wasn't a place in Rockshell that I knew of that looked like this.

Water lapped the shore behind me, and I craned my head around, eventually turning entirely. It was a lake, not an ocean, but it stretched impossibly far. I could just make out the cliff face on the other side, where an enormous waterfall poured into the lake. Hanging in the soft blue sky above the cliffs were several rainbows, some of them touching or overlapping, while others glittered brightly on their own.

The place was beautiful. So beautiful I didn't notice the woman sitting in the lake, a little to the right, perched on top of a boulder five feet from shore. Her auburn hair was twisted tightly off her face, flowing loose in the back in cascading waves. She wore a pale lavender Grecian-style dress. The gauzy skirts rippled, despite there being no breeze. Our eyes met, and the woman beamed, looking happier to see me than even Knox.

"Hi," I said with a wave that hadn't felt dorky until after I did it.

"Hello," the woman replied. Her voice felt like a thousand warm summer nights, like endless Sunday mornings, like a bowl of ice cream that never ended.

Though I felt at peace where I was, I knew I wasn't in the hotel, and that thought was disturbing enough to brush away any warm fuzzies. "What is this place?"

The woman smiled, and my chest felt warm, my lips light. She was happy with me. That was what smiles meant, and that fact was extremely rewarding. "This is your heaven, Jazz."

I gulped. *My heaven?* "Um, no, this is a mistake. My plan was for my father to not shoot me in the head. I was counting on him being a bad shot." Had he let me down again? Terminally?

"You aren't dead. Maybe you should sit down and let me explain."

I thought I had been sitting, but I could see now, no, I was on my feet. Without a better idea, I sat.

The woman dipped her foot into the pristine lake, not seeming to care when her skirts fell in the water. "My name is Sorrows." She paused and looked up at me, smiling at my frown like she'd been expecting it. She looked both ways, cupping her mouth like she was preparing to relay a secret. "That is why I named you Jazz. My name doesn't bring me sadness, but I understand how it does to humans. Archangels get to choose their own names, as everyone knows."

As every— "Literally no one knows that. Okay. If I'm not dead, then how am I in my heaven?"

"We don't get to know when or why, only that I'll be able to speak to you whenever you most need it. It isn't my decision or within my ability..." She quirked her head back, as if indicating the person who made the decisions was located somewhere back there. "I don't plan on wasting any of this time wondering about the mechanics."

Every thought in my brain screeched to a stand still. "Parent? Angel parent? *Archangel* parent?"

I'd hit my head or was I hallucinating as I slowly died?

"You aren't hallucinating," the woman, angel, Sorrows —*mother*—said with a smile. "I've waited so long to speak to you, Jazz. I'm sorry I couldn't stay with you on earth."

Her face fell, and maybe it was the way she'd been smiling since I first set eyes on her, but the fact that she wasn't now felt wrong. As I did with Knox, I found myself searching for something to say to make her feel better. "It's okay. I'm sure you had your reasons..." *For leaving me with a man who only cared about money and would rather I didn't exist.* "Does that mean you had *sex* with my father?"

She snorted, the sound as adorable as it was absurd. "Even angels make mistakes, baby. But I can never regret the actions that led to you." Her sigh was like a soft breeze through a wind chime. "Your father was...very attractive in his time. It's a good thing forgiveness isn't my department because I'll never forgive him for letting you down and letting evil into his heart. When I met him, he was at a crossroads. His future split down two very different paths. I underestimated humans and their propensity to seek power."

I tried to believe this new version of my life. Not left behind. Not rejected. After twenty-three years of believing

I'd been abandoned by one parent and despised by the other, chipping away at the hard layer of hate felt futile.

"You're a nephilim, Jazz. An offspring between a human and an angel. That's why you can do all that you can, why your pregnancy was so much different than the others."

The casual reference to Hollister and the Walkers threw me. She obviously knew the whole story, and it was nice to finally get some answers, but this was... *a nephilim*? I'd heard the word in TV shows and movies but had zero frame of reference for what a nephilim was or the stereotypes surrounding them. I knew I was no angel. I got jealous at the drop of a hat, was possessive, and enjoyed taunting mean people. Especially mean people who had been sent after me. "You've been watching me? For how long?" Had she seen me and Knox... My cheeks burned.

Sorrows nodded, her lips curled in the corners like a cat. "Don't worry. I give you your privacy." She didn't sound very happy about that. "But what does anyone expect from me?" She shook her head. Seeing her get flustered and then soothe herself made her seem more like a mother and less like an untouchable ethereal being. "I don't know what sort of metric they use to decide if you're in enough need because I've watched plenty of situations where you needed me." Her ruby red lip plumped out in a pout.

Her voice made me want to scoot closer to the water and gaze into her eyes, except something tugged at my brain. If I was *here* having an unscheduled conversation with my angelic mother, did that mean Knox was *there* thinking I was dead? My heart tore in two, and the blue sky darkened to a slate gray.

Sorrows clutched her chest and slid off the rock. The water went to her ankles, not nearly as deep as I'd thought. "Please don't feel that way, Jazz." She rubbed the spot she'd squeezed. Directly over her heart. In the same spot my own chest ached. "Nothing that happens here affects what happens on earth. Think of it like a pause. Though you did fool him. He believes your father shot you."

I winced, my chest aching like Knox's likely was. Though the sky had cleared, it began to rain. I hadn't known he'd see my plan firsthand and wasn't sure if I could forgive myself—if it actually turned out I wasn't dead for real.

"I don't have a lot of time, Jazz, even with the pause. You need to know a few things before you go. You aren't the only nephilim in trouble. Others have been attacked. The enemy is rising."

"Who? What enemy?"

Her lips went tight, pressing together though she still spoke, the sound muffled. It was as if she wanted to tell me, but something physically stopped her. "I have rules. Rules I would break in a heartbeat if I could. I can't tell you who, but you're close to finding out. Very close."

"Do you mean the Walkers? Hollister and the others? Are they nephilim?"

She folded her legs under her body to sit on the grass next to me. "No, they are...well. I did that," she said sheepishly.

"You did that? You made me like them?"

"No, precious, I made them like you. Do you remember when you were three and nearly drowned? That man who saved you? His name was Patrick Walker. He pulled you from the water and held you as you cried. He delivered you to your father without ever asking for thanks and stood waiting in the trees for him to notice you and bring you home."

"Patrick Walker? The old Alpha?" I knew that much from my conversation with Hollister.

"The same. I was so thankful to him for saving you, I granted him his dying wish." She ducked her chin. "Maybe I was a little enthusiastic, but I wanted to make his dream come true, to make his son and nephews happy with the one person they were meant to be with. They just needed a little push to set the ball rolling."

"But, if you can influence what happens on Earth, why not help all the time?"

Her lips clamped together, and her eyes rounded with effort. She wanted to tell me. She shut her eyes, scrunching her face into a tight mask of concentration. "It doesn't always work that way. At the risk of sounding uninspired, the stars needed to align. Patrick's wish had to be pure, his faith strong. I wasn't able to save him from drowning, as unfair the death was, but I was able to let his soul know that his children would be cared for."

I didn't know how that should've made me feel. I was glad I hadn't been directly responsibly for Patrick's death and couldn't wait to tell the others what I'd learned. If they would believe me. But this did explain the differences—better than anything else did anyway. Once more, I thought of Knox. Sorrows had said Earth time was paused, but that didn't lessen my desire to see him, hold him.

"Will you please let Knox know something for me?" Sorrows asked, and I had an absurd image of nosy mothers-in-law thinking their child's partner wasn't good enough, but Sorrows didn't seem to be that type. She was a frickin' angel, for one.

"O-kay?"

"Your pregnancy wasn't his fault."

I gulped. "Uhh, he and I were the only ones there. I know it wasn't *all* his fault, but—"

Her laughter sounded like the splash of a child jumping

into a pool for the first time in summer. "He blamed himself for what has happened to you, but he needn't. Unlike an archangel and a human, a nephilim and a human can only reproduce if the nephilim is in love and is loved by their partner. That was what changed, what allowed you to become pregnant. There was never any other option after that. It was predestined, as the important stuff normally is. Stay with him, Jazz. I don't know when I'll be able to speak with you again, but I know you will need him. While you were a child, my blood protected you, but that protection has been gone for a few years, and those who are chasing you won't stop. You need to find the other nephilim. Protect them. The pack survives. Remember that always."

I'd seen enough Disney movies to know what it meant as her image faded.

It hadn't been enough time.

My world went black. I hadn't asked all the questions I'd wanted to ask, but the moment I heard Knox's tortured sob, I was relieved to be back.

My fingers snagged the receiving blanket over my head, and I yanked it off. "Knox—"

I was back in the sitting room, still on the ground, and my head pounded, but I was alive. Knox was here. That meant my father was...

I looked up in time to see a dark red blur leap through the air with a rumbling growl. Dog snagged my father by the neck, and they both went down, yelps and snarls following.

My alpha still had his head in his hands. He braced his weight on his knees, and I swore right then I would never do anything to make him look like this again. "Knox, I'm okay—"

I wasn't sure if he could hear me over Dog's growls and my father's panicked screams.

"Jazz?" Knox lifted his head.

"It was a trick," I whispered quickly. "The blanket, I made it look—"

Knox claimed my mouth in a bruising kiss, and my body came alive. More than anything else, the desire I felt for Knox cemented the truth. I was alive. My father was still here. My mother was an archangel.

I couldn't tell Knox any of that while he occupied my mouth, but I was having a hard time caring. One large hand cupped my nape as the other lifted at my back, helping me sit up. There wasn't a more pleasant feeling than Knox's tongue exploring my mouth, but my father's continued cries wouldn't let me forget Knox and I had things to do before we could have any makeup sex.

I pushed off his chest, but his arms tightened with a growl. It took biting his lip for him to pull away, blinking like he couldn't believe I was there.

My eyes filled with tears. "I'm sorry."

Knox buried his face in my neck, inhaling deeply and holding his breath before he exhaled. His body changed beneath my fingers, swelling with power and authority.

"I left Angus upstairs."

Knox pulled us both to our feet, and we got our first look at what was happening on the ground. Dog held my father down with his jaws around the man's neck. He pressed down as the man wiggled, growling a warning for him to stay still or bleed out.

Dog was already covered in blood from his ear to his tail, but I couldn't see a spot where he was injured.

Knox grabbed my father's gun from where it had skidded over the floor and whistled sharply. I'd never seen Dog respond to anyone but Faust, but he released. "Get up," Knox snarled.

The door slammed open as Huntley and Jagger burst

inside. Both held their swords at the ready and were soaking wet.

Huntley's gaze locked on mine. "Angus, Huntley, he's in one of the extra rooms."

"The last on the right."

Huntley nodded before sprinting up the stairs, while Jagger stepped to Knox's side.

My father clutched his neck, making a big deal out of a few teeth against his jugular. He looked up, spotting me, Knox, and then Jagger. His eyes widened with fear at Jagger and his sword, rounded with terror at Knox, and then narrowed at me. "I can assume my men are dead?" he asked, his nose lifting pompously.

Knox moved like a striking cobra, punching my father squarely in the face.

He fell back, his mouth gaping open like he couldn't believe he'd been punched.

"Yeah," Jagger grunted without remorse. "They're dead." To Knox, he added, "Diesel and Faust are helping Hallie to shore. Should be here any minute."

I had a thousand questions about that but kept them to myself for the moment.

"Angus is fine," Huntley called from the top floor. "I'll keep him up here."

The remaining chunks of fear that clung to the walls of my soul dropped away. My son was safe. His packmate had him.

"What's it going to take here, huh, Knox?" my father sneered. "More money? The rest of the million and let's say, two more."

"How did you find us?" Knox asked without inflection.

"The people *I'm working for,* are powerful, Knox. They've had their men searching for you for a long time.

The men did their jobs. Called me. Guess you aren't as sneaky as you think. You know, I really thought I'd done it with you lot. Immoral, trash, scum of the earth, you prey on people's weaknesses, exploit and—"

It was like he wanted to get punched again, which he did. Soundly.

My father's mouth bled, and he dabbed at it with his sleeve, laughing like a deranged bluebird. "It doesn't matter what you do to me. They won't stop until they've taken care of every freak like him." He jerked his chin toward me.

"You mean nephilim?" I asked.

Knox was silent, but I could feel his curiosity.

"I mean your end, boy. *Portal* doesn't care who you have protecting you. They've destroyed entire towns just to get to one of you. You will choke on hellfire when you die, just like the rest of them."

My father's tirade continued as he explained in detail the reign of terror that was coming my way. He talked so much he didn't notice how his clothes were smoking, his skin blackening.

Knox grabbed my arm and pulled me behind him. My father must've taken that as a sign his taunts were getting to us and, emboldened, continued loudly. "They promised me if I killed you and gathered your blood—demonic freaks— they'd give me whatever I wanted. True power. Absolute. But you were so fucking crafty. I went through the country's top hitmen trying to get rid of you." His eyes darted to Knox before flinching away. "You were supposed to get so irritated you killed him and delivered his body or delivered him to me so I could kill him, and you could do neither!" He screamed as the smoke billowed behind him.

"Portal will never stop until they've killed every last neph —" My father coughed. His face now burned a bright red.

He stuck his finger between the collar of his shirt and his neck, tenting the fabric out in an attempt to cool down. "No —" he gasped, his eyes widening. "No, I won't— please—!"

It wasn't clear who he was talking to. His eyes weren't on any of us, but his panic and fear were both very real.

His skin went from a deep blush to the color of a glowing ember. The skin around his eyes and mouth turned black as he clawed at his throat.

"Whoa." Jagger's whisper sounded from near my ear, but I couldn't tear my eyes away from my father to see.

He screamed, his face flinging upward before his body exploded into a cloud of dark ash.

Knox turned to cover me a moment before dusty bits of my father spread throughout the room.

Jagger coughed, the three of us stumbled from the sitting room into the foyer where the air was clear.

"Did my father just explode? *Ashplode?*"

Dog barked.

I dropped to my knees beside him. Whoever had accompanied my father was clearly dead and matted into Dog's fur. He let me scratch the top of his head, and my fingers hit something soft and rubbery that had snagged in his hair.

The rounded tip of a human ear lobe.

I shuddered but hugged Dog anyway. "You saved my life. I didn't think you liked me."

Dog grunted, resting his chin on my shoulder for exactly two seconds before he lifted it and shook away as if saying, *All right, enough of the mushy stuff.*

"I feel like I missed something." Jagger's voice sounded entirely too amused for what we'd just witnessed.

Huntley piped up from the top floor. "Me too! What's a nephilim?" He brought Angus down the stairs and lifted him into my arms. Immediately, Knox's arm draped over my shoulder, and he held us both close, saying nothing for several minutes.

He inhaled, held it, and exhaled a ragged breath. "I thought you were dead. Why did you *do* that?"

"I was trying to trick him. I knew you were coming but didn't know how quickly you could get to us. I figured he wouldn't be fooled by the wolves, but he's also a really bad shot, so I thought he'd miss me but would think he'd hit me and—"

"What if he *hadn't* missed?" Knox snarled. His pulse visibly pounded at his temple.

I turned my face to Angus and away from my alpha before he could see I hadn't thought of a backup plan.

"We'll discuss that later." His tone offered no room for doubt, and I hunched my head down between my shoulders. Whatever punishment he wanted to give me, I deserved it.

The sound of water dripping against concrete brought my attention forward out the front door. Faust and Diesel hobbled forward, not limping but completely waterlogged. Hallie held Diesel around the neck as he carried her piggyback style.

She saw me and slid down Diesel's back before setting off on a run. At the doorway, she tripped, and Jagger rushed forward to keep her from falling. "You're okay," she cried out, falling from Jagger into a hug even while Knox refused to move.

"You're all wet! What happened? Where are the cars?"

Faust made an unhappy sound. Dog sat by his side, sniffing his companion like he was checking him out. Faust scratched the back of his neck. "The Volvo is at the bottom of the ocean," he snarled. In a much gentler tone, he said to Dog, "You look like you had fun."

Dog huffed.

"I don't know where the rest of that person is," I said, pointing to the carpet near my feet. "Part of his ear is there."

"What's all over the sitting room?" Diesel asked after leaning in to scent all three of us, Hallie included. The action smoothed the wrinkles of concern around his eyes.

"Mr. Walter Whitten." To Hallie I added, "My father."

Either they were stunned or were sharing a moment of silence.

"Hey!" I chirped. "I wonder if this means I'm rich." Nah. That bastard wouldn't have left me anything. Besides, would I want his dirty money?

"Can you explain the whole nephilim thing?" Huntley asked. He'd been patient.

I told them about my plan and how that led to me hitting my head, and then what happened *after* I hit my head. Knox tensed up so tight I thought his bones would snap out his body when I mentioned it had been *my* heaven. I didn't think he liked imagining a place like that would need to exist.

There were smiles all around when I told them about Sorrows, and the Walkers, and how their situation had come to be. But none of those smiles stayed for long after I got to my mother's warnings.

"Staying together won't be a problem," Diesel said. "But what does she mean about nephilims being in danger? How do we stop that?"

"It's connected," Knox bit out like he didn't want the words in his mouth any longer than they absolutely needed to be. "Portal Ventures, our pack, fuck, even Pierce. Walter Whitten and you, Jazz. The only fucking coincidence here is that our team was hired." He snorted. "Though we were far from the first ones."

"Does that mean there was a nephilim in *our* pack?" Faust asked.

The air immediately changed to the consistency of cold oatmeal.

No one offered a suggestion and I didn't think anyone would. Knowing wouldn't change anything, but it might hurt someone.

"I mean, I'd say, all in all, we did a pretty good job protecting *this* nephilim." I pointed aggressively at myself earning laughs from all but one—technically *two* but one wasn't capable of laughing yet.

Knox cleared his throat, lifting me to my feet without allowing any space to come between us. "We'll check the perimeter and then clean up. We still have a lot to talk about. Like *what happens* when you put a gun up to your head *conjured or not.*"

"Technically not a gun," I pointed out, earning myself no points. That was okay. After what I'd put him through, I didn't deserve points. But at least I'd get to live to the day I did.

20

KNOX

I WATCHED my half-angel omega sweat. His body stretched long before bending short, his slick skin glistening beneath the fluorescent lighting.

"Are you going to work out? Or watch me work out?" He grinned at my reflection in the mirror.

"Watch," I grunted.

My omega's gaze burned with desire.

We had about thirty minutes more before Hallie returned with Angus. She'd taken one look at the two of us and sent Jazz down to work out—she didn't seem surprised when I followed him.

I'd never forget thinking I'd never hold him again. Those seconds when I'd thought I'd lost him were moments I never wanted to repeat again. It had been worse than when Pierce had died. Worse than finding out our pack had been destroyed.

Jazz was my omega. His safety landed squarely on my shoulders.

"Stop it," Jazz ordered, still looking at me through my reflection but with a different expression. "I'm here. I'm alive. We all are. We know what we need to do, who our enemy is. They don't know where we are thanks to your killing of their men. We're safe here. Thanks to a legal loophole that I'm fairly sure my mother somehow had a hand it, I'm a millionaire once the paperwork goes through after my father's funerals. We'll be able to fund the pack. These are all good things."

I grunted. Good was in the eye of the beholder. Getting to drive Walter Whitten's luxury SUV into the ocean had been good. Successfully staging his death had been great. Knowing why Jazz was able to do what he did, his ability to create illusions, his pregnancy—that was all good too, but that knowledge came with a tradeoff. My omega was being hunted. Other nephilim were in danger as well. And we had a common enemy, Portal Ventures. The jury was still out on how to explain the way Walter Whitten had met his end. It seemed like magic, but so much of this did.

No one wanted to believe Portal had the time and resources to send teams out to search until their target was found. Faust still believed it was his email that tipped them off. Even now, days later, he waited hand and foot on Jazz and Hallie, jumping to his feet at the slightest sigh or gasp.

"You're still thinking about it," Jazz said with a whine. He turned around and stalked to where I sat on the workout bench. "What happened is done, Knox. There's no reason to brood—about that anyway." He slipped between my legs, and I had to look up to see his face. "Come on, do the thing," he whispered, his voice dipping low enough I felt it stroke my dick.

I pretended to be annoyed.

"Come on," Jazz said, putting a thousand percent more whine into those two words. "Do the thing, Knox. You know you like it."

I rolled my eyes, but not out of actual irritation; this was our pattern. Jazz would suggest I do the thing, and I would pretend I didn't like it, but really, I enjoyed his sexual fantasy. Even if it was a tad cliché.

I gripped his hips, squeezing just hard enough to make him gasp. "You worked really hard out there, sport."

Jazz snorted but quickly fell into his role. His body relaxed, draping against me like I was the only thing keeping him at his feet. "Really, Coach? There isn't anything you think I could do to improve my performance?" He batted his doe eyes.

I cleared my throat, letting the sound drag just how he liked it and Jazz whimpered. His erection poked my stomach.

There wasn't a workout Jazz enjoyed more than when we played *coach* and *eager athlete*. "I'll do anything," he continued. "Anything you say will help me, Coach."

My lips couldn't help their upward stretch. This was silly, we were silly, and I loved it.

That was another thing Jazz's presence had brought back into my life, the ability to joke around and be playful.

I circled my arms around him and squeezed my biceps. Jazz groaned softly, rubbing his erection against me in a gentle, circular motion

"There's one thing that will help you out there," I said. "Your coach's dick."

Jazz dropped to his knees and reached for my waist. "Really? If you say so."

I smirked until Jazz pulled my cock free and stroked it softly.

"Your dick will really make me a better athlete?" he asked with mock innocence.

I nodded gravely.

"I guess if you say I should." He parted his lips and swallowed my length in one swoop. Not even he could keep up the forced timidity once he tasted my dick on his tongue. He moaned, burying his nose into the short hair of my groin.

"Very good. You will definitely run faster now." I buried my hands in his curls but let him keep his same pace.

"I need to jump higher too," Jazz said before doubling down, sucking so hard his cheeks hollowed like he was trying to draw the cum from my dick.

I felt too close to coming and looked away, but now I saw his reflection. Jazz's glorious ass stuck out, the sloping curve of his back creating the perfect trail to his crack.

"Fuck, your mouth feels like hea—" I swallowed the old saying. After hearing about Jazz's experience, it didn't feel like it meant the same thing. "Your mouth is perfect. Look at you, so good, so wet. Who owns this hole, Jazz?" I traced around his stretched lips.

"Mrm," Jazz said, unable to get the sound out around my cock while also refusing to stop sucking long enough to talk. He'd been fondling my balls but lifted his hand to point into my chest. *You.*

I slicked my fingers with the coconut oil—the twins either hadn't noticed or hadn't cared that someone else was using it—and slid my fingers down the tempting curve all the way down to his greedy pucker. It twitched when I brushed over his skin, spreading more of the slick liquid.

Jazz grabbed my hand without stopping and brought it down to cup his jaw. I accepted the silent invitation and brought my other hand to the other side of his face before letting my hips thrust forward.

Jazz's moan exploded down his body, and he shivered while opening his throat. I didn't want to come in his mouth but couldn't resist the opportunity to fuck his face. I didn't have to worry about going to hard or being too rough. Jazz loved it and often spurred me to lose more control. I'd never hurt him, but I'd also never take for granted that I'd found a man who loved being loved the only way I knew how. I didn't have to change, I just had to show him. My fingers continued their journey, probing his pucker as I stretched him out. I thrust forward, watching Jazz's throat bulge as he took me deeper. "So perfect, so good." Our eyes locked. His nostrils flared, his body sucking in air in the moments that he was able. "Your mouth was made for me, Jazz, made for my dick."

Jazz squealed, and the sound sent vibrations up my shaft.

"Made for my dick in your mouth, in your ass. All of your holes are mine, Jazz."

He pulled back, releasing my dick with a squelching pop. "I need you," he moaned, spinning around on his hands and knees to present his ass. "Please, alpha, I need you in me." He brought his head down to the mat, resting between his bent arms. His cheeks spread with the position, revealing the gaping hole, slick and glistening. Ready. Waiting.

I dropped to my knees and entered him in one motion. My head fell back, and I roared, my wolf in the only place he ever wanted to be. I gripped his waist, kneading the flesh while I gave Jazz a moment to adjust.

He didn't want that moment and bucked into me, slapping his skin against mine. His mouth opened, releasing growling groans. His sex noises had changed with his first shift, and I'd never get enough of hearing him. His animal wasn't as close to the surface as mine, both because he wasn't an alpha and was so new at being a shifter, but when I had my dick in his ass, his animal let loose.

He drove his hips back into me, setting a brutal pace that sent violent jolts of pleasure up my spine. I growled, adding the scraping sound to Jazz's keening wails.

"Are you going to come for me, baby? Don't touch yourself..." I slapped his hand out from under his body, earning a sharp cry.

"Please, it aches."

"I'll take care of your aches, baby. I'll take care of everything." Once my fingers wrapped around his dick, I wouldn't be able to hold back the avalanche of desire poised to cover us both. I tightened my hold, taking a mental image of the way his head lolled with every thrust, the soft parting of his lips where he let out the tiniest mewls of need.

My omega.

"Mine." I growled out the word, stroking Jazz in time with my thrusts. He came with a sharp cry, a bowing back, his mouth open to the ceiling in a silent scream. My release gathered in my balls before racketing down as I filled him with liquid heat.

He was limp in a boneless, completely sated way. He humped gently, drawing out the aftershocks that made his body convulse. His back rounded with his inhale and flattened as he exhaled, lifting his face to the mirror, where he gave me a satisfied, well-fucked smile.

"Mmm, that's a good thing," he mumbled, sounding drunk.

Maybe he was drunk on my cum. I didn't hate the thought.

———

HALLIE, Jazz, and Angus sat on a blue-and-white striped sheet in the shade of an umbrella. Diesel, Huntley, and

Jagger were fighting over who could catch the most fish in their wolf forms—though none of them had produced a single one yet.

Faust stayed close to the umbrella. Probably so he was near in case Jazz or Hallie needed something. I had faith at some point his guilt would diminish at least to a level where he didn't frown every time he looked at them. Until then, I'd have to let him work through it the best way he knew how.

It was a gorgeous day to be on the beach, made all the prettier when Jazz stood and threw a handful of sand into the breeze. The small pieces became butterflies, thousands of them drifting in the air.

"Ooh, that's pretty. Do stars next," Hallie urged.

Jazz beamed, pleased to be able to show off. I didn't scowl every time he used his powers anymore. I didn't worry he would try to use them to leave me, but they had been the thing that tricked me into believing my omega was dead. Like Faust, I'd need time to work through that feeling.

His second handful replaced the butterflies. Everyone stopped to stare. He'd created a tiny galaxy. Milky nebulas shone in pinks and purples amidst clouds of glittering stars.

"That's beautiful," Hallie breathed, watching the illusion break apart as the sand fell. "I don't know if I'd call it angelic..."

Jazz snorted. "I don't feel angelic, so that's okay." He searched the blanket for something, and Faust leapt forward.

"Can I get you something? Water? I brought snacks—"

"Faust, no. I'm fine. Hallie is fine. Angus is fine. Nothing was your fault."

Faust frowned but didn't put up a fight.

Jazz stretched his arms over his head. "Is anyone in the mood for a run?"

"You just want to show off that you're faster than all of us," Jagger yelled from waist-deep ocean water.

Jazz's lips twitched as a flock of seagulls gathered over head. "I would never—"

Something fell from the sky, not heavy enough to cause damage. The item landed on the umbrella and slid to the sand. Jazz frowned, leaning over to pick it up.

"Wait—" I growled. Something didn't feel right.

Jazz froze, and Faust swooped in, snagging the bit of paper before Jazz could.

He'd nearly unfolded the small square when another bit of paper fell. I looked up at the seagulls circling the sky above. Without warning, a blizzard of paper fell from the sky, landing in the area on and around where Faust stood.

The others rushed back in, watching the papers fall like snowflakes. Faust unfolded the first note and frowned. He bent over, snagging several notes, frowning harder.

"What do they say?"

He flipped the message around so we could see the writing. The same two words were written on each with increasingly scratchy handwriting.

Help me.

Faust squeezed the notes into a fist and caught my gaze. "Is *this* something?" he asked.

I nodded, remembering the conversation we'd had weeks ago when he'd first started receiving the strange notes. I didn't want another mystery. We'd just recently started getting answers, but it didn't matter what I wanted. Not when someone out there so clearly needed help. "It's something."

The End

Ruler: Wolves of Royal Paynes
Warriors. Outsiders. Alphas.

It all started with a mouse and a note. After that, Faust kept receiving strange messages delivered by forest animals. He's no cartoon princess and this sh*t is weird but not life-threatening. He ignores it until he receives a flurry of notes all with the same message, *help me* and there is no way Faust can ignore the odd messages any longer.

Storri has been locked in a tower for over five years, put there by a man he trusted. The man claims to be protecting Storri from himself and others, but Storri never had any enemies—only a teacher he thought had been a friend. His ability to communicate with animals has helped him stay sane in isolation, but after so long, hope has faded.

Rescuing his prince is only half the challenge. Faust and his pack already have a mystery, and they've never been closer to finding out who destroyed their family and why. But with knowledge, comes danger and the man who took Storri isn't the only one willing to do anything to get their hands on him.

Ruler is the second book in the Wolves of Royal Paynes series. It is an action-packed, magically-infused, swelteringly hot, mpreg romance that continues a world of angels, demons, mystery, and magic. For maximum enjoyment, this series should be read in order.

Wolves of Royal Paynes:
>Hero
>Ruler
>Lovers
>Outlaw

Other series in the Wolves of World:
>Wolves of Walker County
>Wolves of Royal Paynes

Truth: Wolves of Walker County Book One

Chapter One
Branson

"Have you gotten your invitation?" Aver asked. A low but steady beep told me he was on site, hopefully pouring the concrete to reinforce the posts for the Lanser's dock.

"Invitation? Oh, that's right. The winter solstice." The last time I'd seen Aver had been this morning when he'd left for the day. I should've gone with him, but the paperwork was already piled high. The Lanser's was a big job, and they'd opened the doors to us booking up for the rest of the season. Aver hadn't been back to check the mail.

"Don't play dumb with me, Branson. You know what

invitation, just like you know why you've been running us both ragged with endless consultations these past weeks."

"We're running a construction company. I thought that was what we did."

Aver made a sound that was half growl, half snort. "You should've seen it. Hand delivered. Gold foiled edges. The paper was heavier than a rock. Good stock."

I could only imagine the hours Aver's mother would've spent on choosing the card stock. She probably had her spies reporting back to make sure she was the Walker family with the thickest paper.

I scanned the untidy stacks of paper on my desk in the office Aver and I shared in the house we lived in with our two other cousins. Carbon copies of pastel pink, blue, and green fluttered each time a breeze blew from the cracked window. "Maybe mine was lost in the mail."

"You wish. Your mom makes mine look tame. If I know Delia Walker, she's enlisted an entire parade to bring it to your door. Oh yeah, unrelated, I'll be late tonight."

An alert popped up on my computer screen telling me the perimeter sensor alarm had been activated. I groaned.

"Uh oh, is that Mommy Dearest now? Was I right? Is it a parade? Or just a full marching band?"

I yanked open the curtain to the driveway that wound down from the main road. I couldn't see anyone coming. "I don't know. Maybe it was just a raccoon. I'll check it out later. I've got three proposals to finalize as well as updating those numbers for the Forstein addition. Maybe, if you see them, you can try and explain why the granite specially shipped in from Italy would be more than the original locally sourced stone we'd quoted them."

Between the two of us, Aver had a better way with words. His father had groomed him from a child in public speaking, in hopes that it would help him assume leadership of the wolf pack. Now, Aver lived off pack land and co-owned Walker Construction. How the mighty had fallen—according to Aver's father. "If I see them. But I doubt I will. I'll be at the club—"

"Say no more. I don't want to be roped into whatever scheme this is, and I will take no part in you playing this part."

"Things aren't that easy, Branson," Aver replied tiredly.

"It's as easy as 'Mom, Dad, I'm gay, stop setting me up with female shifters you think will lure me back to the pack.' It's what I said."

A knock at the door made me frown. I hadn't heard any of the other sensors. The perimeter alarm had gone off, but not the porch or the door. I pulled up the front door camera but didn't see anything. I'd told Aver that camera was angled too high.

"Awesome, now I get nagged at from both sides. Would you like to also criticize my other choices in life? How many beers I have at the end of the day? The many ways in which I am disappointing my family by living outside of the pack?"

I grinned, but I didn't feel any happiness from Aver's annoyance, just grim acceptance. Which I imagined he felt as well. Sometimes, it was easier to give a mouse a cookie. At least then it got them to stop asking for the whole bakery —for a while. "I'm sorry, you're right. Agreeing to a date now will get them off your backs, but not for long with the Winter Solstice Celebration approaching. Have you spoken to Nana? I have a voicemail I haven't checked from her waiting at the end of my to-do list." At this rate, I wouldn't be getting to the end of my list likely until Aver had returned from his ill-fated date.

"I have a voicemail too. I'm afraid to check it. I never

know with that one. Either she wants us to come over so she can stuff us with pies and tell us we are smart and brave like when we were kids, or she needs to warn us of the latest apocalypse the stars have brought to her attention. It's a gamble I just won't take today. She probably called Wyatt too. Let him handle it."

Another knock sounded. I frowned. "Hold on, there's someone here. That sounds good, about Wyatt. If he is going to claim to be Nana's favorite, he can fend off her endless prophecies." I exited the office, not bothering to close the double doors and walked down the hallway to the front door. "I've been telling you, we need to lower the front door cameras..." I saw the vague outline of a small body through the frosted glass oval insert in the center of the door. So there had been someone there.

The figure was alone, not in a band or parade, so that knocked Aver's suggestions out of the running. I opened the door, my eyebrows lifting as my mouth dropped open.

"What is it?" Aver's voice spoke from far away. Except he was where he'd been the whole time while I'd found myself in a load of shit.

"Who sent you?" I barked, and the young man on my porch flinched.

He was short and slim with silky brown hair and blue eyes. He wore hardly anything, despite the frost on the ground that still hadn't melted from the night before.

"Do I need to come home? What is going on, Branson? Dammit! This camera is too high, I can't see anything!"

"Maybe you should. See if Dave can handle the site for the rest of the day." I slipped the phone in my pocket despite the fact that Aver was still speaking.

The young man on my porch had begun to shiver. My treatment of him could have started the trembling, or the fact that he was dressed like a virgin fit for sacrifice to an angry god. He'd recently bathed, adorning himself with so much cologne I should've smelled him long before the perimeter alarm had gone off. His shirt was white and so thin I could see through it. I imagined that was the intent. But, I couldn't ask him in or even offer him something to warm him up, not if he was sent from my mother.

And he was definitely a shifter.

"P-please, Alpha Walker—"

"Don't call me that," I snarled with more menace than this poor boy deserved. I sucked in a calming breath, shoving my fingers through my hair. "Who sent you? My mother, right?"

"Elder Delia said I wasn't to return if you weren't with me." He clasped his hands in front of his body, lowering his head so deep his chin rested against his chest.

I wished I could believe him, ask him in, give him a blanket, and then send him on his way, but Delia Walker had been trying to bring me back to the Walker family since the four of us—Aver, myself, Wyatt, and his twin brother Nash—left together at eighteen.

An act I'd followed by coming out.

Now, Aver got set up on blind dates, while I got barely legal, or possibly not at all legal, meat offerings.

My lips twisted into a scowl of disgust. I was sure the young man was very nice, and maybe, with a few years and pounds on him, he'd make some man very happy. Right now, he reminded me too much of my nephew, and when I thought of the types of things Delia, my mother, would've suggested to this kid to help him persuade me to return with him, I wanted to throw up. "What's your name?"

It was odd that I hadn't known him by scent, but maybe the cologne was blocking anything familiar about him. He was probably sixteen or seventeen now... Since it had been ten years since myself and my cousins had left, I should have had at least an inkling of recognition.

"Paul, Al—sir."

"Paul?" I didn't remember anyone by that name from the pack families.

"Paul Tyson, sir, I wasn't born in this region. My family comes from the south."

I frowned. "Oregon?"

Paul shook his head. He wore a light coverage of makeup, and as he turned his head, dark blue splotches shadowed underneath. "Texas. I hate it there, and I'm not going back. You can turn me away, but I ain't... I'm not going back." He tugged at his shirt, covering more of his midriff and telling me he wasn't any more pleased to be in that outfit as I was to have him there.

It would have ended my problem, but I couldn't block out those bruises. "Now hold on. Don't go running. I will not be going back with you, but I can't order you into the cold. Hold on." I lifted a finger to tell him to wait while I dug in my pocket for my phone.

He jerked back, toward the door.

"No, just wait—"

"Sir, I don't mean to disrespect you, but I told you I won't go back, and I won't. I thought I'd find safety here, but if that's not the case..." His attention swung up to something behind me. His jaw slackened.

"Fucking fuck, Aver, he's alive. I'm looking at him right now," Wyatt griped into the phone as he moseyed down the stairs. Aver's call had clearly woken him at the early morning hour of eleven forty-five. He wore only holey jeans, and his shaggy hair flopped long enough to cover his eyes.

"And what's this?" Wyatt crooned, coming to a stop at the bottom step. "He's got a friend." Wyatt winked.

I rolled my eyes. Wyatt would flirt with a rock. But Paul had stopped trying to run out the door.

"Wyatt, this is Paul Tyson. I was wondering if you would wait with him while I make a call?" I stepped to the corner, never leaving the two.

Paul's gaze flitted toward me. "Who are you calling?" His tone was unmistakable. He didn't trust me.

That wouldn't change by me lying now. "The police. I know that might not be what you want, but I know the cops around here. They can help you. They won't make you go home."

"I know the sheriff," Wyatt said, but out of his mouth, the words were husky. "He's an alright guy. Can't quite keep up spotting me at the gym, but he tries."

I waited for Paul to start laughing, but the kid was lapping out of Wyatt's hand. "I'm eighteen, though..." Paul said instead in a half-hearted attempt.

Wyatt's gaze flicked to mine long enough for him to turn back to Paul and say, "Still, it's better to go by the book with these things."

I would've mentioned Wyatt had no idea what *these things* were. He was just good at dropping into a situation and assimilating to what was needed. He would've been much angrier had he known that Delia Walker had sent this kid to seduce me. As if I'd find my omega in a shifter who was still a child. She'd crossed the line this time, though. Maybe Wyatt didn't know enough to be angry, but I was livid.

"Sheriff Maslow." Jake answered on the second ring.

"Hey, Sheriff, this is Branson Walker. I may have a kid in trouble here."

"Kid? How young we talking? Are you at home? What's a runaway doing way out there?"

It wasn't like we were in the middle of the woods, but we were a few minutes out of town by car where the Lynx River emptied into Walker Bay. If Paul had come from pack lands, he'd likely run from the other side of the bay to here, but I wasn't going to tell the sheriff that. "Not sure. He doesn't seem like a bad kid, though..." I looked briefly over at the two of them. Wyatt had Paul's full attention talking about some superhero movie that had just released. "He might have been abused?" If my mother had knowingly sent an underaged male to seduce me, I wouldn't protect her. Pack pride be dammed.

"I'll be right there. This is good timing. Well—you know what I mean. That fancy hire from Seattle came in this week. He's been on my ass talking about updating our procedure and policy. I tried to tell him we don't have enough of those kinds of trouble in Walker County to have all that rigmarole." He stopped speaking suddenly and cleared his throat, making me wonder who had walked in on him. When he spoke again, his tone rang with polite authority. "Thank you for calling. We'll come up now. Keep him there, keep him calm."

I hung up, wondering how I was supposed to keep a skittish shifter kid from running, but Wyatt had that under control. His habit for flirting was an advantage at the bar he owned and operated, and, I guessed, it was an advantage when trying to keep impressionable youths from fleeing. I lingered around the border of the room, still keeping an eye, without interrupting. And yes, I got a vindictive amount of pleasure seeing Delia's trap circle down the drain.

If this was the type of shifter she thought would lure me back into her clutches, then she didn't really know me at all.

Suddenly, my driveway was a parking lot. First, Aver in the white work truck with Walker Construction written in blue blocky letters on the side. Behind him was a firetruck, lights spinning but thankfully not the siren, and then Sheriff Maslow in his cruiser.

"Holy shit!" Paul exclaimed when he caught sight of them all.

"It's okay. Only one of them is here to talk to you," I said. "The rest are just nosy." I'd recommended Aver come back to the house, but that was before I realized Wyatt had been asleep upstairs. He didn't always sleep at home, choosing to crash at his bar sometimes instead. And I hadn't meant for Aver to blab to our cousin Nash. He was Wyatt's twin brother and a fireman, as well as the fourth of the Walker cousins to live in this house. And apparently, the town could spare a fire truck. "Stay here," I ordered, mostly to Wyatt.

Aver was already crunching over the gravel. "What's going on?"

At the same time, Nash hopped out of the firetruck and strode over.

"Listen, both of you. Delia sent me... a *gift*," I said with a snarl so they would understand. "He's shifter—"

"If he's shifter, why is the sheriff here?" Nash asked, hackles raised as his dark eyes flit back to where the sheriff was just now getting out of his car.

"Because he's got bruises, and I'm pretty sure Delia sent him for a specific purpose. If he's underaged, I don't care if she's my mother—I'll report her." I'd have reported her even if Paul was of age, but at that point, Paul was responsible for his own decisions in the eyes of human law, and shifter law was just about useless at a time like this. "He might have come from somewhere worse. He said he traveled here to try to join the packs and make a new life, I don't know. But I won't feel comfortable until we check it out."

The sheriff walked too closely for us to continue talking. A second man approached in step beside him. He stuck out immediately in an outfit that was probably called business casual where he came from, but on this side of the bay, he might as well have been in a tuxedo. His light blue button-up and gray wool blazer fit over a broad chest. The creases in his black slacks looked like they'd come straight off the ironing board. With an outfit like that, I expected some shiny loafers or equally impractical leather dress shoes, but I grinned at the tri-colored canvas sneakers.

"Branson." The sheriff offered his hand. I shook it, and then he turned to his partner. "This is our new representative from the Washington State Social Services, Riley Monroe."

I stuck my hand out, but the other man just nodded stiffly in my direction. He had a narrow face and sharp cheeks. His dark brown hair stuck out in a style I could only describe as artfully messy. Already, he had a dusting of facial hair shadowing his chin and jaw. There were faint dark circles beneath his deep blue eyes. A late night? Or early morning?

I pulled my hand away before the moment could get any more awkward. There were any number of reasons why he wouldn't want to shake my hand. It couldn't have been something I'd said—I hadn't spoken to the man yet. But, as the moment stretched on, I needed to say something quick. "Welcome to Walkerton."

The sheriff cleared his throat. "Mr. Monroe, this is Branson Walker."

"I was wondering when I would meet a Walker. Your name is everywhere in this area. I was sure the family wasn't far behind," Riley Monroe said. His tone was pleasant enough, but with an edge I was used to by now.

"Walker is just my last name. I'm afraid you'll have to go to the other side of the bay to meet the impressive Walkers of the family." My great-great-great-great grandfather had helped develop the island. We were one of many coastal islands located between the north-easternmost tip of Washington State and San Juan Island. Accessible from the mainland only by ferry, we lived a sheltered, quiet existence.

Most of the time.

But my ancestors hadn't been all that creative when it came to naming things. We lived in Walker County, the city was named Walkerton, and I looked out onto Walker Bay every morning.

Riley's gaze drifted to the house behind me. "I don't know, this is pretty impressive."

Pride filled me. The four of us had made this home with our own two hands. It had acted as our first symbol of independence from the packs. I rarely had a chance to show it off and had thought that ten years living in it with three other bachelors might've soiled the original feeling, but, there it was again.

I heard the door opening behind me and Riley's expression transformed. When he looked at me again, there was none of the polite friendly demeanor from before. Only judgment. His dark blue eyes narrowed, his gaze searching me with a new purpose. "Is that the child in question?" he asked, his voice all steel.

"I'm not a child!" Paul shouted back, despite the fact that Riley had spoken too quietly for Paul to have reasonably heard. He was either emotional or not used to ignoring his senses around humans.

Riley's eyebrows rose. "Nothing wrong with his hearing." He stepped by me without a glance in my direction. In fact, I got the distinct impression he hadn't looked at me on purpose.

I had no reason to care about what this stranger thought of me. I knew how bad this looked; it was one of the reasons I'd called the police so quickly. I could've sent Paul away with some money and a ticket to the wolf packs in the next territory over. But if he'd been stopped, it would've been harder to explain my involvement at that point.

"Hello, my name is Riley Monroe. I work with Washington State Social Services." Again, Riley skipped shaking hands. Was it a city guy thing? Cold and flu season? He pulled a small, leather-bound notepad out of his pocket and began writing as he asked Paul questions.

The only thing I knew for sure was that I was too busy to be hanging around, especially if my presence was no longer required. And yet, when I turned to make my excuses to the sheriff, what I was said was, "Would you like to come inside? It might be easier for the interrogations to happen in the dining room."

I very nearly clocked myself in the face, I reminded myself so much of my mother. She was vindictive and manipulative, but she would never say a mean word—to your face. Every guest was offered food and beverages, never mind if Delia Walker didn't know how to turn tap water into tea.

Riley approached, having left Paul at the front porch. "I'm going to need a list of everyone who lives in this household. As well as the number to a Mrs..." He checked his notepad. "Delia Walker. Any reason why Paul might've gone to her home? Is she known for housing runaway youths?"

I snorted. Delia Walker was known for being one of

three elder households, garden parties and always getting her way. But I was sure she would've loved being associated with something so altruistic. "Delia Walker is my mother. She lives on the other side of the bay with all the other fancy Walkers." There were four official Walker households: my grandfather, my mother, Aver's parents, and Nash and Wyatt's parents. But once we started splitting the names off, it became impossible to explain without a graph and a bottle of booze.

Riley's eyes narrowed on me again. I wished I could go back to the moment before he'd seen Paul. At least then Riley hadn't looked at me like scum. "Do you know why your mother would've sent Paul here? He's dressed extremely provocatively but claims he got the clothing from your mother."

"I can't begin to pretend I understand my mother. We aren't close, not since I moved from home."

"Hm."

I didn't trust that single noise any more than I trusted the situation at hand. Until now, I'd been pretty polite, but I wouldn't have this stranger thinking something about me that was wholly untrue. "Do I need to remind you that I called the cops here, Mr. Monroe? From my side, I found a young man, clearly down on his luck. And I called the police first. I'm not asking for any sort of reward, but I'll ask you to stop concocting whatever scheme you've decided is at work here. I want Paul safe. That is all."

Riley's eyebrows rose again, only this time, they didn't settle into suspicion. "Forgive me. I'm new and still getting the hang of things. This is unusual, but for what it is worth, Paul has not claimed to have done anything he didn't want to do. I'll need to run his identification through our systems.

If he's eighteen as he claims, that changes my next steps significantly."

He was clearly attractive with a level head. That didn't entirely explain my sudden interest in the man, but I wondered if maybe it had been too long since I'd traveled out of Walker County and mingled with fresh meat. I frowned at the term. I was so out of the game, I'd practically assumed Riley's orientation. He could like women... stranger things had happened.

Riley must've assumed the expression was meant for him. "I'm only doing my job, Mr. Walker. Caring for the welfare of those unable to care for themselves."

I smiled, trying to infuse as much warmth into the expression as I could. We'd gotten off on the wrong foot. I could understand why, but I was still eager to get back on the right foot. "I understand." I pulled out my card. "When you get some answers, please let me know."

Riley took the card gingerly, carefully grasping the very corner between his thumb and pointer finger. "Walker Construction," he murmured with a small smile. His finger traced over the embossed lettering on the card, and I bit my cheek, suddenly wishing his finger would trail over me instead. "I guess it's good to be proud of your name."

Alarms rang in my head as Riley's smile turned sad. I only had about a thousand questions all piled on top of each other. But the longer I stood there, the more I noticed the sheriff standing there with Paul. They were ready to leave.

"Don't be a stranger," I called out as the three of them turned back to the cruiser.

Nash walked up behind me. "Don't be a stranger," he mimicked in a high-pitched tone. I couldn't exactly elbow him with Riley looking. I was still trying to get the man to not think the worst of me.

"Shouldn't you be doing something?" I snapped instead.

Nash's smile never wavered. It hardly ever did. He was the spitting image of Wyatt, except his black hair was close-cut in a military style. "I know what you want to be doing," he teased before shutting the door and ensuring the final word.

Wyatt and Aver waited at the porch. They'd have their own annoying taunts locked and loaded. I sighed, looking back down the driveway. This wasn't the morning I'd planned for, but it was likely the morning I deserved. I could only hope that everything with Paul checked out. And I would secretly hope that Riley was the one to call me when it did.

Continue Reading...

THANK YOU!

Thank you so much for reading Hero! I hope you had as much fun reading about these characters as I did writing them. I can't wait for the next stage in their journey! I'd like to give a big thank you to Kiki's Alphas. You all help me so much with your amazing insight but also, your company! And finally, it wouldn't be a thank you section if I didn't thank my cover designer, Adrien Rose for being so amazing, and my editor MA Hinkle of Les Court Author Services!

———

About Me

Kiki Burrelli lives in the Pacific Northwest with the bears and raccoons. She dreams of owning a pack of goats that she can cuddle and dress in form-fitting sweaters. Kiki loves writing and reading and is always chasing that next character that will make her insides shiver. Consider getting to know Kiki at her website, kikiburrelli.net, on Facebook, in her Facebook fan group or send her an email to kiki@kikiburrelli.net

READING ORDER OF WOLF'S MATE WORLD

OTHER BOOKS BY KIKI

Omega Assassins Club

1. Fervor

2. Quench

3. Behemoth

4. Shatter

Akar Chronicles (Alien Mpreg)

1. CARGO

2. CRASHED

3. CLIP

Welcome to Morningwood (Omegaverse)

1. Gingerbred Lessons

2. Ball Drop

3. Sweet Meat

4. Sack of Gold

5. Hop On

6. Red, White, and Blew

6.5 Labor Pains (Morningwood Novella)

7. Pumpkin Cream Pie

8. Love Nest

9. Picking Cherries

Wolves of Walker County (Wolf Shifter Mpreg)

Wolves of Royal Paynes (Wolf Shifter Mpreg)

Printed in Great Britain
by Amazon

45718495R00189